Mercy's Fight

D0913817

JF
Gray

11-11-2014
#14.95

Mercy's Fight

T.L. GRAY

MARY COTTON PUBLIC LIBRARY
915 VIRGINIA ST.
PO BOX 70
SABETHA, KS 66534

Waterfall
PRESS

This is a work of fiction. Names, characters, organizations, places, events, and incidents are either products of the author's imagination or are used fictitiously.

Text copyright © 2014 Tammy Gray
All rights reserved.

No part of this book may be reproduced, or stored in a retrieval system, or transmitted in any form or by any means, electronic, mechanical, photocopying, recording, or otherwise, without express written permission of the publisher.

Published by Waterfall Press, Grand Haven, MI

www.brilliancepublishing.com

Amazon, the Amazon logo, and Waterfall Press are trademarks of Amazon.com, Inc., or its affiliates.

ISBN-13: 9781477825716
ISBN-10: 1477825711

Cover design by Elsie Lyons

Library of Congress Control Number: 2014940503

Printed in the United States of America

For my family

Your faith is my inspiration.
Your love is my strength.
You make me believe all things are possible.

"A cord of three strands is not quickly broken." Eccles. 4:12

CHAPTER 1

MATT

Disoriented, I blinked repeatedly, trying to get Bruce's face to come into focus. His lips were moving, but no sound penetrated the haze. Attempting to push off the floor, I stopped as pain coursed through my elbow.

"Matt!" Muffled but audible, his voice drifted through the fog. Then my ears cleared with a pop.

"Can you hear me?" Bruce asked, his voice now sharp and clear even though his face still blurred in front of mine.

"Why am I on the floor?"

Bruce let out a relieved sigh and then helped me up and into one of the club chairs he used for counseling. The motions revealed that my elbow wasn't the only part of my body suffering. My back ached and my hip throbbed.

Finally my vision normalized and I recalled some of what had taken place. I'd come in to bring Bruce the file on his new patient, a recovering drug addict recently out of rehab who was coming by stipulation of his parents. We had talked a little about the case and then . . . nothing.

Bruce handed me a bottle of water and sat across from me, still watching me with concern. "If this is your subtle way of letting me know you need some time off, I'd recommend just asking for it next time."

Still a little dazed, I scanned the room, trying to get my bearings. "How long was I out?"

"Minutes, maybe, but you went down hard. I want you to go see a doctor. A healthy twenty-five-year-old man should not be passing out. Are you eating okay?"

Bruce's fatherly tone made me chuckle. I guess he had kind of taken on that role. Although I now ran his counseling practice and side business, a wrestling gym, he still took a personal interest in my life. Of course, he'd also been my counselor for years and the one to lead me to Christ.

"I'm in the best shape of my life. Three square meals."

"What about sleep? Is the insomnia back?"

Finally steady, I eased off the chair and stretched my back, my joints crying out in response. "Sleep is overrated. I've never been a fan. You know this."

Bruce stood, forcing me to look him in the eye. "The nightmares are back, aren't they? I want you back in counseling. No excuses."

This was one of those times when working for a certified counselor annoyed me. I had stopped scheduling appointments for myself over a year ago. "I'm fine."

"Don't make me force you." Bruce crossed his massive arms. A former heavyweight wrestler, he had maintained his girth—all six foot four, 280 pounds of it. Even though I stood only a couple of inches shorter, he still had at least fifty pounds on me. His intimidating stature helped control his patients, but I had seen the softer side of him too often to be scared.

Recognizing the warning look in his eye, I slapped his arm affectionately. "Nice try, old man, but you trained me too well."

"Then I'll just fire you."

I laughed out loud. "Fire me? You don't even know how to answer the phone." I moved to the office door, knowing that Bruce would be lost without me. I kept all the records, transcribed the reports, paid the bills, and did his taxes.

He let out a frustrated sigh, knowing I wasn't going to give in on this one.

But since I rarely denied any of Bruce's requests, I caved a little. "Okay, just for you, I'll get a full physical this week and prove there's nothing wrong with me."

Bruce nodded but placed a heavy hand on my shoulder, his eyes searching mine for answers I didn't want to give. "How long have the nightmares been back?"

I groaned. It always came back to this. "A couple of months."

"What do you think triggered them?"

Turning my gaze to the floor, I felt a sharp sting of loss rip through me. "Her birthday was in April."

"Matt, I'm sorry. I should have remembered." Bruce's sympathetic tone made my throat go dry as I choked down my grief.

Calming myself, I looked back at him clear-eyed. "I'm fine. My mom died almost ten years ago. I've moved past that night."

"Have you?"

Narrowing my eyes, I shook my finger in his direction. "Don't start. I'm fine. Besides, you have your hands full with your ten o'clock." I glanced around the corner to see Rex, a fidgeting teen with a chip on his shoulder, waiting. "And he looks as cheerful as usual."

Bruce shook his head, accepting defeat. "All right. Send him in."

I shut the door behind me and walked over to my desk by the waiting area, catching the eye of my least favorite patient. "Bruce is ready for you."

As always, he flipped me the bird and then stormed into Bruce's office. I couldn't imagine the patience Bruce had to have to deal with punks like that one on a regular basis.

Gripping the side of my desk, I thought about what just happened in Bruce's office. It wasn't the first time I'd blacked out. For months after my mom's violent death, blackouts and vicious headaches were a daily occurrence.

Then the nightmares started.

Nightmares in which I'd witness her death as if I'd been in the room. I chalked it up to guilt. I *should* have been there that night. She called me for help, but I was out drinking like the delinquent I was back then. By the time I heard her pleading message, it was too late. My father had already killed her . . . right before he turned the gun on himself.

Still standing and grappling with frustration, I rubbed my temples. I *was* past this, past the pain and regret. I'd pulled my life together. I had purpose and joy in what I did every day. I wasn't that messed-up kid anymore.

Taking a deep, centering breath, I clicked on my computer and busied myself with court documents and patient reports.

When Bruce's last patient of the day left, I stuck my head into his office to say good-bye. He was buried in his case files, but still reminded me to make the doctor's appointment. Promising again that I would, I headed out to my motorcycle in the parking lot.

I suppose it was cliché that I rode a bike. The muscle machine matched my brawny, tattooed bad-boy look, although I hardly fit the part anymore. Since I'd long ago quit drinking and chose not to date, my nightlife often consisted of training wrestlers or hanging out with the "little brother" assigned to me through the Hartsford Children's Center.

To the average person, my life might seem simple or lonely, but I loved the peace. After years of being driven by anger and emotion, I enjoyed the refreshing calm that had settled over my spirit, empowering me to leave the past behind.

My motorcycle sprang to life, effectively clearing my head as I drove. It was only a few minutes before I pulled up to the doorway of The Storm. Squeezed between a shoe store and a doughnut shop inside a dated shopping center, the small gym brought me a great sense of pride. I'd helped Bruce purchase and outfit the place three years ago and had seen it grow well past our expectations. Now I had a waiting list of hopefuls wanting the one-on-one training we offered.

I walked through the door and relieved Will, the kid I'd recently hired to manage the front desk and make ring reservations. He, too, was one of Bruce's patients, like most of the kids we hired. People so often dismissed troubled kids and rarely trusted them. We found that when we showed we believed in them, they often exceeded our expectations.

Will had already overcome more trials at sixteen than most do in a lifetime. His twin sister died in a car accident while he survived. After her death, Will retreated into himself and didn't speak a word for six months. He started failing his classes and skipping regularly. At a breaking point, his parents had brought him to see Bruce, and after only two months of counseling and gym workouts, Will started to blossom. In fact, I could hardly get him to shut up.

Another victory.

"Anything interesting go on today?" I asked as he packed up his gear.

"Nope. It's been pretty quiet, but you're booked until closing. Oh, and the cleaning crew called. They're running behind and won't get here until eleven."

"Again? They pulled this garbage last week and I didn't get out of here until midnight. Next time they call, tell them to get here at closing. That's ten o'clock, spelled out clearly in our contract."

"Will do, boss. Anything else?"

I pushed my annoyance aside and smiled at him. "How's your mom?"

"She's good. Better. Now that school's out, she's going to take some time off and we're all going to take a trip up to Estes Park in Colorado."

"Well, be sure to take lots of pictures, and let me know when you get some dates so I can mark you off the work rotation."

Smiling again, Will slid on his backpack. "You got it. Catch ya later, Matt."

I watched as he exited and then I headed to the locker room to change. I needed to get in a quick workout and get focused before my first trainee arrived.

Glancing at my watch again, I was getting more and more ticked. I had showered, finished the paperwork, and shut down the computers, and still the cleaning crew hadn't arrived. If they weren't there in fifteen minutes, I was leaving and would personally be calling the owner in the morning.

"Finally," I muttered when a knock echoed through the gym. Yanking open the door with annoyance, I almost berated the poor girl standing on the other side of it.

"I'm so sorry to bother you." She looked around warily. "I have no idea where I am and my phone just died. I know my car charger is somewhere, but it seems I grabbed the wall charger instead, like an idiot." She shook her head in frustration. "Anyway, your place is the only one with the light still on, and I was wondering if I could just plug in my phone long enough to get the rest of the directions."

When she finally stopped talking and looked up at me, she flinched, clutching her phone to her chest as if I were going to rip it from her meticulously polished fingernails. "I-I mean, if it's not too much trouble."

Trying not to be insulted by her terrified stare, I moved out of the way and let her through. A damsel in distress was the last thing I wanted to see at my door. I nodded toward the front counter. "There's a plug by the desk."

She sighed gratefully and then rushed over to the wall, visibly shaken. She didn't look like a girl who was used to hanging on this side of town. Wearing one of those fancy velour sweat suits, she looked dressy even with her hair pulled back into a sleek ponytail.

She plugged in her phone and began punching buttons. "Thank you so much. I'm new in town and really have no idea where I am."

"It's no problem." I turned away and looked outside for the tardy cleaning crew. That's when I spotted the shiny Mercedes E-Class parked along the curb. Oh yeah, this girl was way on the wrong side of the tracks. No wonder she looked so frightened.

Accepting that the cleaning crew was a no-show, I closed the door and studied the girl as she began writing down directions. She was strikingly beautiful, the type who would draw attention wherever she went. I forced myself to look away. Pretty or not, there was a reason I stayed away from girls like her.

After she finished messing with her phone, she gave me a shaky smile and walked over with her hand outstretched. Two deep dimples appeared. "Thank you again. I'm Grace."

I took her small hand and met her eyes. *Wow.* When a woman had eyes that big, that blue, that beautiful, she probably got whatever she wanted without saying a word. Her scent was equally appealing—a mix of flowers and vanilla. My pulse shot up, alerting me that in minutes she'd done what no woman had in years—made me notice her.

"Matt Holloway."

She glanced down, taking in the dark ink that ran up the length of my arm. I pulled my hand back, bothered that I wondered what she might be thinking.

"I promise I'm normally much more responsible and not this flaky." She attempted a self-deprecating laugh, but her hand was trembling.

Heat burned the back of my neck. I scared her.

She looked around, no doubt judging the building I'd put my heart and soul into. A knot formed in my stomach. I shouldn't care what this spoiled princess thought of the place or of me, and it bugged me that I did.

"You know, it's not the best idea to go knocking on strange doors this late at night. A girl like you could get hurt out there." I was trying for sarcasm, a response to her obvious judgment of me, but my voice came out harsher than I intended.

Her mouth dropped open, surprise crossing her dainty features. "A girl like me?"

Something about her shiny dark hair, expensive sweat suit, and perfect, unpainted skin made me feel as if I were in the presence of royalty. The obvious class difference between the two of us irritated me in a way I couldn't explain and had never experienced before.

I leaned against the wall, crossing my arms, and gave her a smirk. "Yeah. A girl like you. Luxury car, fancy clothes, the newest smartphone that's only been out two weeks. You don't exactly fit in around here."

Her face fell, and for a moment she looked downright insecure, but then she regrouped, squaring her shoulders. Without saying a word, she turned to grab her phone before stalking back over.

"I'd thank you again, but since you managed to help me and insult me in equal measure, I will leave with a simple good night."

Noticing that her attempt to be snappy came out as refined as her posture, I couldn't help but laugh. "Night yourself, Duchess, and you be sure to find a more appropriate place to stop next time."

Her gorgeous eyes ignited with fire as she spun around and practically ran to her car. I heard the tires peel out of the parking lot and shook my head when I realized I was still watching long after she disappeared.

CHAPTER 2

GRACE

I was still shaking when I pulled into the parking lot of my new apartment. Granted, I had already been shaking when the phone died, but this reaction wasn't out of fear. I was ticked! How dare he judge me? I hadn't even blinked when he opened the door all moody and unfriendly, his demeanor magnified by the buzzed haircut and black tattoos inching down his forearm.

Okay, so maybe I had blinked a little. Any girl would have when faced with chiseled perfection. But it was his words that really struck a chord, one attached to every insecurity I had about this move. He had nailed my sheltered life with one look.

I rolled my eyes and opened the car door. I wouldn't let some stranger rattle me. I came to Asheville to be on my own for once, to chart my way outside the safety and security of my parents. Oh, I loved them, of course. They were amazing, caring, wonderful people, but I'd spent way too much time trying to be like them. And look where it had gotten me. My precisely designed path had disappeared along with my fiancé and best friend. To say those two deserved each other was an understatement.

The incident did more than just open my eyes to the pretension of my former fiancé. During the months that followed, a terrifying realization crept in—I had no idea who I was. But, I thought smiling, I would soon find out.

Opening the door to my first apartment, I was immediately thrown by the dim lighting and chipping paint. But it was clean, and I could work with the bare windows and dark carpet. This rental was not only a place to lay my head but also my first step toward independence.

A small kitchen stood opposite a square space that would serve as the combined living and dining room. I pictured barstools flanking the long counter, and a round dining table.

Moving to the bedroom, I winced a little at its size, but wouldn't let myself fret over the low ceiling and short distance between the stark white walls.

Contentment is all about attitude. Years of working with nonprofits had taught me that.

Continuing down the short hall, I found a stackable washer and dryer and a compact bathroom. No tub, but the standing shower would do its job.

Walking back along the hall, I opened the rest of the doors, finding only one usable closet—if the three-foot-wide alcove could even be called that.

While determined to be on my own without the luxury of my family's money, I had caved when it came to packing my vast wardrobe. Looking at the closet now, I realized there wouldn't be enough room for everything I owned.

Pushing the depressing thought aside, I went back out to my car and started unloading all the things I had stuffed into the sedan. Mostly clothes, shoes, and linens, but I did think ahead enough to pack an air mattress and some kitchenware.

I'd asked my parents for just $5,000 to help me get the place furnished and keep me fed until I actually started getting a paycheck. They had begged me to take more, but I was determined to pay them back, so I kept the amount reasonable.

By the time I lugged in the last of my stuff, locked the door, and checked all the windows, I realized it was after midnight. Sure my parents would be worried sick, I grabbed the phone and called just as they had instructed me to do.

"Gracie Belle?" My dad's worried tone made me feel guilty for not calling him immediately.

"Hi, Daddy. I'm here, safe and sound. Sorry it's so late."

"That's no problem. I'm just glad to hear from you. Your mother fell asleep a little while ago, but I think it was because she didn't have the patience to wait."

I laughed a little at his delicate way of referencing my mom's fiery personality. She couldn't stand it when things were out of her control. She was taking my move the hardest because we had always been so close. I had remained in our New York high-rise all the way through college and grad school. It was the only life I'd ever known, and I hadn't seen any reason to change it . . . until that night.

"How's the apartment?" my father asked through the silence.

"It's nice. Small. Actually, I think it's smaller than Mom's closet, but very clean. It will do just fine."

"I'm happy to hear that, although I wish you'd let me purchase you that town house your mother found. It's a lovely place."

I sighed. "Daddy, we've been through this. I want to be close to the Hartsford Center. It's bad enough that you got me my job. I want to feel like I'm doing this on my own. I need to find out who I really am without your money."

"Honey, I didn't get you your job. Sam may be a close family friend, but your talent, compassion, and brilliance is what got you the director position. Don't forget that."

Tears stung my eyes. Honesty, love, and godliness defined my father. He adored my mother and me more than his own life, and never missed an opportunity to show us. Stewart looked a lot like my dad on the outside—kind, successful, and generous—but inside he cared only for himself. A strong reminder that the package did not make the man.

"Thank you, Daddy. You always know what I need to hear."

"So when do you officially start?"

My mind cataloged the plans for the upcoming weekend. "Well, tomorrow I'm going to hit every estate sale in town in hopes of finding a decent couch and TV. On Sunday, I'm going to visit that church I showed you online and try not to freak out that on Monday morning I will take charge of one of the most successful children's centers in the state."

Propelled by nervous energy, I grabbed three of the new suits I had just purchased and hung them as we talked. I'd been volunteering for years, so I had plenty of business attire, but it seemed appropriate to pick up a few more. After all, I was in charge now. Hesitating for a second, I asked the million-dollar question. "Do you really think I'm ready?"

"Yes, sweetheart, you are. Sam would not have put you there if you weren't."

"The woman I'm replacing is so much older. She revitalized that center. They're going to think I'm a baby—I'm sure everyone will compare me to her."

"Honey, do you remember the verses I gave you before you left?"

"Yes, of course."

"Say them."

Quoting Scripture was the last thing I wanted to do at the moment, but I did as he asked. "Therefore do not worry about tomorrow, for tomorrow will worry about itself. Each day has enough trouble of its own."

"And?"

"Whatever you do, work at it with all your heart, as working for the Lord, not for men." Despite my reluctance, saying those verses did make me feel better. "Thank you, Daddy."

"Anytime. Well, I'm going to bed. Call your mother tomorrow or she'll skin me alive."

I smiled because I knew he was right, then agreed.

After I ended the call, loneliness crept in. Despite my twenty-five years, this was the first time in my life I'd slept without someone else in the house with me. Wiping the tears away, I reminded myself that crying didn't solve anything. I wanted this. Truth was, a bird would never learn to fly if she didn't leave the nest.

My journey started now.

CHAPTER 3

MATT

"Mom!" I walked down the long hallway to her bedroom, swaying and disoriented. I stumbled, bumping from one wall to the other, searching.

"Matthew?" She was crying . . . again.

"Mom?" Entering her room, I was relieved to see she was packing.

"You were right." She kept her back to me. "I should never have come home." She started crying harder, shoulders shaking. I walked toward her and wrapped her fragile body in a hug.

She cried out in pain and I immediately let go. Gently turning her around, I looked at her face and rage washed over me. Her left eye was a slit, red and swollen. Angry bruises marred her neck and spread down her shoulder.

"He hit you again." I grabbed her suitcase and flew around the room stuffing blouses and pants into the bag. "He's lucky he's not here." Shoes. Socks. "Next time he touches you, I'm going to kill him."

Mom rushed over to me and took my face in her hands. "Matthew, no. You're better than this. Better than him. One day I want you to let go of this anger and make a life for yourself."

Balling my fists, I made her a promise. "We will make a life. You and me, Mom. He will never hurt you again. I won't let him."

"Such a good boy." She kissed my cheek before turning around.

I heard her scream right as the gun went off.

"Mom!"

The screams jolted me out of bed, shaking and sweating. My eyes searched the room. No dead bodies on the floor. I was in my house, my bedroom. A flood of tears came as I dropped to my knees, cursing my father.

When my grief passed, I stood and checked the time—only three in the morning—but sleep would not come again, not when those images awaited me.

The leather from my journal felt smooth under my fingertips as I pulled the book from my nightstand and wrote down everything I remembered from the dream. Comparing the nightmare to others, I noticed more details surfaced each time. Previously, I only walked down the hall or saw her face before the shots woke me up. But tonight, hearing her voice, feeling her touch my face, the dream felt so real.

If only it had been real. If only I'd had those last few minutes with my mother to tell her I loved her instead of missing her call for help. Maybe then it wouldn't be so hard to not look back. I knew that my own guilt drove these nightmares, and once again wondered when they would go away for good.

My past was supposed to stay buried. Wasn't that what I had been promised? A new life? I had one now, so why couldn't I move forward into my future without the scars of my childhood haunting me?

I finished writing, showered, and got dressed. Saturday had been busy and tense, and I relished that today was Sunday. I needed some time with God and the fellowship I'd come to crave from other believers. The nightmares depleted me and I felt my closeness with Him slipping.

Grabbing a cup of coffee and my Bible, I sat on the back porch and read until the sun started peeking out over the horizon. I may have dozed a little off and on, but I wasn't sure. After the nightmares, my sense of time always felt a little off.

But staring out into my backyard with its hint of morning did give me peace. Two oak trees stood proudly, like rigid guards, over the area that had become my sanctuary, their leaves filtering the rising sun. Whenever my life felt overwhelming, I would listen to the sounds of nature and sit in awe of God's amazing mercy.

This house had been one of those blessings. One look at the thick patches of grass and rows of budding flowers, and I knew this small two-bedroom home would be mine. After spending most of my life in tiny, dingy apartments, I had vowed to one day have my own yard, complete with a hammock. I had strung one up my first night as a homeowner, and had since added a fire pit, outdoor grill, and fishpond. I created my own oasis to escape to when I needed serenity, and today was definitely one of those days.

Being up so early gave me plenty of time to hit the coffee bar before service began. Having a fully functional café in our church was one of the perks I loved. After getting my usual—a double Americano—I turned to see Jake and his wife, Naomi, mingling near the tables. Jake was Bruce's former patient and we had become good friends the past year. I even stood up for him at his wedding, a colorful backyard event full of laughter, abundant food, and even some salsa dancing. It was a celebration that fully embraced Naomi's Latino heritage.

Smiling to myself as I remembered the lively reception, I walked over to the happy couple. Part of me envied their joy, but I knew family wasn't in the cards for me. I wouldn't drag anyone into the life I had lived growing up, and I had already seen that the sins of the father reached well into the next generation. No. I made up my mind long ago that I would be walking life's journey on my own.

"Will wonders never cease? You're actually here before service starts." I grabbed Jake's shoulder and gave it a quick squeeze. "And Naomi, you are as beautiful as ever." I gave her a hug, intentionally lingering until Jake pushed me aside and told me with a smirk to back off. I loved getting under his skin.

It took me a second to register the presence of another person in the circle, but my heart dropped the moment her familiar perfume hit my nose. Natural and sweet, the scent was as beautiful as the girl who had admittedly crossed my mind more than a few times since her late-night visit at the gym.

She looked more sophisticated than I remembered. Hair down. Shiny, sleek tresses covered her bare shoulders. Her classy sweats had been replaced with a casual yellow sundress that hugged every one of her delicate curves. She looked put together enough to be on the cover of one of those fashion magazines, and I felt pretty certain that the jewelry and handbag she was sporting cost more than a few of my paychecks would cover. The contrast to my jeans and T-shirt reminded me, once again, that we came from different worlds.

Naomi pulled the girl closer. "Matt, this is Grace. We just met at the coffee bar. She's new to town and visiting today."

Grace looked as surprised to see me as I was to see her, but I had no intention of showing the spoiled rich girl that she got under my skin. Instead, I sent her a cool smile. "I see you found your way."

Hiking up her oversized bag as if it offered some kind of security, she stood a little straighter. "Yes, I did."

"Have you two met before?" Naomi looked confused as she turned to Grace. "I thought you'd only been in town a couple of days."

Grace and I faced off, and I felt the same tingle that had filled my gut the night we met. Irritated by my lack of control, I turned to Naomi. "She got lost and stopped by the gym. Luckily, I was still there."

"Yes, he was very helpful," Grace piped up before turning her eyes back to me. "And not at all rude."

I was rude? Hardly.

Leaning against a nearby wall, I met her challenging stare. "I bet I'm the last guy you thought you'd see here."

Jake raised an eyebrow at me, but I kept my gaze locked on Grace.

She glanced among the three of us, visibly uncomfortable.

Attempting to break up the awkward silence that followed, Jake pointed at me and smiled, but his look told me he'd be asking questions later. "Matt here is what you call a sheep in wolf's clothing." He eyed my faded jeans and work boots. "If you'd get yourself a decent outfit once in a while, you wouldn't scare away all the ladies."

I didn't respond. He knew all about my past, knew that getting ladies to notice me was the last thing on my mind.

Grace let out a forced laugh and Naomi came to her rescue, giving me the stink eye. "We should go in and find a seat before it fills up. Jake?"

"Yep." Jake jumped at her tone. He wrapped his arm around her and stole a kiss.

I moved to follow, but stopped when I heard Grace hiss, "Why would you say that?" She kept glancing toward Jake and Naomi, obviously not wanting them to hear our exchange.

Even though she was embarrassed, the air of superiority never left her. I met her eyes, disgusted at myself for letting her get to me. "Oh, come on. I saw how terrified you were of me the minute I opened that door. I don't exactly look the part of an everyday hero. It's okay, Duchess, I get it."

Her mouth dropped open, and with some satisfaction I watched those large, bright eyes flash. "Is that what you think? Let me assure you that, unlike you, I don't go around prejudging people, and I certainly don't have any issue with the way you look. If I did seem afraid when you answered the door, it was because you practically growled at me."

The retort I'd planned died on my lips.

Others walked around us, some bumping our shoulders as they left the café and moved toward the sanctuary doors.

"You guys coming?" Naomi asked.

Grace shook her head at me and then turned to go into the sanctuary. Feeling slightly humbled, I took a couple of hesitant steps across the faded carpet and followed her. She sat next to Naomi. Although there was an empty seat to her right, I squeezed by and settled on the other side of Jake. There was no way I'd get anything out of today's message if I sat that close to her.

Jake's curious stare matched his pinched smile. "That was interesting."

I didn't respond.

"She sure is pretty. Anything you want to talk about?"

"Shut up."

Jake laughed at my irritation, sending more fire up my back. We all stood as the band started the first praise song. Bowing my head, I prayed for God to empty my racing mind so I could properly worship Him. When I looked up, I found myself sneaking a peek in Grace's direction. She had her eyes closed and her face lifted upward. My heart took on a rapid cadence as I looked at her stunning profile. Closing my eyes, I prayed again. Maybe three seats weren't far enough.

When the service was over, I found Grace waiting for me at the end of the row. Jake kept walking with Naomi, giving me a moment alone with her.

"I'm sorry I snapped at you," she began. "For some reason I made a terrible first impression, so what do you say we just start over and pretend this is a new day?" She stretched out her hand and smiled. Those darn dimples resurfaced. "Hi, I'm Grace. It's nice to meet you . . . again."

Caught off guard by her humility and kindness, I took her hand. The softness matched its porcelain color, which reminded me of a fragile china doll. "It's nice to meet you, too."

I rubbed a small circle on her delicate skin, unable to let go. Our eyes locked on each other, an intangible bond forming that defied all logic or reason.

Chemistry is a sneaky thing, and I appeared to have no weapon against its force. Maybe my reaction was because I had stopped dating years ago, but even before that, I couldn't remember a time when I had been so completely entranced by a woman I barely knew. If just touching her hand drove me this crazy, what would happen if feelings were involved? Nothing good, that's for sure.

I hadn't worked this hard, come this far, to throw it all away on a pretty face.

CHAPTER 4

GRACE

I thought we'd shared a moment, or at least moved past that initial awkwardness. But already Matt was back to his cold stance and terse conversation. Naomi insisted Matt and I both come over to their condo for lunch, and while I enjoyed getting to know her and Jake, Matt's attitude kept distracting me.

Even though he was seated across the table, he refused to make eye contact. Every question I asked was met with a yes or no answer. More infuriating was the fact that his apathy was clearly targeted at me. With Jake and Naomi he was casual, talkative, and affectionate.

"So, Grace, what made you decide to move to Asheville?" Naomi asked, ignoring Matt's rudeness and passing me a plate of soft homemade tortillas.

"A new job. My first, really, so it's a little overwhelming. Before this, it was school and then working with my mother doing volunteer events."

As my words spilled, Matt just sat there, intensely watching and judging me. A familiar surge of insecurity gripped my stomach. Most people my age had at least worked a part-time job.

I tried to justify my lack of experience. "My parents didn't want me working while I was in college, and volunteer work is actually very helpful in my field."

Matt simply rolled his eyes.

Naomi scowled at him before turning back to me. "And what field is that?"

I shifted uncomfortably in my seat. "I work with nonprofits. My degree is in business with some counseling, but mostly I try to help raise money and get support through local governments. It's a lot of grueling, behind-the-scenes work, but I love seeing what happens when a community rallies around a common goal."

Jake perked up at the mention of counseling, and mercifully, the discussion shifted away from me to questions about college classes and case studies. I learned that Jake had recently switched his major from finance to counseling. Jake also mentioned that Matt ran the office for an anger management counselor.

"Is that how you two met?" The question seemed innocent enough, but suddenly the room got quiet.

Jake seemed to be the only one who was comfortable with my question. "Yes, it was. There was a time when I couldn't stand this guy, but that was just because him and Bruce were determined to turn me into a decent guy. I guess in the end they won out."

Naomi smiled warmly at him, squeezing his hand. "You were always decent. Just a little lost."

Jake leaned over and kissed his wife, causing Matt to make some sarcastic comment about getting a room. Laughter erupted at Naomi's beet-red face and immediately the atmosphere felt relaxed again.

"Can I help you clean up?" I offered, stacking silverware on my plate.

"No way—you just moved in." Naomi patted my arm. "I'm sure you have a ton of work waiting at home."

I lowered my head to my hands and shook it. "Oh, you have no idea. I went to estate sales yesterday and hit the jackpot. Got every piece of furniture I wanted. Only problem is, the people dropped everything off just inside my doorway. I managed to move the couch, but the entertainment center is impossible."

Naomi shot Jake a look and cleared her throat.

"Matt and I would be happy to help you move it, if you'd like," he quickly offered.

I spun my head toward Matt. The glare he was giving Jake made it clear that he was less than thrilled about being volunteered for the task.

"It's okay, really," I said. "I found a moving company and I'm going to give them a call tomorrow."

"Don't be silly. Jake and Matt live for this stuff, don't you, boys? They're constantly talking smack about who is stronger or faster, and now they can prove it." Naomi sent Matt a wicked smile before continuing. "I'm sure it's the least they can do after I slaved over their meal."

When both guys reluctantly agreed, Naomi winked in my direction, leaving me to marvel at her persuasive abilities, especially since they saved me from wasting money on a moving crew.

"Okay, great." I gathered some plates to clear. "I really appreciate it."

Naomi shooed us away from the mess, insisting on doing all the work. I gave her a quick hug before stepping outside, thanking her for lunch. Matt was the next one out the door, and he walked straight to a huge motorcycle parked next to the curb. He straddled the massive machine with his strong legs and waited.

Of course he had a bike, because his gorgeous face, strong and cut body, and bad-boy tattoos weren't attractive enough.

My body betrayed me, moving closer to touch the shiny metal. Dangerous. Exciting. Not much different from the man in front of me.

His eyes met mine and narrowed. "What's the matter, Duchess? Never seen a Harley before?"

"Yes, of course I have. I just didn't realize this beast was yours."

"So where are we going?" He pulled out his helmet and leaned against the bike's handlebars while waiting for my response. My heart fluttered. *Why does he appeal to me so much?* Maybe because he had a toughness about his face, a hardness that went beyond his strong bone structure. Or maybe it was the eyes—the sporadic mix of browns, greens, and blues—that would look happy one minute and tortured the next. Whatever the reason, I had to seriously get a grip on myself.

"Um, Raintree Apartments, on Lincoln. Number 154."

He laughed and shook his head. "Nice try. Seriously, where do you live?"

I moved closer, not understanding why he was laughing. "That's where I live. Why is that funny?"

He eyed me closely and set his jaw. "I lived in those apartments a few years ago. It's not exactly the Ritz, nor is it a place I'd recommend for a girl living on her own."

Why did he always insult me? "For your information, I did my research and they are perfectly safe. Residents only reported three cases of theft, all vehicle related, and two of them happened when the owners left their purses in the car."

"The key word there, Duchess, is *reported*. Did your research happen to inform you that they are located only two blocks from the worst street in the city? I've seen some lethal gang action take place in that parking lot. You need to be careful."

His face blurred as fear threatened what was left of my crumbling resolve.

Matt must have seen me falter, because he reached out to steady me, wrapping his calloused hand around my elbow. Startled by the immediate jolt his touch sent, my voice hitched. "I will."

Somehow, despite the mention of gangs and the insinuation of unreported crime, his steady hand made me feel safe and protected.

"You guys ready?"

Matt quickly dropped his grip at the sound of Jake's voice. The brief moment of concern was now replaced with that wall of bitterness that stood between us.

"Yes. Just let me punch my address into the GPS first. I still don't know my way around." I hoped my voice wasn't shaking as much as my hands were.

Matt pulled his helmet on in a huff. "Don't bother. I know exactly where that is. Just follow me."

I fell in line behind Matt's Harley and saw Jake's car move in behind mine. It, too, was a Mercedes, which grated on my nerves. I reasoned that Matt's rudeness was connected to the things he mentioned when we first met—my car, clothes, and accessories. But Jake and Naomi had a great condo and nice vehicles, and yet Matt didn't show any resentment toward their status. He just made no sense at all.

Ten minutes later, we pulled into the parking lot of my complex and I noticed a couple of things I hadn't before. One being that the fence surrounding the complex was missing several panels. Two, the entire building was in serious need of new exterior paint.

Determined not to spook myself, I parked and put on a smile for the boys. I'd picked this place for a reason, I reminded myself. It was only minutes from the children's center, and I needed to understand their world to be of any use to the organization.

Jake stepped out of his car and warily looked around before mustering a fake smile. He had a lot more tact than Matt did, so I wasn't surprised when he just said, "Interesting place."

Matt approached from behind. "It's a dump."

"It's much nicer on the inside." I slid my key in the lock, still trying to get rid of the unease that was now settling in my stomach.

"Watch your step. That entertainment center is literally right in front of the door."

Grateful that the apartment was tidy, I sidestepped the massive piece. The guys followed. "I have some moving straps you can use to get it off the ground. It's going right up against the wall over there."

"Nah, we got it," Jake said, dismissing the offer.

I stepped away, unwilling to argue. Matt and Jake walked around the large console and then, after a three count, attempted to lift. Nothing budged and they both let go.

I tried not to laugh, but a giggle escaped my lips. "So do you want those straps now?"

Jake smiled. "Yeah. This thing must weigh a ton. How did they even get it in here?"

I thought back to the four guys who had haphazardly moved the piece into my apartment and shuddered. "Not very gracefully, which is why it's sitting right there."

Matt still hadn't said a word. Instead, he was looking around my living room as if taking inventory of everything I owned. Had he noticed the missing drapes or cracks on the ceiling? Probably.

His intensity made me nervous but at the same time intrigued me, because it was paired with this unwavering calm. A calm that contradicted the dark storm raging in his eyes. The draw was more than physical. I wanted to get inside his head and figure him out, get past that shield he seemed so determined to raise.

Jake and Matt hooked up the straps and easily moved the piece to the far wall. I was elated. Sure, the green paint hid its beauty, but I could already see how stunning it was going to be.

"Is that it?" Jake approached, pulling me from my thoughts.

"Yep."

Matt noticed the bed frame lying against my hallway wall. "We can put that together for you if you want."

"That's okay. I don't even have a mattress yet."

He turned his piercing hazel eyes to me again. "What are you sleeping on?"

Feeling exposed, I started to stumble over my words. "I, um, brought an air mattress. It'll work fine until I can afford the real deal."

Matt's eyebrows went up at the word *afford*.

Jake cleared his throat and pulled out a card. "Call me if you need anything. I also put Naomi's cell number on the back." He looked around my place, making me realize how run-down it looked compared to his and Naomi's condo. "I mean it. We're just a few minutes away."

I took the card gratefully. "Thanks, Jake. And tell Naomi thanks again for lunch."

He turned to look at Matt, who had moved my TV and was now pulling wires through the back of the new entertainment center.

Matt shrugged. "I'm going to finish this up."

A satisfied grin appeared as Jake retreated. "Okay, well, I'll see you guys around." With that, he walked out and I was left completely alone with Matt, unable to gather any sort of intelligible thought.

"Do you want a drink?" I opened the fridge, desperate for something to do with my hands. "I have lemonade or water."

With the TV all hooked up, Matt took a seat at one of the barstools I'd placed along the counter. He immediately started watching me again, expressionless and with that infuriating calm.

Slamming the fridge door, I crossed my arms. "Why are you looking at me like that?"

"Like what?"

"Like I've grown an extra head or something."

He smiled, and once again my breath caught in my chest. It wasn't the first time I'd seen him grin, but it was the first time he'd directed one at me.

"You baffle me."

Surprised by his words, I let my arms fall to my sides. "I don't know why. I'm an open book."

Matt walked over to me and leaned back against the counter. The kitchen area was small, only a narrow space, and the clean scent of the soap he'd used that morning was undeniably masculine. The hair on the back of my neck began to prickle. He was too close, too appealing. I backed up to the far side of the kitchen. I needed some distance between us.

He watched me carefully as he spoke. "Then explain to me why it is you drive a seventy-thousand-dollar car and yet live in one of the worst apartment complexes in the city. Why you act and dress like you spent most of your life with a silver spoon in your mouth, yet you can't even afford to buy yourself a decent mattress."

I took a deep breath, stalling. I'd never been embarrassed about my parents' money before, but for some reason his words made me squirm. "The car was a gift, as were the clothes. My life is different now." I didn't know how else to explain my situation without going into more detail than he needed to know or I wanted to share.

Matt's face hardened as he pushed off from the counter. "Well, the guy should have at least put you up in a place nicer than this."

He grabbed his keys just as it dawned on me what he was thinking.

"Hey, wait a second!" I yelled, outrage filling my stomach as I grabbed his arm to stop him from leaving. I was much like my father in that way—very, very slow to anger—but Matt had pushed the last button. "My parents gave me that car along with everything else that irritates you so much. I don't know what I did to give you such a terrible opinion of me, but don't you dare imply I'm someone's mistress. Nor am I some snobby rich girl who happened to turn up on the wrong side of the tracks. What I am is someone with feelings. Feelings that you seem set on hurting every time you open your mouth."

As soon as I finished my rant, I was exhausted. I hated conflict, hated losing my temper or even raising my voice. I let go of Matt's arm and turned around. No way was I giving him the satisfaction of seeing the tears trail down my cheeks.

The room fell silent. Thick tension hung in the air, cut only by the sounds of our mutual breathing.

"I'm sorry, Grace." The soft crack in his voice said more than his quick apology.

The front door shut and I turned, feeling the emptiness of his abrupt exit. I realized it was the first time Matt had said my name out loud. I should have still been mad at him, appalled even, but I could only think of how much I liked hearing the word *Grace* spill out of his mouth.

CHAPTER 5

MATT

It was another restless night for me, but not because of nightmares. Instead, I was haunted by the sad blue eyes of a woman who somehow managed to awaken every part of me.

I hadn't meant to be cruel, but anger took hold at the thought of any other guy touching her. And I don't know why I even had that thought to begin with. Grace hadn't given any signal that she was *that* type of girl. While gorgeous to look at, never once did she flirt with me or with Jake. In fact, all evidence indicated that she was sincere and somewhat shy.

Maybe I just wanted to find a flaw, any flaw that would end this quickly growing infatuation.

My mind worked overtime as I lay there trying to fall asleep. Thoughts of Maggie came back to me for the first time in years. I could see her seductive smile as it broke through her fake innocence. Oh, how enamored I had been with her, possessed even. At the time I thought it was true love. But that girl was kerosene to my fire, and her memory was exactly what I needed to remind myself why I'd chosen to be single.

My attraction to Grace yesterday was intense, as was the jealousy that came immediately after I misunderstood her words. Jealousy I hadn't felt since the night I'd kicked Maggie out for good. The night I became like my father.

Feeling a shiver run down my spine, I threw off the covers and found my way outside to the hammock. Stars above me stretched on for miles. The night air was only slightly cooler than the afternoon heat, but it felt fresh with all my landscaping in full bloom.

"My sanctuary." I closed my eyes and listened to the sounds of nature. Field crickets chirped while rustling leaves scraped the rooftop as the soft night breezes swept across my face. A calm fell over me, taking away the stress that had kept me tossing all night. Soon my lids went heavy as sleep finally came.

The rising sun awoke me from my slumber at a grueling five thirty in the morning. I had logged maybe three hours of sleep for the third night in a row, and I felt sluggish and irritable. The shower's hot water massaged my throbbing muscles as I dealt with the aftermath of sleeping in a hammock.

Maybe it was time to talk with Bruce, figure out why I was slipping back into old patterns. I was becoming edgy again and reacting irrationally to even the smallest of things. The thought infuriated me. I'd spent the past year in such a great place emotionally and physically. Call it pride or whatever, but the idea of sitting in that chair opposite Bruce felt like admitting defeat, and I wasn't one to tap out in a fight.

What I needed was to get out of my head, and stop focusing on my life. Derrick, my "little brother," had graduated and was heading off to college. The past three years I had spent mentoring him had been challenging yet completely fulfilling.

Liz Bailey, the tough-as-nails director of the Hartsford Center, had called me two weeks ago about a ten-year-old boy. He'd been through three "big brothers" already and had an enormous chip on his shoulder. She had also taken that opportunity to tell me she was leaving the center and would be replaced by the end of the month.

I didn't want to commit myself to some new kid when I had no idea if I would even get along with her successor, so I quickly declined. She gave me one of her good old tongue-lashings and then said she'd hold his name as a possibility for me until she left. The conversation had ended with her insisting I was the only match for the troubled boy. Maybe she was right.

Grabbing my phone, I listened to Liz's most recent voice mail. She had been trying to reach me every day since we'd talked.

"Matt, you need to stop avoiding me. My last day is tomorrow and I'll be handing everything off to Ms. Covington. I'd like to firm you up on taking Marcus. I don't want him getting lost in the shuffle." There was a long pause. "He was suspended last week for fighting. I hated to do it, but the Hartsford policy is clear—no fighting is to be tolerated. I thought maybe you could relate. Anyway, I'm here until three on Monday. Don't let me down."

A heavy sigh hung in the air as I threw my phone on the bed. Kneeling, I prayed for guidance and almost immediately felt confirmation that taking Marcus as my little brother was the right step forward.

Ten years old, I thought warily. Derrick was fifteen when we'd been paired up. He was eager, studious, and way past the punk attitude of a preteen. I had a bad feeling that Marcus and I were not going to have such a smooth connection.

It was only seven, but Liz would already be at the center. She was a notorious workaholic and an early riser. I figured that I might as well get this over with before I changed my mind.

I lived only fifteen minutes from the children's center and didn't have to pass Grace's apartment on the way, but I still found myself going that direction. Her car was where she'd left it the night before, and the luxury sedan stood out like a sore thumb among the other vehicles in the parking lot.

She didn't belong there. Trash littered the cracked pavement, with the remnants of drugs and alcohol displayed for all the world to see. The mess was a disturbing reminder that the neighborhood was getting worse every year. Revving the gas, I pushed my bike along, reminding myself that I wasn't responsible for her safety.

The scene deteriorated as I approached the center. Most of the homes that still had residents were structurally unsound, their rotting wood exposed to the elements. Run-down duplexes covered with graffiti had sprung up everywhere else. I stopped at the corner, shaking my head as a crew threw out the meager belongings of yet another evicted tenant.

Minutes later, I slid my bike to the curb and locked up all my gear. The neighborhood was known for petty theft. The building had been given quite a face-lift since Liz took over. The crumbling steps had been replaced with fresh concrete and were regularly power washed to avoid graffiti or other forms of "art." While she had done a lot to spruce up the old commercial building, the barred windows and faded bricks still reflected the roughness of the surrounding neighborhood.

In fact, the center had been run by the state until vandalism and lack of volunteers led to funding cuts five years ago. Philanthropist and billionaire Sam Hartsford had bought the property and hired Liz, and together they turned the forgotten place into one of the best private community centers in North Carolina.

Sometimes I wondered how things might have gone differently for me if I'd connected with a big brother when everything went down with my parents, but I wouldn't let myself dwell on the unknown. God had given me Bruce.

I texted Liz and banged on the solid metal doors, knowing they would remain locked until the center opened at nine. When the doors finally opened, Liz scowled at me.

"You dare to come here this time of morning without so much as a cup of coffee?" She was trying hard to look annoyed, but I knew better.

My eyebrows shot up as I turned to look at my bike. "You want me to leave?"

Softening, she stepped aside. "No, I guess I can find something for you to do."

Liz looked the same as she had every day for the past three years. Faded jeans, work boots, worn-out Hartsford T-shirt, and her hair swept back into a low ponytail. If there were any feminine qualities in her, she sure knew how to hide them. Though not tall or heavyset, Liz was intimidating enough to take down even the unruliest of thugs with her arctic glare.

She locked the doors as I looked around. The building had been gutted to accommodate a basketball court. Two areas—a game room and TV/lounge room—were set off to the left, while Liz's office and a couple of counseling rooms were to the right. Bleachers loomed just across the court and were often full during intramural basketball games.

Liz swept by me and continued to her office as if on a mission. That was often how she moved, intentionally and with speed. I'd heard more than one of the kids call her the Energizer Bunny.

"So this is it?" I leaned against the doorframe of her office. A few boxes with personal belongings were scattered around. She shuffled papers while searching for something on her desk, likely the report on Marcus.

"Let's sit." She pointed to the small couch against the wall and spread out the file on the coffee table in front of it. Liz was all about full disclosure, which was one reason why we worked together so well. I trusted her implicitly.

"Marcus hasn't had the easiest time of it," she began after I joined her on the couch. "He was removed from his parents' house at five years old. Then he spent the next three years in foster care until his aunt could finally get custody. From what the counselors tell me, those years were pretty bad, but it appears that he's got some stability now. His aunt's involved, but like most of the single parents we see, she works too many hours to keep Marcus out of trouble."

Liz then pulled out pictures taken by the state that spanned several years. Some were from his biological family. Others were the results of poor foster care. The last picture surprised me. Bruising on his back and arms. His face was filthy and battered. One eye nearly swollen shut while the other, a rich brown, held a bitterness no child should feel. Photographs like that one were rare, since most abusers tend to hit only in places easily hidden by clothing.

"I won't lie to you, Matt," Liz said. "This kid is a hothead and has a massive attitude problem. He shows no respect for authority and is especially aggressive to anyone of the male gender. You're going to have your hands full. But, deep down, I know it's not too late for him. He's scared and hurting. The fighting and tough-guy act is the only thing in his life he thinks he can control."

Listening to her assessment, I knew exactly why she felt I was the big brother he needed. That file could have been about me and would have looked pretty much identical, minus the foster care part.

She looked up at me expectantly, waiting for my answer.

"When do I meet the little monster?" I finally asked, getting a huge smile from her in return.

"He's suspended until Wednesday because of fighting, but I'm sure he'll sneak back over since he knows I'm leaving. That kid loves basketball and plays nonstop. I'll make sure Ms. Covington knows who to look for and introduces you two."

Liz shuffled the papers into the file and stood to get back to work.

"So what's this lady like, anyway?"

She turned and leaned against her desk. "She's young, comes from a dynasty family with tremendous connections, and is exactly what this place needs right now."

I shook my head. "No way. You are what this place needs. I can't believe you're leaving. Hartsford must have lost his mind."

Liz sighed and returned to the couch. "I'm going to tell you something, Matt, and if you repeat it, I'll have you flogged."

I nodded, waiting.

"I haven't been happy here in months. When Sam approached me with this project, I was thrilled. It needed strong hands and my hard-nosed personality. But now that it's running so well, what the center needs is investors, donations, and volunteers. I have a laundry list of needs and no money. My duties went from drywalling to phone calls and charity events, and I'm miserable. I'm not a sweet talker, nor am I politically correct. Leaving is my choice. Don't ever doubt that."

"So where are you headed?"

"I've taken a position at a rehab center in Raleigh. State run, taxpayer funded, and a complete mess. Basically, it's right up my alley." She smiled and I could see the enthusiasm in her face. "I really am excited."

We both stood and I gave her a quick hug. "They have no idea what they've gotten themselves into," I teased. "But seriously, you'll be missed more than you know."

"Well, I better be!" She pushed me back and laughed right as a soft knock echoed through the building. Glancing at her watch, Liz smiled. "Right on time. I guess you'll get to meet Ms. Covington after all."

I followed Liz to the front doors, but stood back in the shadows. Despite hearing Liz's confession about resigning, I was still skeptical about this new lady. Even if she were some kind of fundraising genius, it would take more than smooth words to keep the Hartsford machine running.

The doors opened and Liz's voice echoed through the empty building. "Ms. Covington. It's nice to see you again."

"Oh, please, call me Grace."

Heat flushed my body and sweat prickled on the back of my neck. Liz stepped aside and Grace's eyes met mine. If she was startled, I couldn't tell, because her smile remained unchanged. I could instantly see why she excelled at working investors. Except for the few times I'd pushed too far, she had carried herself with an almost royal air. It was the quality that got under my skin so fast that night at the gym, and was now making me even crazier because I knew what a sweet, sensitive person she was behind the facade.

Carrying on with Grace, Liz pulled me closer. "This is Matt Holloway. He's one of our most dedicated volunteers. In fact, the little brother I just paired him with is at the top of our discussion list."

Grace embodied her name as she shook my hand with a regal ease. "I look forward to working with you, Mr. Holloway."

I aimlessly shook her hand, unable to put together a coherent thought, much less a reply.

Turning her attention back to Liz, Grace calmly said, "Ready when you are."

They both gave me a quick good-bye before Liz swept Grace along to the office. I watched them walk away and couldn't help but stare at their differences. I'd normally find the skirt and jacket Grace wore to be pretentious, but she managed to look both sleek and sexy in the copper-hued getup. In her high heels, she stood a head taller than Liz, and the stilettos clicked rhythmically across the gym floor.

Grace oozed femininity and her warm, floral perfume lingered in the air long after they'd disappeared into the office, closing the door behind them.

I felt an inexplicable need to curse as I slammed the metal doors behind me. Looking up to the heavens, I threw my arms in the air. "Is this your idea of a joke?"

Grace was everywhere. In just a few days, she had managed to infiltrate my gym, church, friends, and now the Hartsford Center. Worse, this need to know her and protect her was beginning to take root. Feelings I hadn't had toward a girl in nine years. Dangerous feelings.

I threw my bike into gear, swallowing the guilt of my bitterness toward God, and drove straight to The Storm. Only one thing could calm the hurricane raging inside me—an hour alone in a room called Apocalypse.

CHAPTER 6

GRACE

I tried not to feel overwhelmed as Liz handed me stack after stack of files—one for each of the registered children and one for their assigned big brothers or sisters.

The system appeared to run exceptionally well. Every person who came through the doors had to check in with a staff member and get an ID tag. Each unregistered child received a guest pass that could be upgraded to a permanent one if he or she followed the rules for ten consecutive visits.

Liz explained that access to the basketball courts, game room, and TV was the only incentive the kids needed to follow the rules.

"We have a zero tolerance policy here, Grace. After three violations, the child will be banned for six months. Consistency is key."

"How do you enforce your decision once a kid is banned?" I asked, wondering if I was equipped to toss out an unruly child.

"There are three staff members besides you who are here from open to close—our activities coordinator and two counselors. All three of them have extensive takedown training and concealed handgun licenses, and they're all ready to react if things get out of hand. In the five years I've been here, we've only had to resort to force one time. Once the kids realized we were serious, they stopped pushing."

I swallowed hard, trying not to look terrified. "None of the parents have complained?"

Liz stared at me for a second. "Most of these kids don't have involved parents. If we happen to have a boy or girl from a decent home, the parents are usually grateful their kids have a safe place to come to after school and during the summers. We had some protesters from around the city when they first found out we were going to carry firearms, but Sam held his ground, knowing we had to create a safe place for these kids. The zealots eased off when Sam reminded them it was private property and he could have them arrested."

I simply nodded.

"Grace, you shouldn't have to deal with anything like that. The Hartsford Center is nationally recognized now and loved by the community. I know your strengths are more political, so embrace those. We need finesse now, not a pit bull like me."

Liz smiled warmly at me before patting my hand. I wasn't sure what I had expected from her. Maybe bitterness or condescension, but she had shown neither, only a desire for me to succeed. Her faith in me was encouraging and just what I needed to calm the storm of uncertainty that was beginning to churn in my gut.

"Okay, well, we've pretty much gone through all the boring stuff. Do you want to meet the rest of the staff and some of the kids? Most will be here by now."

I looked down at my watch and couldn't believe the time. The morning had flown by at lightning speed. "Wow, time just disappeared. How do you get it all done?"

Liz stood and stretched. "The center doesn't open until nine, so I have about three uninterrupted hours between dawn and chaos.

Oh, before I forget, you are never to be here alone after dark. We close at eight, and after cleanup, all of us walk out to our cars together. No one stays . . . ever. Mornings are quiet, though, so as long as you lock the doors behind you, it's safe to come before opening."

Cringing a little, I realized I would need to start going to bed earlier. I'd never been much of a morning person. "No problem. What time does the staff get here?"

"It depends, but usually by eight."

Following Liz out of the office, I was struck by the difference a few hours could make. The once-quiet building bellowed with yells, laughter, and the sound of sneakers scooting across the gym floor. Boys and girls of every race filled the bleachers to watch the two teams chase after the ball. The game room was also in full swing as both TVs blared, battling each other for dominance.

Taking it all in, my heart raced. *Did I even bring tennis shoes?*

Liz tugged at my arm, and we walked around the perimeter of the gym to stop at one of the other staff offices.

A tall, burly man stood to greet us and then approached with a smile. His smooth face glistened like polished ebony, and his confident expression made me think he was someone who could stay composed even during the worst crisis. He was intimidating in stature, but the kindness in his eyes steadied my nerves. "Ms. Covington, I presume? I'm Darius, but you'll also hear the kids call me Coach D."

I shook his hand, hoping the smile on my face would mask my anxiety. "Please, call me Grace."

"Darius runs all the daily operations and makes sure the kids stay in line." Liz turned to him. "Speaking of which, I need a list of all your expected expenses and a wish list for the rest of the year. I want Grace to have a good handle on our needs before she starts pushing for donations."

"You got it, boss. Grace, we're really happy to have you."

Feeling his genuine warmth, I found myself starting to relax. Liz also introduced me to the counselors, who were equally gracious. Either Liz put them on their best behavior beforehand, or all my fears were unfounded. My age didn't seem to be a factor, as everyone regarded me with unearned respect.

"Everyone is so nice," I said as we left the last office.

Liz proudly swept her gaze across the center. "Yeah, we've got a great staff here. You shouldn't have any problems."

Before we moved on to the kid areas, I stopped her. "May I ask why you're leaving? You obviously love this place and it loves you."

Liz looked around and for a brief moment I thought I saw tears, but they quickly disappeared. "My time here is over, Grace. I've done all I can for these kids. It's your turn now."

A sense of pride and ownership filled me. "I won't let you down."

"It's not me you have to worry about. Don't let these kids down." She looked around the boisterous building again.

"I won't."

As we approached the game room, I tried to get my beating heart to settle. The minute we walked through the door, the room went silent and twenty pairs of eyes were suddenly on me.

"Kids, this is Ms. Covington. She is going to be the new director at the center."

Two of the girls approached me.

"How do you get your hair so shiny?" one asked while the other leaned down to look at my shoes.

"Do those hurt your feet? I've only seen shoes like that in magazines."

Soon more kids found the courage to approach, each asking similar questions about my clothes, hair, or makeup. One boy who couldn't have been more than six told me I smelled like flowers, and another asked if I would be his girlfriend.

Trying my best to give each one of them some attention, I found myself repeating "Thank you" and explaining that I was too old to be the girlfriend of anyone there, and promising to paint a few of the girls' nails later in the week. After several minutes, Liz shooed them off and ushered me to the next room. The kids in the TV room had a similar reaction, although I noticed one little boy attempting to duck behind the couch while periodically sending hateful stares in our direction.

When we left the room, Liz leaned over to me and whispered, "The one by the couch, that's Marcus. He's supposed to be suspended, but I figure I'll ignore it if he behaves. Matt should be by later, and I want those two connected as soon as possible."

Just the mention of Matt's name sent my pulse into overdrive. Trying to sound nonchalant as we passed by the bleachers, I pried a little. "So Matt has been volunteering for a while?"

"Three years now. His little brother is one of our success stories. So many of these kids get sucked into gangs or juvie by the time they get to high school. Derrick, Matt's kid, just graduated and will be attending NC State in the fall. Writing Derrick's reference letter for college was one of the most rewarding things I've done on the job. Great kid, that one."

I wanted to ask more questions but stopped when we heard a loud, suggestive whistle behind us and an, "Oh, baby, you are fine, girl."

Liz whipped her head around to find the culprit, but Darius was already on it, blowing his whistle to stop the game and address the crowd.

"This is Ms. Covington," he explained in a loud, authoritative voice. "She is the new director here and you will address her appropriately. If I hear any disrespectful or suggestive comments, including those among yourselves, you will be sent home for the day, no excuses. Do you understand?"

As "yes, sir" flowed through the crowd, Darius blew his whistle again, putting the ball back in play.

Liz continued walking and I followed, trying to act as unaffected as she appeared to be. In fact, Liz was like a stone wall. Nothing seemed to bother her or get under her skin. I'd been close to tears at least five times since we'd begun our walk around the center. Sam had said I would fall in love; I thought he meant with the job. Now I can see he meant with the kids.

The day continued with much of the same fury as when it had started. Between steady knocks on the door and numerous phone calls, we somehow found the time to go over all the files Liz had organized. When I asked about investor information, she winced.

"Grace, I have very little to give you on that one. Sam has fronted all the expenses to date."

"There are no other investors?" I was shocked. In just the little time I had been there, I could see that a place like Hartsford took a lot of money to keep operating. "Have you contacted local businesses? Organized fund-raisers?"

Liz smiled and stood. "That's why you're here, Grace. And with that, I am going to leave this place in your capable hands."

"You're leaving? Now?" I was starting to panic.

"You will never find your place while I'm here. Best we keep this transition short and sweet. I left you all my information, so if anything comes up, don't hesitate to call."

I wanted to hug her, hold on for dear life. Instead, I shook her hand and thanked her. Liz wished me luck before grabbing the box on her desk and heading out the door. I peeked through the blinds that shielded the office windows from the onlookers in the gym and saw that Liz didn't even stop to say good-bye to anyone.

Taking a deep breath, I looked around at the small office that now belonged to me. I allowed myself two minutes to cry, pray, and settle down. Then I stood, opened the door, and began putting the files back into the cabinet, organizing them slightly differently than Liz had.

When I picked up Matt's file, I hesitated. Liz had mentioned his past to me, but we didn't have time to go over details. He was one of the easy ones, she said, and moved on to more demanding volunteers.

Unable to stop myself, I opened the folder, noticing first a picture of him that looked like it was only a few years old. I ran my thumb over his handsome face, and then scolded myself before reading the background report.

What I saw surprised me. He had been arrested at sixteen for breaking and entering, along with theft of personal property. After two years in a juvenile detention center, he moved to Asheville. The addresses listed showed he had lived in the Raintree Apartments for two years, then moved to the Northside Apartments for a few years before settling at his current residence on Spruce Street.

The sound of a throat clearing startled me, causing the file to slip from my fingers. I looked up and saw Matt in the doorway. Moving swiftly, he had the file in his hand before I even reacted. He glanced at the papers for a second before handing them back to me, his face hardening.

"Find anything interesting in there, Duchess?"

Taking the file with shaking hands, I tried to explain. "I-I wasn't trying to pry. I just—" He raised an eyebrow at me. "Okay, yes, I was curious. I'm sorry."

Matt sat on the couch casually, stretching out his long arms. "You trying to decide if I'm good enough for Marcus? Liz didn't have any concerns."

Again, Matt had chosen to assume the worst about me. "No, of course not. I just picked it up to take a peek. No ulterior motive, despite what you're thinking."

"What am I thinking?" Hard and calm, his expression gave me nothing.

"Heck if I know, but you're always thinking something."

Matt leaned forward and lowered his elbows to his knees to glare at me intently. "I'm thinking you're in way over your head, Duchess. I'm thinking you don't know the first thing about the horrors these kids live through every day."

I wouldn't cry. Not in front of him. Luckily, a knock rapped against the door, and one of the older boys entered with a stricken look on his face.

"Ms. Covington, I crashed into the bleachers and my back hurts so bad. Can you take a look?" He hobbled and gripped his side.

Determined to show Matt my qualifications, I gingerly checked him over, noting that his skin was without even a scratch.

"Looks like you're just fine. Give it a little while. If it still hurts, we'll check again."

The boy beamed and turned to give me a big hug. "Thanks, Ms. Covington." Then he left.

Looking smugly at Matt, I crossed my arms. His agitation startled me as he bolted off the chair to shut my door.

"What was that?" he demanded. "How many other boys have hugged you like that today?"

Shocked by his reaction, I stammered, "N-none. Why?"

"Why? Are you really that naive? Fourteen-year-old boys don't come in here to get their boo-boos checked. They come in here to cop a feel and think dirty thoughts while they hug you. How do you expect to gain their trust if you let them disrespect you like that?"

Confusion muddied my thoughts. *Since when is affection disrespectful? It was just a hug.*

"A little bit of free advice, Duchess. Save the affection for boys who have yet to reach puberty." With that, he stormed out of my office.

CHAPTER 7

MATT

I saw the little punk the minute I left Grace's office and pointed at him. "You. Come here." He was laughing and hand-slapping his buddies, no doubt getting a status boost for his performance. Slowly he made his way down the bleachers to stand in front of me.

"What?" he demanded, holding his chin rigid.

I grabbed his ID badge, making note that his name was Trey. "Go home. You're done for the day."

His arrogant smile faltered. "What? Why? I didn't do anything."

"Don't give me that. You know exactly what you did. That crap isn't going to fly around here. You got me? Now get your stuff and go home, and tell your little friends over there the same will happen to them if they pull that garbage with Ms. Covington."

Trey shot me a hateful glance. "What's your deal, man? You tryin' to get with her or something?"

Glaring harder at the kid, I pointed to the door. "Out, before I make it permanent."

Cursing under his breath, Trey grabbed his backpack and spoke to his friends. They quit smiling when they saw my enraged face. Soon he was out the door, hitting the frame in anger on his way.

I shouldn't have gotten this upset over a punk kid. I shouldn't have cared that she was being worked over, but for some reason I did. I hadn't blinked at a woman in nine years and now one was consuming me.

Darius approached as I stood, arms crossed, taking deliberate breaths to calm down.

"You're going to need to cut them a little slack, at least for the first couple of days. Most of these kids have never seen someone like her in person. One little girl even asked me if she was a movie star." He glanced toward Grace's door, which was now shut. "She'll learn her way."

"You just make sure she's never alone here. Word is going to get around real quick, and I have a feeling we're going to have an influx of teenage boys." Still trying to steady my breath, I nodded in the direction of her office. "You may also want to suggest she wear more appropriate attire while she's here."

I immediately thought back to Grace's form-fitting skirt and high heels that showed off her long, lean legs. I sighed. It wasn't the outfit as much as it was the sharp contrast between her and Liz. That soft femininity combined with her vulnerability that she wore like an overcoat.

Darius laughed. "No way I'm touching that. If Liz didn't say anything, then I'm certainly not going to. Besides, maybe her fancy suits will finally get investors to pitch in."

I looked back at Darius, ready to change the subject. "Has Marcus been around today?"

"He's been hiding out in the TV room. Thinks we didn't notice him slip in. Liz said to let him be until you two had a chance to meet."

Nodding, I headed over to the busy room to meet my new little brother. I spotted Marcus immediately. He sat lounging on the far side of the room on one of the couches. He was a good-looking-enough kid, with smooth brown skin and short, coarse hair. His eyes, though, told his story. They had an edge in them, that animal wariness. I'd seen the look often enough in the mirror to recognize it. No doubt this kid would be a challenge.

Tapping a boy next to him to move, I sat down. Marcus glanced at me just for a second before his jaw went rigid.

"Where's your ID?" I asked casually, watching for his reaction.

"Listen, Jack, you don't work here. I don't have to answer to you." I had to hand it to him. Fear showed clear as day in his eyes, but his voice was full of attitude.

"My name isn't Jack. It's Matt. I'm your new big brother, although I was told you wouldn't be back until Wednesday."

Marcus narrowed his eyes at me and moved as far away as the couch would allow. "I don't need or want a big brother, especially some dude who looks like you."

"Well, that's not what I hear. Seems you're having difficulty staying out of trouble."

"Ms. Bailey didn't listen to my side of the story. He started it. I didn't have a choice. You know how it is, man, attack or be attacked."

"You always have a choice, Marcus. In this case, you chose to do something you knew would get you suspended. Now, as much as I'd like to get to know you, you're going to have to leave and come back on Wednesday when your suspension is over."

Marcus lurched up from the couch, his thin frame vibrating with rage. "Fine, whatever. I'll go. Some big brother you turned out to be!" He stormed out the door under the watchful eyes of every-one around him.

I shut off the TV before addressing the room. "Every one of you knew he was in here without an ID. If you want this place to stay safe, you'll have to do your part. Next time this happens, I'm sending all of you home. Understand?"

Muffled "yes, sirs" filled the air, so I switched the TV on again. I hated to send Marcus home when it was obvious he needed to be at the center, but if I broke the rules for one of them, they would all try the same. Discipline and consistency were what made Hartsford so effective.

I glanced one more time at Grace's office before walking out the front doors. These kids were going to eat her alive.

Will stood up, hoisting his backpack, when he saw me walk into the gym. His shift was from three until I showed up, which was usually by six.

"Hey, Matt. You're booked solid again tonight."

I let out a heavy sigh. That wasn't going to work. "Listen, are you interested in picking up some more hours this summer?"

Will's face lit up. "You bet. I'm saving for a car."

"Good. Plan on staying until nine from now on. I'm going to be spending more time at the Hartsford Center, so no more evening bookings. I'll free up some time in the mornings. In fact, I want you to call and cancel the rest of my appointments for the week. Give them each ten dollars off their next session because of the inconvenience."

Will seemed stunned as he set down his backpack. "Okay."

I understood his confusion. Never once in the time he'd worked there had I canceled an appointment. I assured myself it had everything to do with Marcus and not the dark-haired beauty who now ran the place.

I started setting up for my appointments that night while Will made the phone calls. After his last call, I approached the desk again. "One more thing before you take off. I want you to look up a Devon Banks and see if he's still been coming here. If he has, let me know what time."

A few minutes later, Will handed me a slip of paper with some notes scribbled on it. "He comes around lunchtime, usually to use Apocalypse."

Apocalypse was a private room with one punching bag and a stereo system. Knowing the type of rage that existed in his patients, Bruce had created the room to offer a place where they could lose control and get out their aggression without hurting anyone.

I thanked Will and set a reminder in my phone to swing by at lunchtime tomorrow, although I doubted I would forget that detail. The rest of the evening flashed by in a haze of sweat and testosterone until my phone beeped, indicating it was eight thirty.

Turning to Cody, my eager trainee, I halted our grappling. "Listen, I've got to take care of something tonight. Just go ahead and do three miles on the treadmill and I'll add thirty minutes to our next session, okay?"

His face fell but then brightened a little. "Summer tryouts are next week for the varsity wrestling team. Do you think I'm ready?"

I looked at him. Cody had a warrior's heart, but his body had yet to catch up. He'd lost some weight since we started working together, but he still had a good forty pounds to go. A string of bullying had brought him to me four months ago. Overweight, defeated, and spiraling into self-loathing, Cody begged me to take a chance on him. Since then I'd tried to do more than just physically shape him. Using Bruce's techniques, I pushed and pushed until Cody experienced enough victories to make his confidence soar.

Careful of my words, I slapped his back. "Well, I think you could be, but I bet if you wait until fall, you will do more than just make the team. I think you'll wow them."

Cody was thoughtful and then smiled. "Okay, I'll wait."

"Good call. All right, I'll be back soon."

With that I grabbed my keys and headed straight to the Hartsford Center. Parking off in the shadows, I waited until the four employees came out the doors and then locked them. Grace stood talking to Darius for a few minutes before getting into her car. As she drove out of the parking lot, I casually followed, being sure to keep my distance.

She stopped at a drugstore and then headed to her apartment. I watched as she parked her car and then leaned in to grab her bags. Shaking my head, I noticed she never once looked around to check her safety before opening the door to her apartment. I heard the alarm click on her car and then watched as she shut her door. I swung through the parking lot to make sure no one was casing out her place. There was a gaggle of drunks bumping to music from their car, but they seemed too absorbed in the party to notice Grace. After watching them for a few minutes, I finally felt comfortable enough to head back to the gym.

That night the nightmares came again.

The smell of burnt grease and cigarettes turned my stomach as I clocked out for the night. I hated this job.

Busing tables at the nastiest dive in town wasn't exactly how I'd pictured my life, but they paid me under the table, so I took the work.

Sadness hit. I missed my mom. Had it really only been six months ago that she died?

Refusing to spiral down that hole again, I thought of Maggie. She was my future now. We would make a life for ourselves. One better than what we both grew up with. That jerk would never hurt her again.

Smiling, I pushed harder on the gas, my sad excuse for a car puttering along. I couldn't wait to see her. Couldn't wait to officially make her mine. Eighteen would come soon enough and we'd be married and get out of here for good.

Turning the lock, I pushed the apartment door open. Maggie scrambled half-naked off the couch.

She wasn't alone.

The dude she had with her raised his hands. "I don't want any trouble."

Driven by a rage I didn't know existed, I had the guy pinned and wailing as I beat him senseless. After throwing him out of the apartment, I slammed the door and turned to Maggie. She screamed at me, asked what I expected when I left her alone all day.

"Someone has to pay the bills!" I yelled back, still too enraged to see straight. "Unless this is your new day job, Maggie. Is that it? Are you selling yourself now?"

She hollered at me again and barreled forward, crazily slapping my face and chest. I tried grabbing her wrists to stop the attack, but she continued to curse and beat me until my anger snapped.

As if in slow motion, I whipped my hand across her face and watched as she crumpled to the ground in tears. Horror and regret instantly engulfed me. I looked down and saw my father's hand at the end of my arm. Terrified, I reached out to Maggie's crumpled body only to see Grace's teary blue eyes staring up at me.

I heard myself scream "NO!" as I bolted out of bed. My breathing was strained and my chest ached as I gasped for air. This couldn't be happening. I wouldn't go back there . . . not now, not ever. I had to get Grace out of my head. I couldn't care, couldn't feel. It was too dangerous.

My peaceful, calm life was disappearing before my very eyes and all I could do was desperately fall on my knees and pray that the Lord would save me from myself.

CHAPTER 8

GRACE

I hadn't seen Matt in three days. I should have been glad, since the last time we spoke he pretty much said I wasn't cut out to do this job. Even so, I still found myself watching for him and wondering why he'd disappeared.

Marcus returned yesterday and I got my chance to officially speak to him. He hardly said a word or made eye contact, but Darius told me that was pretty normal behavior from him. I had been spoiled with how all the other kids seemed to treat me with awe and even reverence. Marcus looked as if he hated me from the get-go. Liz was right. He and Matt were the perfect match.

I rolled my neck as I sat, trying desperately to work out the pain that had been there all morning. My poor excuse for a bed had deflated on me in the middle of the night and I woke up achy all over. Oh well, I guess the couch would be my bed for a while. The secondhand piece wasn't much, but the board I put under the cushions really helped the sagging.

Rubbing my aching neck, I realized that today was the first time I'd missed home. I longed for a comfortable bed and hot, luxurious bath. Not the nasty, chipping, rusted-out shower stall I used every day. Remorse stopped my pity party. It hadn't even been a week, and there I was thinking of what I left behind. Shameful.

The sound of someone approaching yanked me from my thoughts. I winced in pain after turning my head too quickly to see who was there.

"Rough day?" Matt was leaning against the doorframe again, and I had to swallow the large lump that suddenly formed in my throat. *Did he have to always look so good?*

"More like rough night. My air mattress decided to spring a leak." I could hear the strain in my voice and prayed Matt didn't notice how nervous he made me.

He pushed off the door and strolled casually over to my desk. I tried not to watch him but failed miserably. His shirt hugged every muscle in his chest and arms, and the black design creeping down his forearm called to me, left questions that begged to be answered. What did it mean and why had he chosen it?

When he positioned himself next to me, I took a deep breath and tried to look like a professional and not some teenage groupie.

"May I?" His voice was soft as he placed his hands on the back of my neck. I could only nod for fear that my voice would give away how much his closeness affected me. Then all thought was gone as pain tore through my neck and down my back.

"Ouch!" I tried to pull away, but his strong hands kept me immobile.

"It will only hurt for a second."

Tears sprang to my eyes as the pain continued, but soon the ache gave way and all I could feel were Matt's skillful hands massaging my neck and shoulders. I relaxed into him, forgetting for a moment that he hated me or that I wanted to cry every time he insulted me. My head fell back, strands of hair brushing along his solid stomach. I closed my eyes, enjoying the forbidden connection far more than I should have.

The massage stopped abruptly. Seconds later he was on the other side of my desk with his hands shoved deep into his pockets.

I stood, rolling my neck to ensure the pain was gone. It was. "Thank you. Where did you learn to do that?"

He was still in complete control, while I was a mass of jittery hormones. "I wrestle a lot, which means I'd either have to hire a full-time chiropractor or learn a few tricks. You really should get yourself a decent mattress."

I willed myself to toughen up. "So I met Marcus yesterday. I got a growl and a grumble out of him, but I guess that's a start."

Matt smirked slightly. "I'm going to have my hands full with that one." He walked over to the couch and sat on the armrest. "I'm still trying to figure out where to begin."

It was unspoken, but I sensed a truce between the two of us, as if his willingness to talk about Marcus showed his support in some way. Feeling empowered, I walked around to the front of my desk and leaned against it, facing him. I tried to match his relaxed stance, but immediately missed the familiar barrier when his eyes drifted down the length of me and back up again. His face gave nothing away and I forced myself to continue.

"I called his aunt yesterday just to talk and introduce myself."

One eyebrow shot up in surprise. "How did it go?"

"Great, actually. She's a wonderful lady and I could tell she loves Marcus very much. She works the swing shift six days a week, so she thanked me for giving Marcus a safe place to be." Emotion gripped my heart when I remembered her appreciation and tears, but I quickly pulled myself together.

"Anyway, she said that he's become more and more withdrawn over the past several months, but he won't tell her what's going on. They used to be close, but now he hardly talks to her. She was hoping maybe you could break through to him. He hasn't had any positive male influence in his life, ever."

Matt watched me so intensely that I couldn't stand still any longer. I started to fidget, pretending I was looking for something on my desk. For what, I had no idea, but I needed to get away from that stare. Finally I saw the notes I'd taken while talking with Marcus's aunt and grabbed them.

"I can make a copy if you'd like." I held the notes out to him.

Matt walked toward me slowly, but didn't take the paper from my trembling hand. Instead, his gaze fell over me like a caress and I found myself wanting desperately to touch him.

"You were smart to make the call, Grace. I wouldn't have thought to include her."

His words brought an immediate smile, partly because they were kind, but mostly because he said my name in the sweetest way. We were inches apart now and I couldn't stop myself from glancing at his lips. *Would they feel as soft as they look?*

My heart thudded against my chest as we stood there, silently watching each other. He stepped closer and adrenaline surged through me. Ever so slowly, his hand touched mine, removing the paper from my grip, and all I could think of was closing the gap between our bodies.

The shrill of the phone caused me to jump.

Matt immediately broke contact and walked out the door without a word. I stood, paralyzed, scandalously wishing he'd done more than just look at me.

The phone continued its demanding chirp until I reconnected with reality and grabbed the receiver.

"Hartsford Children's Center, this is Grace."

"Gracie Belle! How are you?"

I couldn't help but smile at Sam's delighted tone. Only my family and close friends ever called me Gracie Belle.

"Hi, Sam. I'm good. Just trying to get myself settled in."

"Excellent! I spoke to Liz earlier and she thinks you are going to be fantastic." Somehow I doubted Liz used those words, but the praise still made me smile. "So what's first on your agenda?"

Despite his friendly demeanor and our close relationship, Sam was still my boss, so I immediately went over some of my observations and ideas.

"This place runs great, but we're busting at the seams. Darius thinks we may have to turn some kids away if the trend continues."

"How is Darius? It's been a while since I've been down there."

"He's working too much, for starters. He's here every day for at least twelve hours with no assistance. If we don't hire him some help, then I'm afraid he's going to run out of steam."

"Darius? Not likely. I've never met a more dedicated man. Are the counselors complaining?"

"No, but there's two of them. Regardless, we've got to get more staff in here. I was thinking, if we could share hours, maybe we could start opening the doors on Sunday, even do some church services here."

"Won't that ruin our chances at those federal grants you told me about?"

I hesitated for a second, not wanting to sound argumentative. "Sam, your firearm policy already disqualifies you, so it really doesn't matter. Also, I know you don't want to hear this, but we need to renovate the rest of the building."

I could hear Sam quietly breathing on the other end while he processed everything I had just thrown at him. When the center opened, they only renovated half of the building, leaving the back of it closed off. Darius had walked me through it the other day, and I knew the renovation would be a million-dollar project.

"Gracie, there is no money outside of the operations budget. I'm sorry. We had two investors fall through last year, and I've already committed to the new center in New York. Without that grant, we may even need to cut our hours, not extend them. I'll be honest with you, the center's future is rocky."

"What if I could raise the money? Would you give me the go-ahead to hire two new positions?"

"Of course. In fact, if you could get the money for the renovations, I'd gladly come down and help you oversee it. Don't get your hopes up too high, though. You know I want that place to succeed, but by now the operation should be self-sustaining. The city loves us, but they have yet to support us."

Excitement shot through me. "That's all I needed to hear, Sam. We're going to get that money. You just wait."

I heard his bellowing laugh. "Your unending optimism is exactly why I hired you. Just let me know what you need on my end."

"I definitely will, and thank you, Sam, for believing in me."

"You know I always have."

I hung up the phone feeling total elation. After spending the next hour going through figures and the wish list that Darius gave me, I circled the bottom line with a red marker: *$2,000,000*. It would be a challenge, but I knew I could do it with the right strategy. Grabbing the phone again, I dialed the one person I knew who was capable of raising that kind of money.

"Mom? I need your help."

CHAPTER 9

MATT

I needed to be shot.

No, I needed to be strung up on the highest mountain so the world could see what a complete idiot I am. I almost kissed Grace! At the center . . . with her door open . . . right in front of hundreds of kids. Luckily, no one seemed to notice us, or the way I bolted from her office, barely able to catch my breath.

Three days away from the center should have been enough to get my head screwed on straight. I had even traveled back to my hometown and driven by my mother's disgusting apartment in hopes of putting the past to rest for good. It was the first time I had seen it since that horrible day. Nothing had changed except it looked more run-down.

I drove away before the nausea made it to my throat, remembering the bright yellow police tape that had been placed in an X across the door. Next I went by my old apartment, the one my mother moved us into when we ran from my father the first time. The closure I'd hoped for didn't happen. Maggie still haunted me, and the nightmares of my mother's death were getting worse and terrifyingly vivid.

Finding an empty spot in the bleachers, I lowered my head to my hands. I was losing control. I could feel it in my training and even with Bruce. I'd been testy and short-tempered, lashing out for no reason.

Yet there I was, drawn to Grace, when I knew I needed to stay away.

A hand settled on my shoulder. "You all right, man?"

I looked up to see Darius watching me, his eyes full of concern. We had known each other awhile and never once had he seen me so disheartened.

Standing up to stretch, I found my center like Bruce taught me to do. "I'm good. Just tired."

"It's open gym right now, and Marcus has already started running his mouth. The boys are getting agitated, so you may want to get over there."

Glancing at the little boy who was taunting everyone around him, I couldn't help but smile. That's what I used to do whenever I felt afraid or insignificant. Heck, I was still doing that with Grace, so I obviously hadn't grown out of the defensive behavior.

Jogging over to him, I jumped up for the rebound before Marcus had a chance to get the ball.

"Hey, man!" he yelled as the boys around him snickered.

My scowl silenced them. "You boys find another hoop. Marcus and I have this one."

Disgusted, the boys moved over to one of the other five hoops in the gym. I could see why they were annoyed. The gym was packed.

"I don't want to play with you," Marcus grunted, folding his arms.

I locked eyes with him. "Then go sit out." I held his stare, unblinking and direct, until Marcus finally looked away and squirmed.

"Fine. Make it, take it, and I get the first ball."

I swallowed a laugh at his annoyed expression and tossed the ball through the hoop. Marcus caught it and then backed up to start the game. Standing in front of him, I wondered what he was thinking. He was small for his age and I stood at six foot two, with long arms poised and ready to swat the ball away at any moment. His determination won out, and like a raging bull, he charged and had the ball through the hoop before I'd even reacted. I grabbed the ball and tossed it to him, getting ready again. *Time to pay attention.*

After three straight shots, I finally blocked his attempt and got the ball. The boys from earlier started laughing when I sank two straight from the free throw line.

"You gonna stand there and shoot the whole time like a girl or actually play the game?" Marcus taunted.

I shrugged before landing my third perfect shot. "I can't help it if you're vertically challenged. Why don't you at least attempt to block me?"

Marcus threw the ball back at me, his face contorted with rage. I dribbled twice and he charged. Knowing immediately that he was thinking with his emotions and not his brain, I easily sidestepped him for a layup.

He cursed and the other boys laughed harder, catching my attention. I glanced up just in time to hear Marcus tell them very colorfully to back off. When they responded in much the same way, Marcus charged in their direction. I was on him in three easy steps and hauled him back to the side.

"You need to calm down," I hissed in his ear as I held him.

He struggled against my firm grip. "Get off of me! Don't touch me!

When we were a safe distance from the court, I let him go. Tears pooled in his hard eyes. "I don't want you to touch me." Marcus's breath was gone. Panic sweat slicked his skin. "I don't like being touched."

I knew how he felt. It took years before a man could touch me without me wanting to jump or throw a punch. I did my best to make my voice calm, nonthreatening. "I'm not going to hurt you. You lost your cool. If you get in another fight, your next suspension will be two weeks. Is that what you want?"

Marcus swiped his eyes with the back of his hand before throwing his ID on the floor. "What I want is for you to leave me alone!" Then he was out the door in a sprint.

I grabbed his ID and placed it on the counter before going after him. He made it across the street to a bus stop and then slumped down on the bench. I gave him a minute to collect himself before sitting down next to him.

"Sheesh, man, take a hint." He scooted as far away as the bench would allow.

"I get why you don't want to be touched, Marcus." My voice was calm. "My old man, he knew that I hated him touching me, and so he'd mess with my head, just to see what I would do. Sometimes he'd pat my cheek, smiling when I flinched, and other times it was a backhand, just to let me know who was still in charge."

I waited for his reaction. He glanced my way, making eye contact, but didn't say a word.

"Why don't you come back in, finish the game at least? It beats sitting out here in the hot sun."

"You gonna stop messing with me and actually play the game?" He jutted his chin defiantly.

"I don't know. Are you gonna stop playing like a crazy person and get your head straight?"

Marcus squared his shoulders and turned to me. "It's called playing with heart."

"People like you and me, we've got more heart than most. We're driven by it, but we can be ruined by it, too. What you have to do is think." I tapped my head for emphasis. "Then, your opponent has nothing on you."

Marcus stood and crossed his arms. "Where's your old man now?"

"He's dead."

"You kill him?"

"Nope." I stood and headed back toward the center. Marcus trailed behind but was following me. It wasn't a huge victory, but at least it was a start.

I spent the rest of the evening at the center. Marcus and I played two more rounds of ball before Darius closed the court for intramurals. When I asked Marcus why he wasn't on a team, he just shrugged and headed off to the game room. Not wanting to push the little trust that we finally had, I gave him some space and busied myself helping Darius referee the games.

Grace spent most of the evening in her office on the phone. I tried not to look, but couldn't help but glance in when no one was watching. She joined us for the last game, though, and found a seat on the bleachers. Warmth spread through me when the kids surrounded her and she talked with each of them. Her smile was pure and sunny and never failed to light up her face or set off the dimples around her mouth. She affectionately ruffled the kids' hair or patted them on the back. I was struck by her ease with them, as if she'd known each of these kids their whole life.

I rubbed my hands over my face, felt the scrape of a day's growth of beard, and reminded myself again that I needed to stay away.

Darius blew the whistle and yelled, "Time-out!" bringing me back from my thoughts.

"Yo, ref, that guy totally fouled me! Are you even paying attention?" a kid yelled as he brushed past me in a fit of anger. Normally, I'd take the boy aside and have words with him, but he was right. The minute Grace stepped out of her office, my head left the game.

"Watch your tone," was all I said as I jogged off to grab a cup of water.

Struggling to keep my eyes off Grace the rest of the game, I focused on the players. The game ended up coming down to the last second, when the same kid who yelled at me sunk a three-point shot before the buzzer went off. His team stormed the court and lifted him up with cheers. His face beamed with pride, and his joy was contagious. These kids didn't get many moments of victory.

I wondered if Grace saw it, too, that look on his face. Hope. It was the look that kept me coming back to this place. The look I prayed I would get to see on Marcus's face one day.

My eyes sought her out, only to find her high-fiving the superstar and laughing. The winning coach joined them and then sent the boy back to the team. I expected the man to follow, but he lingered, standing much too close to Grace for my comfort. I'd met him before. He was a nice enough guy, but in that moment I wanted to rip his hand off, especially when I saw him lightly touch her arm.

Seeing the kids huddled by the bench, I blew my whistle. "Coach, finish up with your boys so we can close up."

He touched Grace's arm again before jogging back to the bench.

I knew what was happening the minute my stomach filled with heat, and I closed my eyes to get control of myself. Hearing Bruce's voice in my head, I went through the steps to calm my erratic heartbeat and stop my shaking hands. On the fifth deep breath, I finally felt peace return and was able to open my eyes again. Just my luck, Grace was the first thing I saw and she was staring right at me, no doubt seeing my weakness. When she saw me notice, she quickly turned away and scurried back to her office, leaving me to start the process all over again.

CHAPTER 10

GRACE

Matt was still at the center, helping with the final cleanup for the night. It was the first time he'd stayed that long, and I couldn't help but wonder if the moment we shared earlier had anything to do with it. My mind ached to talk to him, get to know him, explain this crazy infatuation I had with him. The way he watched me all night had me believing he felt the pull, too.

"You ready?" Darius asked as he hit the gym lights.

"Yes. Just let me grab my bag." I ran to my office and gathered my stuff before turning off all the lights. The rest of the crew was waiting for me by the front doors with Matt. My heart picked up pace as I approached them, wondering again why he was still there.

We exited and Darius made sure the doors were secure for the night. Tired of feeling so much anxiety, I turned to Matt as we walked to our cars.

"I'm starving. Have you had dinner already?"

Surprise crossed his handsome features and he paused, no doubt considering whether he wanted my company, since I'm sure he knew whether he was hungry.

"If you don't want to, that's fi—"

He interrupted, glancing at my suit. "The place I have in mind is casual. I don't suppose you own a pair of jeans."

Only Matt could excite and infuriate me in one sentence. "Yes, I have jeans. Why don't you follow me to my apartment so I can change real quick."

He nodded and started his bike, waiting for me to get into my car. The picture of him straddling that huge motorcycle sent flurries in my stomach. I wondered what it would be like to ride with him.

I pulled out of the parking lot, silently scolding myself. I was crushing hard on a guy who barely tolerated my presence. A guy who embodied the words *dark* and *mysterious*. A guy who, to my dismay, I could not stop thinking about.

Matt was already off his bike before I opened the door to my apartment.

"You should really look around before you just open your door like that."

I turned to him, confused. "What do you mean?"

"I mean if someone is casing you or this place, you are a walking target. You should do a loop around the parking lot, make sure no one's following you. Always be aware of your surroundings. Aren't you from New York, Duchess? Didn't your parents ever teach you this stuff?"

He was mocking me again in that condescending tone of his. And how was I supposed to respond? Tell him the truth? That I had a driver until a week before I came to North Carolina? That my doorman opened my car door and escorted me inside every time I arrived home? Yeah, he'd have a field day with that one.

"We lived in a pretty safe area," I choked out instead, pushing hard at the door.

"Well, you don't anymore." He followed me in, glancing around at the disarray in my living room. The place was clean, but the sheets were still on the couch I had crawled onto at five that morning, hoping for at least an hour of restful sleep. If he noticed, he didn't say anything.

"I'll be just a second." I hurried off to my room, happy to escape his suffocating presence in my apartment. For some reason his being there made my home seem smaller, dingier. I knew he would notice every crack or broken tile, things I never saw until the day he and Jake helped me move.

Rushing around, I found a pair of jeans and a casual blue tank top. It was conservative and hung gently, so I hoped he wouldn't find the silky fabric too pretentious. The jeans were designer with fancy pockets, but there was nothing I could do about that. I owned expensive clothes, always had, and never before felt a need to apologize. But Matt made me feel as if wearing them marked one more strike against me. I exchanged my heels for some sandals and made a mad dash to the bathroom to touch up my makeup and brush my teeth. This wasn't a date, just two friends having dinner, yet I was more nervous than I had been four years ago when Stewart took me out for our first official night as a couple.

The lights above my vanity flickered, making me scowl. They had been doing that since I moved in, and the office manager had yet to get them fixed. I was half tempted to go to a hardware store and replace the silly lights myself.

Finally ready, I took a calming breath and headed back to the living room. Matt had found a seat on the couch, having moved aside my bedding, and was looking through one of my fashion magazines. I cringed internally, wishing I had a *National Geographic* or something equally impressive.

"Okay, I'm ready." He glanced up at me and then I noticed his mouth open slightly before it closed again. Two creases formed above his eyes as he stood, never taking his gaze off me.

"Your couch has seen better days."

"Huh?" I had been so lost in his eyes that I hadn't heard a word he said. They looked green just then, with only a slight blue hue.

"Your new bed," he explained, gesturing toward my run-down sofa. "That can't be comfortable."

"It's better than the floor." My curt tone was intentionally dismissive. I was tired of having to explain my choices. Matt followed me out the door and waited while I locked it behind me. Next thing I knew, he was straddling his bike again and offering me a helmet.

I glanced quickly at my Mercedes. "Y-you don't want to take my car?"

He grinned and my whole body responded. "That car doesn't really fit in where we're going. Come on, Duchess. I'll make sure you're safe. Unless you're worried about your hair."

Matt was toying with me now, waiting to see how I would react to riding with him. I tossed back my hair, grabbed the helmet, and took a seat behind him. He started up the monster machine and wrapped my arms tightly around his waist before taking off.

As he accelerated, my body tensed with fear and excitement. But soon I found his rhythm and was able to move with him along the curves. Being this close to him, I could smell his cologne and the shampoo on his hair. The scent was clean and masculine, yet so uniquely Matt that I wondered if he even knew how appealing it was. Any question I had about our connection was answered. The electricity between us was undeniable.

He stopped in front of an old building that had a lit-up sign flashing "Pit Stop." Except the second *t* was burned out, so it looked like "Pit S op" from the road. The parking lot was full of beat-up trucks and a few other bikes like Matt's.

"This place may not look like much, but they serve the absolute best barbecue in the state."

I nodded and Matt locked up our helmets before guiding me inside. The minute he pushed open the door, I was lambasted with the smell of smoked barbecue. The air felt about ten degrees warmer, and I realized why as soon as I saw the open-pit grill right outside the back doors. Long tables were covered with brown paper, and everyone sat on benches like they were all part of one big family.

My head snapped around at the sound of a shrill female voice. A girl no taller than five foot two was enveloping Matt in a huge hug.

"Matt Holloway! It's been way too long. Where you been hiding, my love?" She glanced at me and I tried not to scowl. "And who is this?" Her words were suggestive, making me blush.

Matt simply chuckled and released her. "Carol, this is Grace. She's new in town, and I figured she couldn't become a true North Carolinian until she had some of Max's famous brisket."

I had been holding my breath for his answer, eager to see how he would refer to me. Of course his response gave me nothing except the knowledge that once again Matt was warm, affectionate, and friendly with anyone who wasn't me.

"Ain't that the truth!" she agreed, flapping one hand with a flick of her wrist before handing us each a menu. Matt nudged my back a little so I would follow her, and we sat at the far end of one of the back tables. As he settled in across from me, I feared I would have no escape from his intense stare all night.

A few seats down were two huge men with overflowing plates and paper towels tucked in their shirts like bibs. I tried to glance away before they caught my shocked stare, but Matt noticed and started snickering.

"I told you it was the best barbecue in the state."

"I guess you come here often?" I asked.

Matt shrugged and smiled. He seemed relaxed in this environment and I silently prayed he'd stay that way the whole evening. "I used to. Bruce took me here when I first moved to town and we'd come for lunch at least once a week. Now we're both so busy it's hard to find the time."

I didn't know who Bruce was and wondered if I should ask. After a back-and-forth battle in my head, I just thought, *Forget it. Stop analyzing every word out of your mouth and relax!*

"Do you still get to hang out with him? Bruce, I mean."

Matt casually leaned forward on the table, removing some of the distance between us. "Bruce is my boss, so I pretty much see him every day."

The way Matt was positioned, I could clearly see the tattoo design on his forearm. The pattern made no sense to me. It twisted and curved sporadically, following no clear path. Matt noticed me staring, and the muscles along his forearm flexed.

I darted my eyes away, feeling slightly embarrassed for ogling him.

"I got it when I was sixteen. Body art was a way to express all the things going on in my head."

I studied the black ink for a moment before looking into his eyes, which had suddenly turned sad. "Why did you choose this one? There doesn't seem to be any sort of pattern to it."

"Exactly. It represented chaos."

I waited for more, but he didn't offer anything. "And the others?" I had seen some ink on his neck and a small line that was barely visible on his other arm when he had been wearing a T-shirt.

"The others were first. Little ones that represented my mood or state of mind. I got my last one right before I came to Asheville, a parting gift."

"What is it?" I didn't know when I'd become so bold, but knowing Matt, the defensive walls would go up again at any minute, and I wanted so desperately to understand him.

"A cross, right here." He pointed to his heart. Tears flooded my eyes. He was giving me a glimpse of himself, this man who had overcome mistakes and terrible circumstances. I wanted to know more, wanted to know every moment in his life that had turned him into the complex guy in front of me.

"You guys ready?" Carol interrupted the connection, a hand on her hip.

We hadn't even glimpsed the menu. "You pick for me," I offered, looking up again at Matt. His vulnerability was gone.

He gave our order and turned back to me when she left. "Now it's my turn. Why North Carolina?"

Surprised by his quick change of topic, I played with my rings as I answered, a nervous habit I had. I touched the empty space where there had once been an engagement ring, then quickly lowered my hands to my lap. "The job, of course."

"Yeah, I'm not buying it. Darius mentioned that Sam is starting a new center in New York, which is why funds are so tight. Why not just work up there with him?"

"Well, for one he didn't offer me that option. But truthfully, I wanted to get away from my family, try something new."

"Get away?" Matt asked, pondering my response. "You don't like your family?"

"Oh no, it's not that. My family is great. I just wanted to see if I could make it on my own, chart my own course." I smiled shyly at him, hoping he wouldn't make me feel like a spoiled little kid again.

He didn't. Instead, I almost melted from his warmth. "That takes a lot of guts, Grace. Most people spend their whole lives trying to achieve what you walked away from."

I loved it when he said my name. He only seemed to do so after I'd say something to impress him. "Thanks."

Our eyes met again, creating that surge of tension that so often choked out any coherent thought. Clearing my throat, I gazed around, trying to look at anything but Matt. "What about your parents? Do they live in North Carolina, too?" I knew from his background check that he was born about an hour away, but there was no information about his family.

Matt's warm expression disappeared and the hard wall was back with a fury. "Both my parents are dead." His voice held no inflection or sense of grief. The words just rolled off his tongue as if he were saying, "My parents are teachers." I immediately felt terrible for asking.

"Matt, I'm so sorry." I hope he could see that I meant it and that I wasn't downplaying the significance of his loss.

He just shrugged and changed the subject. Soon we were talking about the center and Marcus. All personal talk was over. But the divisive line between our two worlds had been crossed. He'd let me see past the armor around his soul, offered me only a glimpse. And like a drug, I wanted more.

CHAPTER 11

MATT

Grace was beautiful. Even with that small spot of barbecue sauce above her lip. In fact, it only added to her beauty because it made her seem real and not untouchable in her perfection. I made her laugh several times tonight and found myself drowning in the wonderful sound of it. She finally relaxed, and despite the warning bells ringing loudly in my head, I liked her ease.

With a slight brush of her napkin, the spot was gone and she sat back, holding her stomach.

"Oh my goodness, I'm stuffed. I've never tasted anything so delicious."

"What? No room for banana pudding?"

Her expression was almost pained. "Not a chance. Ugh, I hurt just thinking about it." She giggled slightly, making her already bright eyes dance, the blue in her shirt setting them off perfectly.

I had planned to say something to her about how she dressed for work, but one look at her in jeans and I quickly realized that the form-fitting skirts and suits were the lesser of two evils. Her body was stunning and I doubted if anything she wore could hide that.

Carol brought the check and I quickly handed her cash, not liking the smirk she gave me whenever she looked at Grace. In seven years I had never stopped in with a girl, and I knew Carol would chew my ear off the next time she caught me alone. She'd tried to set me up at least five times and felt it was her personal mission to see me attached.

I should have thought of Carol's nosiness before I brought Grace along to the Pit Stop, but then again, I liked seeing her in my world. She fit in better than I ever thought she would. For all of Grace's family's money, she didn't have a snobby bone in her body.

"You ready?" I stood, tossing a few more bills on the table.

Grace smiled as she moved away from the table, too. "Thank you for dinner. Best meal I've had since I moved here."

Strolling next to her, I offered my hand. She shot me a look of surprise but slid her delicate hand in mine. I laced our fingers together before guiding her out the door. As much as I knew touching her this way was a mistake, I couldn't find the strength to fight it anymore.

Reluctantly letting go of her when we reached my motorcycle, I moved a piece of hair away from her eyes before carefully slipping the helmet onto her head. She watched me without a word, but there was no need to say anything. Sometimes our shared moments of silence said more than our conversations did.

I mounted the bike and felt her slender arms wrap tightly around me. I could have stayed there forever, with her body pressed up close to mine, her helmet lying softly against my back. I couldn't even remember the last time someone had held me the way she did. She gave everything, total trust, never once stopping to question if a monster lurked below the surface. Her world had been all light, mine darkness. How could I ever expect to be with her and not ruin the rose-colored glasses she looked through?

Sadness overwhelmed me as I drove Grace home. *I can't do this.* Her body moved closer as she snuggled up next to me, and I cursed my father for making me this way. Cursed him for leaving a legacy I couldn't break free of.

Pulling up to her door felt like saying good-bye, because I knew deep down we couldn't do this again. I was falling, hard and fast.

I didn't take her hand again as we walked to her door, but I sensed the longing in her gaze and the way she hesitated before putting the key in the lock.

Stuffing my hands into my pockets so she'd know my intent, I nodded toward the door. "I'll wait till you get inside."

"Oh, okay." She quickly opened the door and slid in, closing it halfway. "Thanks for tonight. I had a wonderful time."

I nodded again. "Get some sleep."

She shut the door and I slapped my palm to my forehead, wanting to kick anything in my path. I was such a jerk!

That night I knew the nightmares would come . . . even as I closed my eyes.

It was the same dream as before. I was walking down the long hallway, only to find my mother beaten and packing. The difference this time was that she looked terrified, as if she knew that she would die that night.

After I threatened again to kill my father, she rushed over to me and took my face in her hands. "Matthew, no. You are better than this. Better than him. One day I want you to let go of this anger and make a life for yourself."

Shaking as I tried to get control of the fury, I made her a promise. "We will make a life. You and me, Mom. He will never hurt you again. I won't let him."

"Such a good boy." She sighed and kissed my cheek before turning around. We hurried faster, with her urging me along.

"Where is he?" I asked, zipping the last suitcase and throwing it over my shoulder.

She shook her head and her eyes filled with tears. "I don't know, but tonight was different, Matthew. We need to leave now."

She picked up the other bag and we both walked out the door, ready to leave the nasty apartment for good. But he was standing in the hallway, gun pointed straight at us. "You're not going anywhere."

I pulled my mother behind me and defiantly faced my father. He curled his lips up and then the shots filled the air. I looked down, feeling a searing pain rip through my chest as I tried to breathe. I was falling, but there was no apartment, no floor. Closing my eyes, I was ready to surrender until the ground hit hard beneath me, forcing my eyes open.

I lay on the floor, stunned, then grabbed at my chest and took deep, desperate breaths. My back hurt where I had hit the ground, forcing me to slowly crawl to the nightstand to get my journal. Each dream held more information, like a puzzle coming together piece by piece.

When I first shared my nightmares with Bruce, he explained that sometimes dreams were memories and other times they were the subconscious mind revealing desires, fears, or hopes. The pain in my chest felt so real, so terrifying. But wasn't that my deepest desire? That it had been me who took the bullet that night instead of my mom. Despite my many promises, I'd failed to protect her.

I pressed hard on my aching back, pushing and grinding the lower muscles until they relaxed. Dragging my body to the bathroom, I let the hot water in the shower wash away another restless night.

. . .

"That's not it!" I yelled, pushing Cody aside as I stood to get some water. I could see the hurt in his face and tried to get myself under control. His confidence was still so fragile.

"I'm trying, Matt. That double leg snatch is too hard for me."

"That's because you're not strong enough. I gave you that workout routine for a reason." I gripped the ropes and forced myself to breathe.

Cody stood stoic, looking at his feet. I hated myself for yelling at him, knowing how sensitive he was and how hard he tried.

Finally calm, I faced him. "I'm sorry. I've been getting very little sleep lately and it's making me edgy. Let's just call it a day and pick up here on Monday."

He didn't move, just nodded while I jumped out of the ring, still feeling like my skin was on fire. I barreled through the gym and threw open the door to Apocalypse, knowing I needed to hit something or I would explode.

An audible growl escaped my lips when I heard the music and saw the bare back of a man punching the bag. In two strides, I had turned off the stereo. "You have to schedule an appointment to use this room."

The man turned and I immediately ran my hand over the short strands of my hair to absorb the surprise. "Devon? I was beginning to think you were avoiding me. Why aren't you on the books?"

He pulled off his gloves and grabbed a towel to wipe the sheen of sweat off his face. "I heard you were looking for me." His stance was defensive, but his eyes were remorseful. Devon and I had been tight back in juvie. His connections and fierce fighting skills kept me untouched while in the joint. Wanting to offer him what I had been given, I begged Bruce to try to mentor him. Devon hadn't been receptive.

"You've been back in town awhile. Why haven't you come by to see me or Bruce?" While I still cared about his well-being, my questions were more than just friendly small talk. I needed his help.

Devon threw his towel and picked up his T-shirt. "Ah, Bruce don't want to see me. I'm one of his failures. Listen, if you don't want me coming here, it's okay. I get it."

He carefully put on his shirt, his dark muscles bulging as he tugged. Despite the different paths we'd taken, Devon had been there for me, protected me when I needed it.

"Devon, you're always welcome here. I'm glad to see you. Not only because it's been a while, *but*"—I hesitated—"it turns out I need a favor."

His dark eyes met mine as his eyebrows shot up. "What favor am I gonna help you with? You're all straight and sober now, living the high life."

"You still have some influence in the neighborhood?" I tried to be careful with my words, not wanting to give too much away.

Devon nodded. "Yeah, but my cred went down while I was in lockup. What's up, bro? You need me to deliver a message?" His eyes turned cold, and I knew he'd do anything I asked, even if it meant breaking the law. He was built that way—loyalty and brotherhood came first.

"Actually, I need you to put out a 'no touch' order . . . for the new director at the Hartsford Center."

Devon gave me a sly smile, telling me he knew more than I wanted him to. "Yeah, I heard about her." A low whistle escaped his lips and it took everything in me not to pummel him.

"What have you heard?" I growled, barely keeping my arms pressed against my chest.

Devon raised his hands up and chuckled. "Whoa. Stand down, man. I'm just hearing the same stuff you're hearing. It's all good. I'll put out the 'no touch' order for your girl. But it's only gonna take care of half the problem."

I furrowed my brow. "Half?"

Devon stepped close to me, his voice low and serious. "There's a new guy in the hood and he's got a following, if you know what I mean. Not sure how he does it, but his supply never dries up. He's taking over parts of the city no one's even touched before. He's even supplying for half the price to his loyal regulars in the neighborhood. It's pissing off the other suppliers."

He walked toward the door but stopped to say one more thing. "There's a war brewing, and that children's center, along with your pretty lady, is sitting right in its path."

I absorbed his warning as he disappeared, and then took all my anxiety and frustration out on the bag.

"Matt." The sound of Bruce's hard voice pulled me from the computer screen, and I looked up to see him standing in his doorway. "Let's talk."

He stepped back into his office and I begrudgingly followed. I knew this was coming. I had snapped at Rex earlier in the day when he'd smarted off. If Bruce hadn't stepped in, I'm not sure what would have happened. Thank goodness it was Rex's last appointment. He'd go into the column of kids who'd had a second chance and thrown it away. I had no doubt that kid would spend most of his life in jail.

Bruce was already seated when I took the other chair. He kept his back rigid and his eyes focused on mine.

"We've known each other a long time, and I've always considered you more than just an employee. I see you like the son I never had, and because of that I can sense that something is going on in your head. Something you aren't talking about."

I ran my hands down the sides of my face. "I'm not sleeping well. It's getting to me."

"This is more than sleep deprivation. You're moody, you're hot-tempered, and you look like you could jump out of your skin at any moment. Tell me what's going on." His voice was firm, but I could see the concern in his eyes.

Where did I start? I wasn't ready to talk to him about the nightmares or Grace. Admitting my weakness was like admitting defeat. I could handle it on my own. I just needed to keep my distance from her while I worked it out. But I knew Bruce, and I had to give him something. He wouldn't let up until I did.

"I've got a new little brother. He's a punk kid from the neighborhood. His file looks a lot like mine, and I'm not really sure what to do with him. He doesn't trust me."

Bruce sat back and I could see that he knew I was deflecting.

"And that's it?" he pressed. "There's nothing else you want to talk about?"

"That's it." I hated lying to him, hated what a failure I was turning into. Bruce had spent a year with me, working through my issues. He'd declared me healed, freed. But now I was back in chains. It reminded of me of that verse in Luke, about the man who was freed from his demon. The demon roamed the earth, and when he came back to the man, the demon found his house in order. Getting seven friends more wicked than himself, the demon returned and the man's condition was worse than before he had been freed. I felt like that man.

Bruce steepled his fingers. "Well, if it's really about the boy, maybe his situation hits close to home. Is he still being threatened?"

I shook my head. "I don't think so. He lives with his aunt now, although she admits that he's become more withdrawn and hostile this past year."

He nodded and got that Counselor-with-a-capital-C look on his face. "When he sees you are constant, he'll start to trust you. I suggest you go up there every night at least for a while. Let him see you're serious about him."

Slumping in the chair, I knew Bruce was right. I'd just have to find a way to be at the center without being near Grace. I stood up and sighed. "I better get going then. There's only an hour left of open gym before intramurals start."

Bruce stood, too, and rested a hand on my shoulder. "I know there's more, Matt. I'm here when you're ready."

I simply nodded and bolted out the door.

CHAPTER 12

GRACE

My cheeks actually hurt from so much smiling. From the moment I had placed my hand in his, a whirlpool of possibility spun in my stomach and still hadn't cleared. Last night made everything so clear—the short words, the distance. He had been fighting the attraction. I guess I could understand. We were so different, and yet somehow last night felt perfectly right.

I sighed as I leaned back in my chair. I couldn't concentrate. Glancing at my watch, I knew he'd turn up soon to play basketball with Marcus. Maybe he'd stay and help us clean up again. After all, it was Friday. Surely, he'd want to go do something with me on a Friday night. My mind raced with the possibilities until the phone rang.

I answered in the dreamy voice I'd had all day. "Hartsford Center."

"This is Mattress Shoppe. We have an order here for Ms. Grace Covington."

Sitting up straighter, I replied, "This is Grace, but I didn't purchase any mattress."

"Well, ma'am, I have an order that says one was purchased for you. I just need to schedule a delivery time. Are you available tomorrow?"

"I'm sorry, did you say someone already paid for it? Who?"

She told me to hold on and soft music filled the phone. After a beep, her voice returned. "I'm sorry, ma'am, he wished to remain anonymous."

A smile crept across my face. *Daddy.* I don't know how he knew, but as always he was coming to my rescue. I should refuse the gift, but after another horrendous night on the couch, there was no way I could turn down the comfort—and sleep—a good mattress afforded.

After scheduling a delivery time, I stood to check again if Matt had arrived. The air left my lungs the minute I stepped into the gym. He and Marcus were engaged in an intense game of two on two. They were easily outscoring their opponents, and I smiled at the way they high-fived and encouraged each other. I had never seen Marcus without a scowl on his face, but he was laughing and cheering. I didn't think it was possible, but watching the way Matt handled the troubled little boy, I fell even harder.

The game ended when Darius blew the whistle to clear the floor for intramurals. The girls were playing, and several of them had asked if I would be staying to watch. Of course I'd agreed, and I silently hoped Matt would join me in the bleachers.

His eyes met mine from across the gym and I smiled, sending him a small wave. He turned and walked away. Feeling a pit start to form in my stomach, I followed him to the kitchenette just off the gym.

His back was to me and he stood gripping the counter with his head raised toward the ceiling.

"Hey," I said shyly as I stepped into the small alcove.

He slowly turned around and leaned against the counter, crossing his arms. His blank stare gave me chills, and not the good kind.

Swallowing hard, I moved a little closer. "I was thinking since it's Friday, maybe you could show me later what there is to do around here."

Matt closed his eyes for a second and then started toward the door. "Sorry, Duchess. I've already got plans. I just came to see Marcus, not be your personal tour guide."

My mouth dropped as I watched him walk away. He didn't look back as he dropped his ID badge at the counter and pushed through the front doors. I fell into one of the chairs, hurt and frustrated. I had completely misread him.

"Ms. Covington, the game's about to start. Aren't you going to come watch?"

I turned to see Olivia standing by the door. She was an eager sixth grader with big brown eyes and a contagious smile. Neglected by her parents, she attached herself to anyone who showed her the least bit of attention.

Sending her a smile, I stood and wrapped my arm around her shoulders. "Wouldn't miss it."

As we walked to the gym, I glanced wistfully at the front doors one more time before taking a seat in the bleachers.

I was restless and agitated, and getting more so with each passing second. I blamed it on being home on a Friday night, but deep down I knew the source was a hazel-eyed man who was taking me on a roller-coaster ride.

In my attempt to be productive, I tried fixing the flickering vanity light, only to have the stupid thing go out completely. Now I had no light in the bathroom at all. I called the office manager again and got more promises that he'd handle it. Yeah, right. He hadn't fixed one thing I'd called in and there had been a list.

I walked back to the kitchen and stood staring at Jake's business card on the fridge. What would it hurt to call? When I'd stopped by Naomi and Jake's condo for lunch, she had stressed how much she wanted to get to know me. Mustering the confidence I needed, I grabbed my cell and punched in the number.

"Hello?"

"Yeah, um, Naomi? This is Grace. Grace Covington." I couldn't believe how shaky my voice was.

"Grace! Hi, how are you? I was hoping you'd call. Silly me didn't get your phone number."

Her welcoming tone put me at ease and I let out the breath I was holding.

"What are you up to tonight?" Her voice sounded hopeful. Maybe she was feeling the same restlessness that I was.

"Nothing, actually. That's why I'm calling. I'm sure you and Jake have plans, but I thought maybe you could give me some suggestions on what there is to do around here."

Naomi laughed. "Your timing is perfect. Jake is gone all weekend for work and I hate staying alone. Normally, I'd go see my parents, but—anyway, why don't you come over? We can sit in our pj's and get to know each other."

Smiling from ear to ear, I agreed and was knocking on her condo door in less than an hour. She greeted me in a pair of flannel pajamas and pulled me inside as if we'd been friends since childhood. The feeling took me aback. I'd had a friend like her once, and I still missed her even though I knew we'd never be close again.

"So tell me all about your week. How did your first day go?" Naomi settled into the couch opposite me with a glass of water and waited for details.

I laughed at her eagerness. "How long has Jake been gone?"

"Since Wednesday and I'm dying for company. I've grown so spoiled since we've been married and now I hate to be alone." She laughed and took a sip of water. "So spill."

"Okay. My first day was great. My staff is amazing and those kids, Naomi, they steal your heart the minute you walk in the door." I hesitated, careful not to sound too earnest. "You know, Matt volunteers there."

Interest lit up her eyes. "Really? Where do you work, by the way? You never said the other day."

"The Hartsford Children's Center, downtown."

Naomi's eyes got even bigger. "Wow, Grace, that's amazing. Everyone knows about that program. That neighborhood gets worse every year. It's so wonderful that those kids have a place to go to that's safe and fun. I bet you love working with Matt. He's such a great guy."

I choked on my water as she said that, and took a minute to get back in control. Naomi watched me skeptically and I wanted to ask her a million questions about him. Have her tell me everything she knew and how I might possibly get past that cold exterior of his. Instead, I pushed thoughts of Matt aside, unwilling to spoil this new friendship by putting her in the middle.

"I'm organizing a banquet and silent auction to raise money for renovations and new staff. You don't happen to know of any venues that might be affordable, do you?"

I had successfully changed the subject and Naomi seemed none the wiser. She looked at me apologetically. "Not really. I did attend one banquet last year that the Winsor football staff hosted. The company was miserable, but the room was beautiful. You can try there. It's the Hotel Mayan. They're locally owned, so maybe they'd cut you a deal."

My hands flew to my heart. "That's perfect. If the city is as crazy about the center as I am, I know I can get them to host us. Thank you."

The night continued much like that, the two of us talking about every subject—from our childhoods to our most embarrassing moments. Our new friendship was as easy as the conversation.

"So what about boyfriends? Did you leave someone special behind when you came here?" Naomi asked.

"Not exactly," I deadpanned, but Naomi quickly realized there was more to the story.

"I told you how Jake and I met and all our crazy drama. Surely you have something that will make me feel better."

Stewart's face filled my thoughts. "You have no idea."

"Oh yeah? Do tell."

I wanted to decline, but she had been so open and honest with me that I couldn't hold back. Sitting straighter, I forced a smile. "Okay, I'll tell you, but please don't mention any of this to Jake. It's pretty humiliating. For weeks after everything went down with Stewart, my ex, people looked at me with this pitying expression. I never told anyone why we broke up, but there were rumors. I don't want to see that look again."

The lighthearted air we'd had until then suddenly felt heavy as Naomi agreed not to say anything.

"I'd known Stewart since high school. Our parents were good friends and we hung in the same circles. There was always an attraction and a lot of flirting, but he never pursued anything with me. He was a year older and going off to Stanford while I was staying in New York, so I think we both knew the bigger picture was better left alone.

"He'd call periodically through college, and we'd go have dinner when he'd come home for the holidays. But it was always just friendship, nothing more, at least on his end. I'd kind of had a crush on him since high school. Then he graduated and came home to work for his father. The calls came daily and soon we were dating. Our parents were thrilled. A few years later, he proposed and I said yes, of course. Everything was perfect. I thought Stewart was just like my father. He was warm, funny, and affectionate. We'd go to church together and he treated me like a princess."

Naomi clutched a pillow in one hand. "So what happened?"

"After we got engaged, Stewart started pressuring me, you know, to sleep with him. He knew my conviction and my boundaries, but we'd been together three years already and were looking at another eighteen months for our engagement."

"Eighteen months!" Naomi's eyes got really big. "I can totally see why that would be hard. Jake and I were only engaged for two months, and there were several times we pushed the envelope. If he hadn't made a promise to my dad, I'm not sure we would have made it." She suddenly quit talking. "I'm sorry, go on."

Taking a deep breath, I continued. The next part still crippled me with regret. "In my social circles, long engagements are the norm. Weddings are not just a moment but also an event, and the grander the better. I had planned that day since I was a little girl and knew exactly what I wanted. But the waiting was getting to him. He said he had needs and I wasn't meeting them. I talked with my friends about it and they all said that I was crazy to wait. That we were engaged, and no one waits until they're married anymore. So I gave in."

Silence hung in the air as tears filled my eyes. Naomi didn't say anything, but she patted my leg for reassurance.

"After a few times, I couldn't stand the guilt. I put my foot down and told him I wanted to wait till we were married. I explained that I couldn't enjoy being with him when I knew our relationship was outside of God's plan. We argued about it for weeks, but finally one day he just conceded. The irony is that I actually respected him more because he put me first. The only problem was that while he agreed to be abstinent with me . . . he didn't stop having sex."

Naomi's hand flew to her mouth. "Oh, Grace. How did you find out?"

"My parents were hosting a dinner party and everyone was there. The wedding was only a few months away, so it turned into a couple's shower as people kept handing us cards and money. At one point during the night, I spilled something on my dress. I went off to try to clean up in the bathroom and saw Stewart and Lacey, my best friend, making out in the hallway. In my house, of all places. They didn't notice me. But I saw them disappear behind the guest room door."

Naomi stood, her face fired by fury as she paced. "I can't believe he did that to you! What did you do? Please tell me you hit him and then her and then hit him again."

I laughed as I watched her. Her reaction was the same as my mom's had been.

"Nope," I admitted, shaking my head. "I'm just not wired that way. I hate conflict, especially when it's highly emotional. After I got over the shock of what I saw, I went back to the party and carried on as if nothing had happened. Twenty minutes later, Stewart was by my side, as if it had all been in my imagination."

My eyes followed Naomi as she dropped back down onto the couch. "That wasn't the first time he'd been with her, was it?"

"No. I met Stewart for lunch the next day and confronted him calmly. He tried to deny it at first, until I told him I'd seen him and Lacey with my own two eyes. Then he confessed everything. I guess they'd been fooling around for a few months. Stewart insisted that she'd seduced him and that he'd wanted to stop, but he didn't know how to without her telling me. He begged and pleaded for me to forgive him, but I just couldn't. He swore to me she was the only one, but I often wonder if there were more while we dated. Either way, I knew I'd never trust him again, and that is no way to start a marriage. I just gave him back his ring and left the restaurant. That was two months ago."

Naomi looked surprised. "Only two months ago? You seem so calm about it. Most girls would still be crying their eyes out."

"Oh, I did cry, for about two weeks, but then I stopped crying and started really examining my life. I realized that I didn't know the girl in the mirror. Everything I had planned out for my life was a carbon copy of my parents' lives. In my effort to be just like them, I had totally forsaken my own path. This is one of those cases where what man intended for evil, God used for good. If I had married Stewart, I wouldn't have accepted the job at Hartsford. I'd never have had the chance to make a difference in all these kids' lives. I know this is where I'm supposed to be."

Naomi's face was full of awe. "You amaze me. You don't seem bitter at all."

I shifted on the couch and rested my head on a cushion. "It takes too much energy for me to stay angry, and I've never been able to hold a grudge, even when I've wanted to. Obviously, my relationships with Lacey and Stewart are over forever, but I don't wish them ill. They aren't bad people."

"Are they together now?"

I shrugged. "Not really my business anymore. I've seen each of them at different places but never together."

After a long swig of water, Naomi grinned at me. "So you are available and obviously tough as nails. You know, I have four handsome brothers and three of them are still single."

We both fell into a fit of laughter and moved on to much lighter topics. It was pushing one o'clock when we finally called it a night, and Naomi insisted I stay in the spare room. The minute I crawled into the soft bed, I felt my muscles sink into the mattress. Making sure to thank God for my new friendship and all He had helped me through the past few months, I closed my eyes and enjoyed the best night's sleep I'd had all week.

CHAPTER 13

MATT

I saw him in the hallway with a gun pointed at us. "You're not going anywhere."

Acting on instinct, I pushed my mother behind me and stared into the vicious eyes of my father.

His lips curled upward. "You always were an obstinate little brat."

I now understood my mother's terror. He had snapped. His eyes were too wild, his voice too calm. I pushed her and we slowly backed into the bedroom. I needed to find a weapon, something that could defend us from him.

My father followed slowly, never lowering his gun until he was standing in the doorway and we were trapped inside.

"Marcie, come here," my father demanded.

My mother started to move around me, but I blocked her. "No, you aren't going back to him. Never again." I turned to my father. "This is over. Either let us go on your own or I will make you."

He let out a wicked laugh. "You know, I never wanted you. Told your mother to take care of the problem, even beat her a few times to help the process. But no, she just had to have her little boy. What a disappointment you turned out to be. You'll probably never graduate and will end up being a drain on society just like you've been a drain on me for the last sixteen years."

I wanted to lash out, scream at him that I was better than he was, always would be, but fear for my mother held me in check and kept my mouth tightly shut. My eyes darted around the room, looking desperately for anything I could find that would disarm him.

"Worthless, Matt. That's what you are and what you always will be." My father's eyes snapped to hers and I moved again so his vision was obstructed. "Remember what you promised me?" he yelled. "That I wouldn't even know he was here. That nothing would change. But you always loved him more than me, and why? He's a nothing, a nobody."

My mother was gripping my arm and I could feel her teardrops as they landed. She was shaking violently at this point. "We'll be okay. Just trust me," I whispered, hoping she would calm down.

I turned when I heard my father rack his pistol. "Marcie, I'm losing my patience. I'll shoot him. I swear I will, and society will thank me for it!"

The shaking stopped and my mom pushed off me, getting around my body so she could face him. "No, stop!" I yelled, gripping her tighter.

"Marcie, this is your last warning . . . Get over here!"

I heard the shots, but all I could see was darkness. I screamed and screamed her name, searching desperately for her until suddenly the lights were on.

My screams were deafening when I sat up in bed, completely wet with sweat and gripping the sheets as if they were a lifeline.

I raised my fists toward the ceiling. "WHY?!"

I began hurling everything I could find—lamps, pillows, the shoes I had left on the floor. Ripping the sheets, I tugged and pulled until the bed was completely stripped and my room looked as if a rabid animal had been set loose in it.

Falling to my knees, I gripped my head and cried. "How long, Lord, how long?" I begged, rocking back and forth. I couldn't take the pain anymore.

I woke up a few hours later, still huddled on the floor in the fetal position. The tears had dried on my cheeks and every inch of my body screamed in protest. The clock brightly displayed 5:15 a.m., and I slowly pulled myself to the shower, avoiding the mess on the floor.

I'd go to the early service at church. I didn't want to see Grace. Didn't want to look into those hurt eyes again. She thought me cruel and harsh, yet she had no idea what I was capable of. No idea that walking away from her was a gift I was giving her so she'd never know the kind of darkness I faced.

The morning passed in a daze, until I found myself seated in church, still stiff from the night before. The music played, but I barely heard any of the sound. My mind was too busy asking God why and demanding to know what His purpose was in all of this mess.

Pastor Davis was as eloquent as always, but his words made me angry. He was talking about joy in the Lord and contentment. I wanted to know where my joy was. Where did my contentment go? I felt like a spoiled child demanding answers, but I was entitled. I'd turned my life around. Gave up everything I knew for Him, and I felt abandoned.

At the end of the service, I was no more settled than I had been when I arrived, and pushed aside the nagging voice that said it was my fault. I managed to make it two feet from the door before I saw Grace sitting with Naomi at the café.

She was laughing with her head thrown back and she looked stunning. My eyes followed the line of her finger as she tucked a strand of hair behind her ear. I could feel the tug, even from across the room. She was as bad as the nightmares. Sent to torture me with the knowledge that the one thing I wanted most, I could never have. Turning quickly, I pushed the glass doors open and left before she could see me.

CHAPTER 14

GRACE

I tried not to look distracted as I glanced at each person to come through the doors. Service would start in just a few minutes, and he should have been at church by then.

"Doesn't Matt usually come to this service?" I asked Naomi.

She glanced around, looking for him. "Yeah, he does. Regularly, too. Huh. I wonder if everything's okay."

I slumped down in my chair, but tried to maintain an easy air. My emotional side said he was avoiding me, while my practical side reminded me that he did say he had plans this weekend. Maybe I was just being too sensitive, which is what happens when one dates the same guy for four and half years. My guy radar was completely malfunctioning.

Naomi and I finished our coffee and headed into the service. The music was fantastic and Pastor Davis's words really touched my heart. I loved how going to church could get me so grounded when life and temptations started to pull me in too many directions.

When church let out, I felt empowered and motivated. I even stopped by the hardware store and picked up a replacement light for the vanity, determined that I was independent enough to fix my own hassles.

Three hours later, I wanted to scream my head off and throw the light fixture out the window. When I'd finally managed to get the old one down, using the emergency tool kit in my car, I thought the hard part was over. Then I opened the box and saw I had to completely build the new light. I should have known that was why the thing was half price. Worse, the directions were impossible. I could have been reading the French instructions, for all the ones in English helped me.

After another frustrating hour, I gave up and wanted to curl into a corner and cry. I'd thought I was so ready to be on my own, yet every day something happened to show me how completely naive I was.

When my pity party was over, I conceded that in this case I was just going to have to call someone for help. The building maintenance was a joke, so that wasn't happening, and Jake would be gone until late that night. I had a contact list of all the people who worked with the center, but I couldn't bring myself to call Darius on his one day off.

Whether he was my last option, or I just wanted to believe he was my last option, I don't know. But somehow I convinced myself to call Matt and just ask. I mean, what was the worst he could say? No? Make me feel stupid? He'd already done both of those and I survived.

My hand shook as I punched in his number. Voice mail. I pushed my disappointment away and attempted a lighthearted tone.

"Hi, Matt, this is Grace. I'm so sorry to call you, but I need help. If you don't get this, no worries—I'll figure it out."

Ending the call, I felt satisfied. My voice was a little shaky, but at least I didn't sound desperate.

I kept the phone near while I worked on the list for the fundraising banquet, trying hard not to get discouraged when an hour passed without hearing from him. Then a loud banging on my door sent a jolt of panic through me.

"Grace!" someone yelled, pounding again.

I rushed over, peeked through the peephole, and quickly opened the door when I saw Matt's agitated face.

He took one look at me and pushed through the entryway. "Are you okay? Did something happen?" He walked around the apartment like a cop, searching for some unknown threat.

I shut the door in confusion and followed him. "Yes, I'm fine. I just couldn't get this light fixture together," I said, pointing to the heap of metal and wires I had piled on my bed. "And I thought you might be able to do it."

He turned to me, his face a mixture of shock and fury. "Are you serious? Do you have any idea how terrifying the last fifteen minutes have been for me?"

"It was just a phone call. I never claimed I was in any danger. You're acting as if I called you screaming." My voice got higher as I defended myself.

He ran his hands down his face. They were shaking. Suddenly he dropped down on my bed and exhaled. The motion made the light fixture noisily clank around on the bed.

Calm again, he turned his tortured eyes to me. "Grace, you said 'help' in the message. I take that very seriously. When I thought I'd missed your call . . ." He closed his eyes for a second, then reopened them. "When someone needs help, I go. Immediately. Not an hour later. Not the next day. I go immediately because you never know what can happen when you wait."

Somehow I knew he was no longer talking about me. Stepping forward, I ran my hand over his arm for comfort. "You don't have to stay. I'm sorry if my phone call was misleading."

He turned to look at the mess I'd made of the light and grabbed the instructions. "I'm already here. I may as well take care of this for you."

He worked in silence for a few minutes, and I stood back, not wanting to crowd him while he expertly managed to do what I had found impossible.

"I see you put your bed together and finally got a mattress." His mouth twitched but settled back in as he resumed concentrating.

"I did. I slept like a baby last night."

That time he definitely grinned. I ignored the tingling it caused. Matt's smile had a lethal effect on me. I continued to watch him work. He was so different from Stewart, but I liked that. I liked that he didn't care about fashion and wore jeans and T-shirts everywhere he went. *Chest-hugging T-shirts*, I mused, averting my roaming eyes.

"You ready to put this up?" He lifted the large piece, and I was thankful he hadn't noticed how closely I'd been checking him out.

"You're done already?" I didn't know whether to feel overjoyed or completely furious that he was able to put the light together in less than ten minutes.

"Come on. Grab a flashlight."

I followed Matt to the bathroom and held the flashlight for him while he twisted the wires and manually tightened the screws. I'm sure he would have given his left arm for an electric drill, but he didn't say anything.

When he hopped off the chair and flicked on the light, a small drop of perspiration ran down his forehead and along his cheek. I followed it with my eyes, staring at his lips until I realized what I was doing. I quickly glanced up, only to see a look that matched my own—a look that made my throat go dry and set off a wave of butterflies in my stomach.

Then the moment was gone.

I moved away from him and escaped to the kitchen, grasping for clarity. I wanted to pace, or maybe hit the wall or something. I couldn't explain this feeling, this fire that was moving up to my chest. I wasn't like this. I wasn't a fighter. I was a peacemaker, but at that moment I just wanted to scream at him.

Still fuming, I turned away when he came in the room.

"Any more slave labor needed before I head out?" His voice was mocking and snapped the final straw.

I spun around in a fury. "Why don't you like me?" I demanded. "Everyone else is nice to me and treats me with at least a little respect. But not you. No, you have made it your mission to jerk me around. One moment friendly, the next so hurtful I want to pull my hair out. What did I ever do to you?"

"I'm not having this conversation." He grabbed his keys and started to leave.

"NO." I'd probably lost my mind, but I clutched his arm, forcing him to turn and face me. "You're not going. Not until you tell me what I did to make you hate me."

We were both breathing heavily, overloaded with adrenaline, or at least I was. His eyes got that tortured look again, as if he were fighting himself more than me.

He moved forward and I instinctively backed up until my backside hit the counter. His arms slowly reached around me, gripping the edge of the Formica while they caged me in. My heart raced, desire raging inside of me as I stared into the depths of his eyes.

"I don't hate you, Duchess, but I hate what you do to me." His voice was so infuriatingly cool that goose bumps spread across my arms. "I hate that it takes me days to recover after seeing you, that every time you smile or tuck your hair back, I want to pull you into my arms and kiss you until you can't stand up. I hate that I think about you, that I worry about you constantly, when there is absolutely no way anything will ever happen between us."

I tried to consider the consequences. But there are times when desire simply overpowers logic. I cradled his face between my palms and dragged his mouth down on mine, releasing every pent-up emotion I'd felt for him since we'd first met. His entire body tensed with the contact, but he didn't let go of the counter or kiss me back. I moved closer, making my body flush against his, my mouth demanding his to respond.

I ached for him to hold me, to kiss me back the way I knew he wanted to, but instead I felt a rush of cold air as he pushed off the counter and away from me.

My eyes begged him not to reject me, to let this thing between us happen. He looked stunned and frazzled and completely off guard, but he shook his head no.

"I'm not doing this." His harsh words immediately brought tears to my eyes. I didn't see him walk out, only heard the door slam behind him.

CHAPTER 15

MATT

I hadn't spoken to Grace in almost a week. In fact, despite being at the center every day, I barely even saw her. When she did happen to walk into the gym, she simply went about her business with Darius or the kids. She was perfectly polite to me—so polite that I felt the chill for hours after each encounter. I told myself the distance was what I wanted. That her longing stares and infatuated eyes were too hard to resist. But I missed them.

The worst part was that now, instead of being haunted by the unknown, I had gotten a glimpse of what it would be like to let myself love her. She was passionate and challenging, yet refined and sensitive. She could set me off in a blaze one moment, and later calm the storm with just a slight touch of her hand.

I pressed my palms to my eyes before swinging off my bike. At least one good thing happened this week. I had a breakthrough with Marcus. We'd been playing basketball together faithfully every day. I didn't demand that he talk or ask a lot of questions. I just kept showing up and hanging out.

Yesterday he got the rebound, stopped, and looked up at me. "I'm glad you're my big brother."

I grinned and rubbed his head. "Yeah, me too, kid. Now shoot the ball."

Just thinking about the smile he gave me was enough to make all the time invested worth it. Hot air blew on my face as I strolled across the parking lot toward the large metal doors of the center. I spotted Marcus in my peripheral vision and stopped. I didn't like his stance. His shoulders were tense, defensive. A tree was in the way, so I couldn't see whom he was talking to.

Before I could approach him, Marcus turned and headed my way, oblivious that I was watching him wipe his eyes. He halted when he saw me. "You're early."

"It's Saturday. I thought maybe we could change it up a little, go do something fun."

Marcus shook his head quickly, his eyes full of distrust. "Nah, man, let's stay here."

I nodded and followed a stiff Marcus into the building. I understood his hesitation. He wanted to feel safe.

The next hour was a nightmare. Marcus was back to being moody and withdrawn. He didn't want to play basketball after we lost the first game. I challenged him to an Xbox game. He declined and sat pouting with his arms folded, watching some stupid TV show.

He turned to scowl at me. "Don't you have something better to do?"

Seeing Marcus was like watching a movie reel of myself. Something had happened outside, and he was fighting the feeling of helplessness by being short and guarded with me.

Done playing his game, I looked him square in the eye. "Who were you talking to outside, Marcus?"

"What are you talking about? I didn't see nobody outside." Defensiveness tightened every word as he turned his face away from mine.

"I put up with a lot from you, Marcus, but don't lie to me." My voice was stern enough to send a message, and Marcus's chin jutted in defiance.

We sat in stony silence until he pushed up from the couch and lumbered across the room, looking out the window. Every muscle in his body appeared bone stiff. I recognized the stance—he was braced for a blow but ready to fight back.

I found a spot next to him and spoke low enough that the other kids couldn't hear. "Tell me what's going on. Is someone hurting you?"

Marcus turned, his voice angry. "You think you know about my life because your old man hit you around a little. You don't know nothing, man. Nothing! This stupid center is a joke. Y'all don't even see what's going on right in front of your eyes!"

I felt stung as he turned back to look out the window.

"Just leave me alone."

Sheer frustration drove me from the room. I took a moment to glance around, skeptically watching each kid for a clue as to what Marcus was talking about. I noticed a group of boys huddled on the bleachers in the gym. They were all wearing white T-shirts, but a sleeve had been ripped off each one. The center had banned headgear or any other accessory that could be taken as gang paraphernalia, but a sharp pit formed in my stomach as I studied their matching shirts.

Darius was in his office when I approached him. "I think we have a problem."

Instinctively, he barreled out the door, looking immediately for the chaos. The kids were all in their areas, with no issue to be seen. "Everything looks fine to me."

I nodded toward the group huddled together. "Look at their shirts. It's a sign, Darius. I know it. They're making a statement and trying to be sneaky about it. Marcus said something is going on. And I've heard the same thing from another reliable source," I added, thinking of Devon.

Darius groaned. "I can't go suspending kids for tears in their T-shirts, Matt. This place would be empty. Besides, I'd need Grace's approval before making a sweeping announcement like that."

I clenched my hands into fists. "So ask her. She'll do what you suggest, I'm sure. It's not like she even knows what a gang is."

Rubbing his chin, Darius looked at the boys again. Even I had to admit they didn't look threatening, but still, my instincts were screaming. "I'll keep my eye out and if I notice more kids picking up the fashion trend, I'll say something to Grace. She's been so down the last couple days. I don't want to do anything to push her over the edge."

I couldn't believe my ears. Darius was dismissing a possible gang threat because he didn't want to upset Grace's delicate feelings? I'd seen him and Liz having heated arguments time and time again, and he never backed down.

"You're making a mistake," I said.

Darius glanced at the boys one more time and shook his head. "If I am, I'll own it, but for now I'm not going to put this place in a panic, especially when your source is Marcus."

He suddenly shifted and stood a little taller. I followed his line of vision and saw Grace walking in our direction, her heels tapping on the gym floor. She didn't seem tense or nervous, and her fluid movement made my stomach flip like a smitten teenager's.

"Good afternoon, Matt." Her tone was easy and casual as she turned to Darius. "I'm sorry to interrupt, but I'm starting tours today with possible investors and need to get those back rooms a little more presentable. Do you have a free second?"

"Of course," Darius replied, giving me a warning look. "Matt and I are finished."

They walked off together. "I can help," I called toward their backs.

Grace turned, her ease faltering a little. Our eyes met and I could see the hurt despite her attempts to hide it. "Thank you, Matt, but we're good. Enjoy the rest of your day."

I watched them retreat and then disappear through a doorway. Heart thumping, I stormed out the front doors. I wanted to hit something, anything. I didn't need this garbage in my life. If none of them wanted my help, fine. But even as I drove furiously to the gym, a sense of loss settled over me. How was it possible to miss something I never even had?

CHAPTER 16

GRACE

The plans for the banquet were going better than I ever could have imagined. Thanks to my mother's contacts and my father's business associations, I had almost two hundred thousand dollars in donated items for the silent auction. All I needed was something that would draw people in. Something or someone they'd be willing to pay fifteen thousand dollars a plate to see.

I'd racked my brain all day for another option, but kept coming back to the same solution—Carter Fields. A world-renowned author and motivational speaker, he had written six bestsellers that had practically reinvented the role human resources played in the business world. If I got him, we'd sell out of tickets. The problem was, nobody could get him. When he turned sixty, he retired and refused to do any book signings or speaking engagements. His position hadn't changed, no matter how much money was offered.

I lowered my head to my hands. If I wanted him, I'd have to call her. I stood, looking out into the gym, which was packed with kids. We had to get those renovations. The crammed environment was already creating problems. Each day there seemed to be more and more tension in the air. Resolved to putting the center above my hurt feelings, I pulled out my cell phone and tapped in her number.

"Gracie?" Her voice was surprised, breathless. "After fifty messages, I kind of gave up on you ever calling me back."

I took a calming breath. "Hello, Lacey. This isn't a personal call. I need a favor, and you can appreciate I must be desperate if I'm calling you."

"Anything, Gracie. You have no idea how much I miss you. How sorry I am." I heard her start to cry and closed my eyes. I wasn't going to let myself be affected by her tears.

"I know Carter Fields is a close friend of your father's. I'm putting together a charity banquet and I need a speaker no one can get. If you ask him, I know he'll at least take my call and hear me out. Can you do that for me?"

Her voice was broken from the sobs. "I-I'll ask. Y-your mom s-said you m-moved. I-I'm so sorry. I-I wish I could t-take it back."

I'd heard her apologies before. But she couldn't take it back. We'd been best friends since kindergarten and she'd had an affair with my fiancé. There was no recovering from that level of betrayal.

Before I could respond, she continued, calming just a little. "He's heartbroken, Gracie. We don't even talk anymore, but I saw him at Brook's Café, and he looked miserable. We both are. It was a mistake, a stupid, selfish mistake. If we'd known we'd lose you, I swear . . ."

"Lacey, please. I don't want to talk about Stewart. Just text me Carter's number after you talk to him. Try to persuade him if you can. It's the least you can do for me." My voice cracked a little at the end, irritating me. I wouldn't cry.

"I'll do everything I can, Gracie. I promise."

I thanked her and ended the call.

Despite my steady demeanor, my heart felt heavy with loss. As I had often done over the past few months, I quietly prayed for God to soften my heart so I could truly forgive both of them. I was past the bitterness, but conversations like that one showed me the hurt was still there.

"Penny for your thoughts?"

I slowly looked up to see Jeff, one of the counselors, at my door. He gave me the same look the entire staff had all week. Concern, pity. As much as I appreciated that they cared, I hated that look. I also hated my transparency.

Sending him a reassuring smile, I stood. "What's up?"

"You have a visitor who says he's here for a tour."

Excitement surged, making me forget all about my heartache. "Yes! I'll be right out. Can you get him a visitor badge?"

I'd sent invitations to hundreds of business professionals in Asheville and the surrounding area, inviting them to tour the facility. I wanted us to be the first nonprofit on their lists when end-of-year tax deductions were needed.

Straightening my suit and quickly checking my makeup, I headed to the gym to meet my guest. He was an older gentleman, maybe in his early sixties, and appeared to be enjoying the conversation he and Jeff were having.

As I approached with a smile, I glanced quickly at his guest tag and reached out my hand. "Mr. Jacobs, I'm so glad you stopped by. I'm Grace Covington, the director here at Hartsford."

He returned my warm smile, but looked slightly surprised. I was sure my age threw him—it usually did that to people.

"I'd like to take you through the facility and answer any questions you may have," I offered, hoping he was there for more than just curiosity's sake.

"That would be great." Turning to Jeff, he shook his hand. "Very nice to meet you."

I gestured for him to follow me. "As I mentioned in the invitation, Hartsford Center is entirely privately funded. The generosity of investors has allowed us to create a unique environment targeted to the needs of the kids in this specific area. Jeff is one of two counselors who not only provide emotional counseling for the kids but also help with getting these kids financial aid for higher education, and have even tutored on occasion." I pointed toward the gym. "Our activities director, Darius, makes sure that there is enough positive activity in the center to keep the appeal high. The sports program also gives these kids a sense of accomplishment and teamwork." I paused for a second, giving him a chance to ask questions.

When he remained silent and looked back at me, I continued. "We also have a very successful big brother and sister program, and currently have eighty kids assigned. We'd like to do more, but volunteers are not always easy to come by. Every year we have more, though, so considering we've only been open five years, I think we are definitely moving in the right direction."

We walked as I talked and showed him each room. The kids watched suspiciously but didn't approach us. Once the main building tour was over, I guided him to the door connecting the space I hoped to renovate.

"Back here is the expansion area, if you have a few more minutes?"

Mr. Jacobs glanced at his watch, looking rushed, and then back at my hopeful face. When his expression softened, I knew he'd stay, but I also knew I'd have to make it quick. I got him in and out of there in less than ten minutes, and we headed to the front doors.

"Well, Grace, I must say it has been a delight and very informative," Mr. Jacobs said. "I'll be speaking to my board and will contact you if we can help in any way."

"Thank you, Mr. Jacobs. I know your time is valuable, and I am honored you gave me such a large chunk of it. I look forward to hearing from you."

As soon as the doors closed, I wanted to fall to the floor in relief. I'd done it.

Jeff walked up after hovering nearby. "Nice job, Grace. Did he commit to anything?" His voice was hopeful. We all knew the future of the center depended on my ability to get funds.

"Not yet, but he was listening, and I got the impression he wasn't just some lackey sent to check off a box or save face. I can usually spot those. I guess time will tell."

Jeff sensed my frayed nerves and draped an arm easily around my shoulders, guiding me into the kitchenette. He offered me a celebratory Coke while he filled me with stories of past events at the center. After only a few minutes, I was laughing and somewhat relaxed.

"What's with the guy in the money suit?" The voice made the hairs on the back of my neck stand up. Even with my back to the doorway, I knew exactly who it was.

Jeff stood, lighthearted and completely oblivious to my unease. "I'll let Grace fill you in. I've got to get back to my office."

The air seemed to follow Jeff out of the room. I didn't turn, not yet ready for a confrontation. His steps echoed in the space until I saw him in my line of sight, filling the chair Jeff had just vacated. Our eyes met, which of course meant my body reacted in ways that screamed his rejection hadn't changed my attraction to this insufferable man.

"So that's the plan?" Matt's tone was accusing. "To let the high and mighty come through here and decide if we are worth anything? You going to start dressing up the kids, too? Put them on display?"

I straightened my suit coat, irritated by his lack of faith in me. "People want to know details before they hand over their hard-earned money. I'm simply giving them those details in a way that makes us more than just one more charity on a long list of possibilities. I've done this before, Matt, and it works."

I was so tired of fighting with him. So tired of the whirlwind of emotions that churned every time I saw him or spoke to him. As the director, I knew his value, but as a girl, I just wanted him to go away.

His face softened as he took in my resigned posture. "You look tired."

Shaking my head, I just looked away. I wanted to roll my eyes, but refused to look like a spoiled child who didn't get what she wanted. "Thanks."

The silence lingered, getting more heated as we sat there.

"Listen, Grace, about the other day . . ."

"It's okay. You don't have to say anything. I know it was out of line. It won't happen again." I stood, unwilling to stay that close to him.

He grabbed my hand before I could flee. As he stood to face me, his eyes looked sad, remorseful. "There's so much going on in my head right now that you don't want to know. You're knocking on doors you can't possibly be ready to open."

"Once again, Matt, you underestimate me." His hand seared mine, and I could feel the steady beat of my heart as I challenged him.

He stepped closer, his breath hot against my forehead as he leaned in. "That's just it. I know exactly what you're capable of doing to me. What you're already doing to me." His words were soft, tortured even, and hung in the air as he retreated, leaving me behind in a daze.

CHAPTER 17

MATT

Things were getting easier. I started setting my alarm at two-hour intervals every night, so I never fell into a deep enough sleep to dream. It made for long, weary days, but with the nightmares gone, I began to relax again. Finally I was backing away from the cliff I had been in danger of falling from just weeks ago.

It helped that Grace and I had settled into some kind of a truce. My honesty with her in the kitchen took away the cold shoulder she'd been giving me, and I was finding ways to interact with her that didn't send me into a tailspin. My cool had been tested a few times when some of the yuppie businessmen were more interested in getting a look up Grace's skirt than touring the center. But she seemed to handle them without my interference. I'd learned that while Grace was warm and sweet, she could also deliver a dressing down when needed. And she did it with that aristocratic air that must have been ingrained in her since birth.

I often wondered what she'd look like if she completely let go. Breathtaking, no doubt. Pushing the thought aside, I reminded myself that ship had sailed, and I was the one who sent the vessel out to sea.

Getting Marcus's trust was a little harder, but he was coming around. The first day back after our fight, Marcus looked surprised to see me. Then he just ignored me the rest of the night. I persisted, coming every night for basketball, and eventually he started talking to me again, laughing even. Bruce thought that if I could just get him out of the neighborhood, then maybe he would share what was going on.

Something was happening around us. The center felt like a ticking time bomb just waiting to implode. I continued to argue with Darius about the way the boys were dressing, but he wouldn't back down, saying the tension was from all the investors coming around, not because of some fashion statement. But I knew I wasn't seeing things. The guys had come up with different ways to match their clothing each day, sometimes subtly, sometimes not so much. Their numbers were growing, too, as I counted fifteen boys today who had their socks pulled all the way to their knees.

"Yo, Matt, you gonna shoot?" Marcus's sharp words brought me back to the present, and I jumped, sending the ball easily in the net. We were playing a game of twenty-one, and Marcus had five points on me.

"So I have some Asheville Tourists tickets. I know you're more a basketball man than baseball, but those games are a lot of fun." I watched for Marcus's reaction, noting that he was trying to hide his excitement, and shot the ball again.

When I missed the shot, he rebounded and held the ball, shrugging. "I guess I could go, so you don't waste a ticket. Aunt Mave won't mind."

"Great. Then I'll meet you here tomorrow at four. Sound good?"

Marcus started dribbling the ball and then stopped. "You gonna make me get on that bike of yours?"

"Yep."

He shook his head as if I'd taken away his puppy, but I didn't miss the grin on his face as he made his next shot.

I couldn't have asked for a better day for the game. A northern front came in, lowering the temperature to a perfect seventy-seven degrees. The stands were more full than usual and the air was charged with excitement. Minor league games are fun, but on days like this one, they become unforgettable.

Marcus was all smiles, as I had given him free rein at the concession stand. Now trying to balance nachos, a hot dog, and popcorn on his legs, he screamed with the crowd as the Tourists took the field.

By the seventh inning they were up by three runs, and Marcus had eaten more food than I thought possible by a ten-year-old boy. It also didn't escape me that the past few hours, watching the game, had been the most peaceful time we'd spent together since we met.

Spying the ice-cream cone another fan was eating, Marcus turned to me. "Hey, can I have one of those?"

"You're gonna make yourself sick. Let's just give your stomach a minute to rest before we put something else in there."

Marcus looked disappointed, but soon forgot all about the ice cream when the ball sailed in the air, sending a runner to third base.

The next batter sent a sacrifice fly out to right field. Once the ball was caught, his teammate on third base bolted toward home plate, expanding the Tourists' lead to four.

When the cheers ended, Marcus took his seat. "I'm glad they scored and all, but I'd hate to be guy who had to get an out. That totally jacks his stats."

"It's all part of being a team. Everyone has to do their part." I hoped Marcus could sense the double meaning in my words.

He sighed and looked down at his lap. "I shouldn't have yelled at you the other day."

"Hey." My sharp voice caused him to look up. "That's the most honest you've been with me. Don't apologize for that. Like these guys, we're a team. I can't do my job if I don't know what you need."

He looked back at his lap, not even glancing up when shots boomed and the crowd started screaming, indicating another run for the home team. His shoulders were slumped and he was playing nervously with the edge of his shorts.

"Something scared you that day, didn't it?" I pressed.

He nodded.

"Is your aunt aware of the situation?"

"No way," he promised, his eyes becoming protective. "And you can't say anything! She's already done so much for me."

"I'm not going to say anything to her, Marcus, but will you tell me what's going on? Or at least tell me why you said what you did about the center?"

Marcus shook his head and looked away. "It will only make it worse."

"Is someone at the center hurting you, Marcus?" I held my breath, praying that wasn't the case.

He didn't say anything, but shook his head no before turning to me. "Are you and Ms. Covington friends?"

Hesitantly, I answered, "Sort of, why?"

Marcus smirked, letting me know we were moving away from the earlier subject. "I see the way you're always panting after her. You've got the hots for her, don't you?"

Taken aback by his words, I pushed on his arm affectionately. "I've never panted in my life."

He laughed. "Hey, I don't blame you. She's the prettiest lady I've ever seen, but you don't look like her type. She probably likes those rich, snobby dudes she's been bringing around. She always gives them those big smiles."

"Well, aren't you just full of compliments today? See if I take you to another game. Besides, what do you know about Ms. Covington's type or about women at all?"

"Hey! I have cable." Marcus laughed some more and turned his attention back to the game.

Even a ten-year-old could see it. There was no scenario that put Grace and me in the same league. Marcus was just stating the obvious.

The game ended soon after with a decisive five-run win by the Tourists. Marcus talked nonstop about the players, giving a recap of the game, play by play, as we made our way to my motorcycle.

He got on confidently this time, a huge change from the terrified look he'd had when I picked him up. I took him straight home since the center was closing in a few minutes, and then headed back there to wait for Grace. My habit of following her home hadn't changed, even with Devon's "no touch" order. And it didn't look like I'd be able to stop anytime soon. Despite my warnings, Grace was still careless about her safety.

The familiar flashing blue and red lights knotted my stomach as I pulled into the parking lot of the center. Not even bothering to lock up my gear, I bolted to the front doors, rushing through with one thought in mind: get to Grace.

Heart pounding, I took in the scene in front of me. Three guys lay on their stomachs, with their wrists handcuffed behind their backs. There was blood pooled on the gym floor not far from them, and Darius was giving a statement to one police officer while the other talked into his radio.

"Hey, that door was supposed to be locked!" Steven yelled, coming over to me. He had blood on his shirt and looked completely spent. Steven had been a counselor at the center for two years, and he and I still hadn't developed camaraderie. Fact was, I just didn't like the guy.

"Where's Grace?"

"Her office, but—"

His words fell on deaf ears and I sprinted to the edge of the gym. The cop slid his hand to his holster until Darius stood him down. I wasn't surprised. *Thug* was usually the first thought that came to mind when others saw me.

The moment I spotted her, I was at her side. She was sitting on the couch with her head cradled in her hands. They were trembling.

"I'll be back out in a second. I just need a moment to pull myself together," she whispered.

She hadn't looked up or opened her eyes. Taking note that she wasn't hurt, I very gently reached up and touched her cheek before pulling her into my arms. She fell willingly, letting me hold her while she gently cried.

Stroking her hair, I whispered, "It's okay to cry, Grace. You can tell me what happened after you calm down."

A few minutes later, I heard footsteps and eyed the door as Darius entered. One look at his guilty face, and I knew the answer before I even asked the question. "It was that group of boys, wasn't it?"

Grace stiffened when she heard my demanding voice and moved away from me, subtly wiping her eyes. "What are you talking about?"

Darius crossed his arms as he approached. "One of them was taunting Melissa. When her brother reacted, they all jumped him. Eric fought hard, but they eventually pinned him. It took five of us to stop the beating and most of them took off right afterward. We were only able to detain three."

Grace stood now, fully back in control. "Have you heard from Jeff yet? I need to go over to the hospital and see how Eric is doing."

"I'm assuming that pool of blood belongs to him?" My voice was still harsh and accusing as I kept my eyes locked on Darius. "Are you going to take care of this now or is it going to take another fight to get you to hear me?"

Whether it was guilt or fury I wasn't sure, but Darius came at me, fists clenched. "You know I didn't mean for this to happen! They weren't breaking the rules!"

Grace stepped between us just in time. "Stop it, now. We won't solve anything if we're fighting among ourselves. Darius, what is he talking about?"

Darius backed down, but his eyes were still heated. "Matt noticed several of the kids altering their clothing. He wanted them talked to and suspended if it continued. I thought we should wait and keep an eye on it. Obviously, I was wrong."

Grace turned to me. "Why would they alter their clothes?"

Realizing once again how naive she was, I looked at the ceiling to hide my frustration. "Because they're a gang, Duchess, and they want everyone to know that if you mess with one, you mess with all of them."

Pressing her fingers to her temples, Grace took in a deep breath. "Okay, from this point on, any kid who alters his or her attire in any way that matches a kid or group of kids at the center will be suspended for no less than seven days. Darius, make an announcement tomorrow and put up signs. I'll call Sam tonight and let him know what happened. Now, if you both would excuse me, I need to call the media, before speculation ruins all my fund-raising efforts."

Her clipped tone made it clear she was dismissing us. Darius walked out first, but I was right behind him.

"Don't push me, Matt. I'm already at the end of my rope," Darius warned when I followed him to the kitchenette. He picked up a bucket, slammed it in the sink, and started filling it with soapy water.

"What if she had been standing there?"

Darius turned, his face in agony. "You don't think I've thought of that? You're not the only one who cares about her, Matt. We all do. Gangs haven't been in this center since the first month we opened, okay? I wasn't being irresponsible."

The pain on his face said it all. Nothing I could say to him would be worse than his own regret. Calming my voice, I walked to the counter to get the other cleaning supplies. "There's something bad brewing in the neighborhood, man. Whatever it is, Marcus is terrified of it, and obviously it's coming through our doors. I think it's time to put this place on lockdown. Zero tolerance."

"Oh, trust me, big changes are coming."

We moved in comfortable silence after that, both working to erase the evidence of the horror that had taken place there tonight.

CHAPTER 18

GRACE

The hospital felt cold and ominous as we approached the elevators. Matt had followed me from the center, but kept to himself. Already vulnerable and a little embarrassed over my breakdown earlier, I stepped in first, glancing away as he entered.

The elevator doors shut, leaving us in uncomfortable silence. Matt was stoic as he leaned against the metal wall. We were side by side, but didn't look at each other. I should have said thank you or given some other indication of my appreciation for his comfort, but the words stayed lodged in my throat. This was the guy I threw myself at, and his rejection still stung, no matter his reasons.

Second floor.

Third floor.

A resounding *ding* meant freedom and I practically jumped out of the stuffy space.

Antiseptic lingered in the air as I walked slowly to room 316, praying for strength with each step. Eric would need me to be strong, not to act like some blubbering fool. Forcing a smile, I entered and zeroed in on his battered face. Both eyes were bruising now and the cuts on his lip and eyebrows were an angry red. The blood was all gone, though, which did take away some of my earlier terror.

"Hi, Eric. How are you feeling?" I crossed the room and took his hand. His fingers felt cool next to mine, reminding me again of his vulnerability. Melissa was by his side, her mascara smudged against her milky skin. A lady who I assumed was his mother slept soundly in a corner chair. Her long, stringy blonde braid rested casually on her thin, unhealthy frame.

Eric squeezed back and attempted to grin. "A few more minutes and I could have taken them."

"I have no doubt you would have." I pulled up a chair, getting closer to him. I thought of his sweet disposition and fiercely protective nature. He was a great kid, an example to others at the center. This shouldn't have happened to him. "Did Jeff talk to you about pressing charges?"

Eric's smile faltered, his eyes turning sad. "You know I can't, Ms. Covington."

I didn't know anything. I didn't know how ten boys could so viciously attack one, or how others stood around and let it happen. The idea that they'd get to simply walk away infuriated me. "Eric, I know it's scary, but if you don't press charges they are going to get away with hurting you and will probably hurt someone else."

"I'm sorry, Ms. Covington. I know what you want, but I just can't." His voice sounded so resigned, so hopeless, that I felt my shoulders stiffen with determination. I'd convince him.

"But if—" Matt's hand on my shoulder stopped me midsentence. His squeeze was gentle but distinct. My frustrated glare was matched by a warning one as he shook his head.

Tears burned in my eyes, distorting the image of the young boy before me. I stood to get myself under control, moving quickly to the one window in the room.

Matt casually examined the injuries on Eric's face and then his knuckles. "How many hits did they get on you?"

Eric's smile returned along with some feigned confidence. "Not as many as I got on them. Well, until they pinned my arms down."

"I can teach you some things, ways to get free if you're ever pinned again. You interested?"

"You bet!" Beaming, Eric practically jumped out of bed.

"All right, get yourself all healed and then I'll take you out to The Storm." He turned to Melissa, who slunk back with her eyes downcast when Matt noticed her. "You, too. Every woman should know basic self-defense."

A shy smile appeared on her face. "Okay," she whispered before looking down again. Earlier Darius had explained to me that Melissa's awkward shyness was targeted often by the boys, but never to the degree that it was today. Apparently, the boys were throwing her things around to each other and calling her "Carrie," until Eric intervened and demanded they leave her alone.

I watched as Matt effortlessly defused the tension I'd created with my insistence about pressing charges. Eric was laughing and Melissa actually smiled more than once.

I wanted to flee. I was messing everything up. Matt was right. I had no idea what these kids went through daily. Looking at the woman in the chair, sunken cheeks, ugly dark circles under her eyes, I knew she'd likely been high or drunk before getting to the hospital. I wanted to shield these kids from all the horrors in the world, but how was that even possible when events like those today were their normal?

Forcing myself to calm down, I stepped closer to Eric's bed. "You be sure to come see me when you get out of here, okay? That is, if all the love-struck nurses will let you."

Eric grinned at me sheepishly, and I patted his leg before retreating. Tears blurred my path to the elevators, but I managed to let the door close before they spilled over. I'd never felt so helpless in my life. I always believed that I could make a difference, that changing the world happened one person at a time. But the world was much darker than I ever realized.

When I finally escaped the hospital, I dropped onto a nearby bench and closed my eyes. I wanted Eric's strength, the ability to smile in the face of horrific circumstances. To take life in stride, grasping only the positive. He inspired me.

The bench creaked in protest when someone sat next to me. I didn't have to open my eyes to know it was Matt. The current surging through my body was confirmation. His thigh brushed mine as he rested his elbows on his knees.

"Why won't he press charges?" I demanded.

"Retaliation, Grace. He has to consider his mom and his sister. Remember when I emphasized the difference between reported crime and actual crime? Well, here's your real-world lesson for the day."

I was growing tired of his "lessons." Tired of him always having an opinion, and especially tired that he was right almost every time.

He nudged me, his voice softening a little. "Come on. I'll follow you home."

"Go ahead. I'm not ready to leave just yet."

"You can't sit out here all night." His tone was stern, fatherly.

I lowered my head to my hands. "Please, Matt, go easy on me tonight. I just can't face my apartment yet, okay? It will make the events of today too real, too hopeless."

The silence echoed, cut periodically by sirens or distant voices.

"Let me take you somewhere, then."

I glanced at him, exhausted and confused. "It's okay. I don't need you to take care of me. I'm going to be fine."

Matt scooted closer and ever so lightly ran his thumb over my cheek, leaving a trail of fire in its wake. "I *want* to. Please, come with me." His eyes, more brown than green at the moment, pleaded as he gently took my hand. I knew I should run. Guard my heart like a fortress. But I had no ability to resist.

Riding the bike in a skirt was difficult, but I managed to get situated without flashing passing cars. I held on to Matt for safety, but carefully created as much physical distance as possible during the ride. The city lights faded in the distance as we traveled, wind ripping against my helmet. I thought about the difference between tonight and the first time I rode with him. Back then I was excited, hopeful. Now I knew better. Jaded and discouraged were all I could feel as we sped toward what appeared to be a plateau overlooking a valley.

The rumble of the engine suddenly went silent, and I immediately dropped my hands from Matt's waist and dismounted. Walking toward the edge of the plateau, I was struck by how visible everything stayed, illuminated by the full moon. The city lights reflected from the valley, making what I'd always considered a small city look grand and alive.

Leaves crunched as Matt approached, my body heating with each step he took. He stopped behind me, but I knew if I just leaned back slightly, I would touch him. And I wanted to, wanted his comfort and reassurance.

Instead, I crossed my arms. "I'm screwing everything up. Nothing like this ever happened when Liz was here." Defeat rang louder in my voice than I intended.

The motion was gradual, carefully gauging my reaction. I felt his body touch mine and then his slow, deliberate hands slipped around my waist, tugging me back securely. "It's not you, Grace; it's just bad timing."

I fit perfectly in Matt's arms, and relaxed into him, letting go of the fear. Tomorrow I would hurt. Tonight I just wanted to escape. "Why did you bring me here?"

"I come here when I feel overwhelmed. The peace calms me, reminds me that God is bigger than my circumstances. I thought you might need some reassurance that you weren't in this alone."

Large trees glimmered in the moonlight and stood proud and steadfast. I looked back at the city. The buildings seemed smaller, the scene less intimidating. From this angle, it was as if nature prevailed and the hand of God rested over the city and the lives of the children I loved so much.

"Thank you," I choked out as his lips pressed against the back of my head.

Matt pulled me closer, dropping his head to my neck. "Grace." The longing and pain in his voice ripped at my heart, even as his lips started to trail down my neck. His grip tightened as if he were drowning, and yet I was the one gasping for air. Lost completely in his touch, I turned in his arms.

His face said it all. The longing, desire, and attraction. It matched mine, only Matt seemed sad, while my heart raced with anticipation.

"Tell me what you're thinking." I searched his eyes, waiting. I wouldn't initiate this time.

One arm pulled me closer while the other carefully touched my flushed cheeks. "I'm sorry. That's what I'm thinking." The huskiness in his voice stirred more hunger through me, making the small distance that was left between us feel like an eternity.

"Why?" I weakened enough to let my gaze skim down his face and linger too long on his mouth, which was a mere inch from mine.

"Because I should leave you alone. I'll only hurt you. But yet, here I am, completely powerless, knowing exactly what I'm going to do."

With that, Matt brought his mouth down hard on mine, taking me over the emotional cliff I'd been hanging on to all day. He demanded and I gave, snaking my hands up his chest until his short hair tickled my palms.

"You don't know the real me," he whispered, breaking contact, but only by a fraction.

"Then let me." I cupped my hand at the back of his neck, dragging him back to me. It was a plea, and I had never before begged a man, but I was willing to do anything to have him kiss me like that again. His grip tightened on my clothes, clenching my blouse while he devoured me with another toe-curling kiss.

I wasn't innocent. I understood intimacy and lust, but never had I known such need. The way he kissed me, touched me. It was as if his life depended on it.

He suddenly dropped his forehead to mine. "Tell me to stop."

His breath was as labored as mine. We were both so lost in desire that I actually considered giving myself to him right then.

Shame snapped through me—sharp, painful, and with a scorching burn. I was no better than Lacey or Stewart, who let passion and lust rule their decisions and ruin years of trust. "I'm sorry. I lost myself for a moment."

Forcing me to look at him, Matt shook his head. "Never apologize, Grace. You have no idea how beautiful you are under the moonlight, looking at me the way you do. It makes me crazy." He pulled me into his arms and held me reverently as he stroked my back.

"Are you going to disappear tomorrow? Go back to pretending this doesn't exist between us?" My voice was muffled against his chest and part of me didn't want his answer.

His body vibrated with a short, harsh laugh. "Oh, Grace, haven't you realized yet? I'm incapable of staying away from you."

I held him tighter, silently praying he was telling the truth.

"It's late. I should take you back to your car."

I shook my head against his chest, tightening my grip. I didn't want to go home, didn't want to let go of this moment. "Just a little longer, please."

He leaned down, still holding me tightly, and kissed my head. "Okay, Grace. We'll stay as long as you need to."

Matt held me while I cried, while I prayed, and while I silently contemplated the ugly world I now saw on a daily basis. He didn't say a word or force me to talk. He was just there for me, my rock in the storm, until I finally had the strength to stand on my own again.

"Okay, I'm ready now." I stepped back and wiped away the last of my tears. Cupping my face, Matt pulled me back into his arms and showed me once again why I'd fallen so hard for him. The kiss was intimate and soft, bonding us as two people sharing mutual hope—a hope that this was only the beginning.

Trepidation weighed heavily on my shoulders as I turned the bolt at the center the next morning. The previous day's events had made for a restless night, as I feared what would come in the new day. Would the center remain empty? Would the kids be too afraid to come? Would Matt give me the cold shoulder again as he was prone to doing? After last night, I could never go back to how things had been between us. He had awakened something in me, something I buried long ago.

I shook my thoughts aside, pushing the heavy doors instead. It was early, just barely after sunrise, but I wanted to make sure the center was prepared for the new policies we planned to put into action. The doors shut with a bang and I turned back the lock before heading to my office.

The sun glistened through the high windows, but still the center seemed brighter than usual. Suddenly realizing a few of the lights were on, my heart sank. We turned everything off when we left each night, a practice that helped reduce our high electricity bills. Glancing quickly at the offices, I soon discovered that only mine was in use, with light streaming through the blinds and creating a striped mosaic on the gym floor. I slowly walked forward. I must have left a lamp on in the confusion of last night. We had all been a little off.

"Hello?" My voice sounded weak, annoying me. No one answered my call.

I continued forward until I could peek into my office without being seen. The view of a man stretched out across the couch sent my pulse skyrocketing as I dropped my keys with a startled squeal. The echo made him stir. As if in slow motion, he sat up, rubbed his eyes, and stood.

It took a while for my brain to function, but once it processed the image in front of me, I let out all the breath I had been holding and stepped through the door. "Sam? What are you doing here?"

He turned to me and smiled, stretching his arms high above his head. "Gracie Belle! I wondered if you would keep the same crazy hours Liz did." His brown hair fell lazily over his forehead as he glanced at his watch. "I guess you do."

My body still recovering from the shock, I stepped forward, dropping my bag on the desk. "You scared me half to death."

Easy as ever, Sam strolled to the doorway and picked up my forgotten keys. Watching him, I understood why he'd been named New York's most eligible bachelor the past few years. Only ten years my senior, Sam had a youthful playfulness but still had the imposing demeanor of a Fortune 500 CEO. Most of my girlfriends had crushes on him, but I'd known him since I was sixteen and always saw him as more of the young uncle type. Besides, back then I only had eyes for Stewart.

"You don't sound happy to see me." He handed me the keys while giving me a look I couldn't read. Working for him had changed our dynamic and I still hadn't quite adjusted to it.

"It's not that. I just wasn't expecting you until Saturday, for the banquet."

His arms crossed, but his smile reappeared, sending me mixed signals. "Well, consider yourself lucky to have an extra pair of hands for the next few days."

I took in his intimidating height and tried to ease the gnawing sensation in my gut. "Sam, if this is about yester—"

"Gracie." His warning voice stopped me as he lowered one hand to my desk and leaned forward. "My being here doesn't discount the amazing job you've done, okay? I need to know my staff is safe and, well, your father needs to know you are."

"You told him?" I felt like a little girl all over again.

"I sent his only child hours away, put her in the hood, and then left her to fend for herself. I'm already on thin ice." He laughed. "My only restitution is that I promised to keep him informed. I don't break my promises."

I nodded, understanding. So much for charting my own course.

"You look good, by the way. I think being in charge agrees with you." His tone changed back to its normal cheery candor as he pulled up a chair. "Speaking of which, why don't you show me everything you've been doing around here."

Pulling myself together, I grabbed the banquet files and investor information, proud that four businesses had already promised us a monthly stipend that would cover the salary of an assistant for Darius.

Sam listened closely, never interrupting but asking questions when he wanted details. I was surprised by how easy he was to work with. I'd heard others say he was demanding and aggressive in his business dealings. But then again, this wasn't his business. It was his passion.

The Hartsford Center had been his father's idea, but Sam carried that dream to fruition. George Hartsford, Sam's father, lived the ultimate American success story, pulling himself up the ranks to become one of the richest men in the United States. He died when Sam was in college. I always wondered if that was the reason he and Daddy were so close. Though he'd never admit it, I knew my dad had always wanted a son and Sam needed a father.

An hour passed quickly, and soon we heard the doors unlocking as Darius and Jeff came in together. Sam cocked his head toward the sound and smiled at me. "Looks like the rest of the crew is getting here. Let's see if I can stun them half as much as I did you."

I nudged him playfully. "You've always been incorrigible."

He winked. "Only with you, Gracie Belle."

CHAPTER 19

MATT

Reds and oranges filled the sky as the sun peeked over the horizon. I sipped my coffee, struggled to loosen the knots in my shoulders, and tried to concentrate on the beauty of the sunrise instead of on my next steps. I'd become resigned that keeping my distance from Grace was impossible, yet I knew that last night was only a taste of how things would be with her. I had been consumed, so lost in her that I moved solely on instinct. Even this morning, I wondered where she was, what she was doing. I wondered if she'd wear the copper suit that set off her eyes. Eyes that saw past my sarcasm and distance to the deepest parts of my soul.

I shifted, frustrated by the yearning that had only deepened for me after holding Grace in my arms. Was this how my father felt? I remembered his jealousy, his rage. My mom couldn't even talk to another man without consequences.

"No!" I said aloud. I wouldn't hurt her. I didn't want Grace to be weak or afraid. I wanted her strong and empowered. I wanted to cherish her and protect her. My father had done neither of those things for my mom. His love was selfish and cruel.

I stretched my weary back and went to get dressed. Maybe I'd stop by the center for just a moment this morning before heading to Bruce's office. The idea of seeing Grace's beautiful face made me smile. I'd just take things one day at a time.

I rapped on the door, waiting for someone to let me in. Bruce's first appointment was at eight thirty, so I only had a few minutes. Unfortunately, I'd already imagined several things I could do with Grace in those few minutes, making me antsy when no one came to the door.

Finally the lock turned, but Steven stood in my path. "You do know you don't work here? Center opens at nine."

My hard stare forced him to back away as I stepped through the door. Liz's decision to hire him was one of the only things I questioned. "Grace here?"

"Yes, but she's busy. You can come back later." His snotty voice grated, and I cracked my neck in an attempt to calm myself.

Stepping near him, I almost laughed as he cowered slightly. "In case you haven't figured it out, I'm not the kind of guy who gets told what to do. *Capisce?*"

He huffed and slammed the doors behind me but didn't say another word as I moved toward Grace's office. Signs were already posted outlining the new policy on clothing and alterations. Irritation swirled in me as I thought how last night would have been avoided if Darius had only listened to me. The anger quickly vanished, however, when I saw Grace.

Standing in her doorway, I noted she wore a gray pantsuit that hugged every one of her beautiful curves. She was focused on the file cabinet in front of her, carefully placing files back in their appropriate spots. I considered surprising her, sweeping her off her feet, but I was enjoying watching her too much to move. She tucked back some hair when it fell over her face. The motion must have clued her to my presence, because she suddenly stood straight, looking nervous.

Sending her a warm smile, I shut the door behind me. Within seconds, she was in my arms again, my lips kissing hers as if I hadn't seen her in years, not hours. She eagerly responded and all hesitation melted away. There would be no day by day. I wanted it all.

"Good morning," I whispered as I planted kisses along her jawline. She smelled like heaven.

The look she sent could have taken down a legion of warriors. "Yes, it is."

Squeezing my eyes shut for a moment, I forced myself to step back. I didn't want her to think I only came by to kiss her, although there was some truth to that. I laced her fingers with mine as I leaned back against the desk.

"Are you worried about today?" I choked out, refusing to be one of those guys who reduced his relationship to only a physical one. It had been a long time since I touched a woman, and my self-control was weak at best.

"I was, but I feel better now that you're here." She moved in to lightly peck me again. "I didn't know what to expect."

I pulled her closer, her body now pressed up against mine. "Expect to see a lot of me. I may take things slow, but once I'm in, there's no halfway."

There was no mistaking the intensity in my voice or the possessive way I held her. Her heart was drumming hard against mine, her breath catching. She trembled as I ran a finger down the length of her hair before taking her mouth in mine again. Electricity coursed through me as my instincts once again overshadowed my good judgment. I shouldn't be kissing her like this, not in her office, but my mind and body were not communicating.

Her hands pushing against my chest cooled us both down as she took a step back and smoothed out her suit. With her cheeks flushed and hair disheveled from my hands, she was by far the most beautiful thing I'd ever seen.

Attempting to brush her hair back into place, she lifted a hand to hold me off. "You and I may need to set some boundaries early."

She was absolutely right. I took the hand she raised and brought it to my lips, a reassurance to both of us that my intentions went way beyond the undeniable physical chemistry. "We can do that."

Just then her door flew open and Grace jumped back. "Gracie Belle! I have a great idea for that back room." The man entered as if he owned the place and stopped short when he saw me. His smile wavered as his eyes moved back and forth between us.

Standing slowly, in vast contrast to my racing heart, I pushed down the fire igniting in my gut. *Gracie Belle?*

Grace was back in director mode, looking poised and regal as she approached the man. "Sam, this is Matt Holloway. Matt, Sam Hartsford." She emphasized his last name as if I wouldn't catch the importance. That grated. I wasn't an idiot.

For some reason, I'd always pictured the center's benefactor as an old man with white hair and a cane. The man in front of me was anything but old. In fact, he and Grace matched in both style and presence, making me feel as if I was the intruder, not him.

He stepped forward, casually draping his arm around her shoulders, a gesture that seemed far more intimate than was appropriate between a boss and employee. The look he sent me wasn't casual, nor was it friendly. "Matt. Very nice to meet you."

Grace must have sensed the tension, and went overboard explaining how I'd worked with the center for years and how far Marcus had come since meeting me. Call it hurt pride, but each word she spoke felt like she was trying to justify why she'd even be talking to a guy like me. She didn't need to explain herself to him, nor did I appreciate how much she seemed to value his opinion.

Unable to stomach any more of her flustered explanations, I moved toward the door, stopping just long enough to shake his hand. "Sam, it's nice to finally meet you. Liz always speaks highly of you." Turning toward Grace, who remained at his side, I nodded toward the door. "Come walk me out." It was a statement, not a question.

She hesitated, eyes wide, and appeared to be battling with herself. That was all I needed to see, and I turned to leave without a look back. I didn't need that crap in my life.

I was already out the front doors when Grace caught up with me. "Matt, wait. I'm sorry."

Turning, I waited until she was only inches away before speaking, my voice harsh. "Do you want to be with me, Duchess? Yes or no?"

She let out an exasperated sigh. "Yes. You know I do."

"Then don't ever make me feel like that again. I'm not your dirty little secret." I was too angry to trust our closeness, and started back toward my Harley. Driving off before Grace could reply, I wondered once again what I had gotten myself into.

CHAPTER 20

GRACE

I watched until Matt disappeared, berating myself for the way I'd just handled things. Of course he'd be upset. He finally let his guard down and I acted as if we were mere acquaintances. I wasn't prepared for my two worlds to collide, and obviously my ability to think on the fly was dismal.

Sam was still waiting when I stepped back into my office. I grabbed a clipboard and smiled. "Show me your idea for that room."

He merely lifted an eyebrow. "What is he to you?"

Leave it to Sam to get straight to the point. His innate ability to read people had no doubt contributed to his success. "I don't know yet. It's still very new."

He moved closer, making me uncomfortable under his stare. "What about Stewart?"

"What about him? We're not together anymore." My voice raised an octave, making it sound like I cared more than I did.

"Hey, I'm not saying you should be. But Gracie, you've been in love with him for as long as I've known you. This Matt character can only be a distraction and not the good kind. You need to let yourself heal."

I was getting angry. "Sam, I am perfectly capable of knowing what my needs are. Now, would you like to discuss the back room or are we done for today?"

Sam's bellowing laugh filled the room. "Yikes, Gracie, you almost sounded like your mother just then. I didn't know you had that kind of fire in you, but I like it."

Crossing my arms, I could feel the anger dissipating already, and couldn't help but return his grin. He gripped my shoulders and then turned me around, affectionately pushing me toward the door.

Suddenly we stopped, and Sam leaned in. "You know I'm going to check him out."

Easing out of his grip, I turned, feeling uneasy. "We already have a background check on him. He has a past, but it's just that. His past. He's a great guy and I like him. A lot."

"Gracie, your wholehearted love for others is what makes you so special. But it's also what makes you vulnerable to people who want to hurt you."

"People like Stewart and Lacey?" My clipped voice challenged him.

"Yes, to name a few. But they aren't bad people, Gracie."

"Neither is Matt."

His mouth was set in a thin line. "We shall see."

I suddenly understood why people were intimidated by Sam. The way he spoke those last three words made it clear he was ending our conversation, but he also made it clear the subject wasn't going to be dropped. He'd look into Matt's past and see a record. He wouldn't see the kind, compassionate man I knew. The man who made me feel treasured and safe. My stomach knotted as I realized things were going to get a lot more complicated.

I was relieved and exhausted by the time Sam left, saying he had some business to take care of. He had promised to be an extra pair of hands, but as I looked down at my now doubly long to-do list, I realized he was just finding more and more for us to tackle. He was excited about the renovation plans, and even more excited that there was a good chance we'd have the resources to do it. He admitted to having all but given up on the center's viability. When I asked him why he hired me when he was practically sure the center would close, he just changed the subject, commenting again on how much older I seemed since leaving New York.

The whistle blew. Intramurals would be starting soon. I had seen Matt come in earlier, but didn't go talk to him. He was involved with the center for Marcus, and I had no intention of our new relationship, or whatever it was, getting in the way of those two bonding.

As if he could sense I was thinking about him, I heard a rap on my doorframe. "Have you eaten yet?"

I looked up from my desk and studied Matt's face to see if he was still upset, but he remained completely unreadable. Typical.

"No. Are you asking me to dinner?"

He grinned, warming my insides. "Come on."

Looking at my watch, I saw it was only six. "The center doesn't close for another two hours."

"Grace, you've been here since dawn. Darius and Jeff can handle cleanup. Come on, we need to talk."

His words made me nervous, as if he was setting me up to say good-bye. I wasn't ready to end this thing between us, no matter what challenges were lurking in the shadows. Matt made me feel things I never had before.

Standing slowly, I grabbed my bag. "Okay."

He was right as usual, and Darius had no issue with doing cleanup. To my surprise and delight, the center was bustling as if yesterday's turmoil had never happened. I guessed one incident wasn't enough to keep the kids away, but I knew in my heart there couldn't be a second one.

We drove by my apartment so I could drop off my car and change into casual clothes. Matt wouldn't tell me where he was taking me, but I knew without asking that it wouldn't be anyplace fancy.

We drove out of the city again, but to a different area from last night. This place was surrounded by trees, and we had to walk awhile before I saw a clearing come into view. A large blanket with a picnic basket was waiting for me along with a single rose.

"When did you do all this?"

"Before I came to see Marcus." Matt was watching my reaction and then laced his fingers with mine. "This is my way of apologizing for this morning."

Walking toward the romantic setup, I smiled. "You're good at it."

We sat cross-legged and faced each other. Matt took my hand again, rolling my palm around in his. He seemed nervous.

"Let's talk about boundaries. You go first." He waited, giving me full rein to place any demands I had on our relationship.

Swallowing hard, I realized I'd never had this kind of conversation before. Stewart and I never talked about boundaries. He'd just push until I said no. It was always on me to stop things.

"I firmly believe that sex is for marriage. I know that's old-fashioned in today's world, and I'm not saying I think we're going to get married or anything. But it does mean that I don't want to take things so far that it's hard for either one of us to stop. I know I won't change my mind on this issue, so if that is a deal breaker for you, I understand." It had been a deal breaker for Stewart and I wasn't going down that road again.

Matt grinned, his hazel eyes sparkling. "It's not a deal breaker." He waited in silence for me to continue.

"Okay, um, I think in light of this morning, we should forgo any affection at the center. It's my workplace."

"Completely agree." A mischievous grin spread across his lips. "But that means I get to kiss you everywhere else."

"That's only fair," I conceded with a smile. His walls were completely gone and I adored this new, affectionate Matt.

His hand, roughened with calluses, wrapped around my neck and pulled me gently forward until we were touching. The kiss was sweet and endearing, without the desperation we had experienced earlier but just as remarkable.

"I'm sorry, go on." He sat back, waiting.

I took in his face. He intimidated people. They'd move out of the way when we approached, or watched him from the corners of their eyes, but I had seen his gentleness. I found his short dark hair sexy. In fact, I found every inch of him to be sexy, even the tattoos that subtly told his deepest feelings. "I think that's it. What about you?"

"I only have one."

I waited, nervous for some reason.

"It's you, me, and no one else."

Now I was pulling him to me until we were falling as we kissed. Somehow I knew the struggles I had with Stewart wouldn't exist with him. Matt wasn't a pretender, nor did he make promises he wouldn't keep. I didn't wonder if he would respect my limits or if he would be faithful. I trusted him completely.

He adjusted his weight so he was beside me and not on top. I could already sense he was being more careful when we touched. With his elbow bent and his head propped up against one hand, he ran a finger along the bottom of my shirt in a slow, seductive manner. The gesture seemed innocent enough, but it was driving me crazy.

"Why does Sam call you Gracie Belle?"

The mention of Sam's name quickly doused my fire. I sat up and Matt followed.

"I really didn't want people to know this because it makes me look unqualified, like I only got the job because of my connections."

He was watching me, hanging on my every word. "Go on."

"Sam and my father are very close. Truthfully, he's close to all of us. He's like an adopted member of the family. I've been called Gracie Belle since I was a little girl, and since Sam spends so much time with us, he just kind of picked it up."

Matt took my hand in his again, running his finger along each one of mine. He stopped at the ring on my right index finger, examining the way the ruby caught the light. "Grace, anyone could tell from the way you two interacted this morning that there is history there. There's chemistry. I overreacted the way I did this morning partly because I assumed it was romantic."

"With Sam?" I shuddered. "He's like a brother to me."

Matt grinned, clearly happy with the answer. "So how did you get the name Gracie Belle?"

I covered my face. "Ugh. It's so stupid."

"Tell me," he prodded, laughing. "I want to know everything about you."

Peeking through my fingers before lowering my hands, I caved. "All right, fine. When I was a little girl, I loved the movie *Beauty and the Beast*. Belle had dark hair like me, and she was strong and determined. I wanted to be just like her, so I told my parents that my new name was Belle and I wasn't going by Gracie anymore. I even stopped answering when they used my real name. I don't know, somehow Gracie Belle took hold and I've been called that ever since."

I pushed him when he started laughing, feeling even more embarrassed. "Stop."

"So do I get to call you Gracie Belle?"

"No, absolutely not! Only family calls me that, and obviously a few friends who have known me forever. *Gracie* makes me feel like I'm still a child."

He lay back, pulling me on top of him, his hard body in vivid contrast to my soft one.

"Besides . . ." I paused, feeling light-headed from the way his mouth felt moving up my neck. "I love the way you say my name."

Suddenly I was on my back, my eyes locked with Matt's adoring ones. "Then I'll be sure to say it all the time . . . Grace." He barely got my name out before he lowered his head to mine again, sweeping me up in a kiss so passionate I could hardly breathe.

CHAPTER 21

MATT

I have a girlfriend, I thought, smiling. More amazing was that being with Grace no longer scared me. The feelings I had for her were different than with Maggie. More real, more mature. Sure, I still wanted to protect her and could spend every waking minute with her, but she didn't make me crazy the way Maggie had. In fact, she did just the opposite. Grace calmed me, centered me.

Cody was already waiting when I strolled into the gym, whistling.

"Hey, buddy, how's your week going?" He watched me suspiciously as I put on my headgear and mouthpiece, still smiling.

"Fine, I guess." He was understandably distant. Our last session hadn't gone well, and I had lost my temper with him. I'd have some rebuilding to do today, that was for sure.

We got in the ring and Cody's stance was defensive, like his tone had been. I took him through moves he had mastered, giving him the opportunity to pin me several times and praising him along the way. As he became more confident, I switched to some of the harder moves, the ones he'd struggled with last week. Once again he had the technique perfect, but lacked the strength to finish the job.

Throwing his headgear down, Cody turned and grabbed the ropes. "I'll never make the varsity team. I'm just a fat kid who's fooling himself. Why did I ever think I could do this?"

"Cody, over here. Now."

He turned, tears threatening to fill his eyes.

"Down here." I got in the push-up position, waiting for him to join me. Finally he did, and we held ourselves there, face-to-face. "Now a little lower," I said, showing him what to do. He followed, and I could see his arms shaking a little. "Lower." I continued until I knew he was ready to collapse. I then pushed back up to the ready position, nodding for him to do the same.

Standing, I offered him my hand. He took it begrudgingly and stood.

"I want you to do fifty of those every day, counting five seconds between each position. Break it up all you want, but at the end of the day, you make sure you have fifty."

I walked closer, squeezing his bicep, which was firmer every week. "Cody, you're almost there. Don't give up now because you have to work a little harder. Every day you get stronger, and soon that move will be as easy as the others. That vulnerable kid you once were is gone. In fact, I've never been more proud of a trainee than I am of you."

His head shot up in surprise because I rarely dished out compliments like that, but I meant every word. He had heart and determination, an unstoppable combination.

"You don't think they'll mess with me when school starts again?"

"At this point, Cody, if they do, I'll enjoy hearing all about how you took them down. Come on, let's do two miles and then try again. We still need to get your stamina up."

Cody followed me to the treadmills and finally smiled as we started jogging. "It's good to have you back." His words meant more than he could know, and I realized how much I had let the chaos in my head affect every part of my life.

"It's good to be back."

My time with Cody went a little long, keeping me from stopping by to see Grace before I headed to Bruce's office. I settled for texting.

Me: Morning. Running late, so I won't get to stop by.

Grace: Probably better. Sam has us running around like crazy people.

I stared at her text, feeling a little sting. Where were the *I miss you* and *Think of me* comments? The girlie stuff that all us guys say we hate but secretly expect from the girls we care about?

Shrugging off the disappointment, I tied my bag down on my bike and headed to the office. Bruce had a full load scheduled, starting an hour earlier than usual. He was becoming more and more in demand. With all the court-appointed cases and word-of-mouth referrals, I could hardly find available booking times. I mentioned hiring another counselor, but Bruce was territorial and dismissed the idea completely. Maybe he'd change his mind when we had to start refusing new patients.

He was already there when I came in, but his door was shut. I knew from experience he was likely reading and praying before his first patient, a practice he said was essential. Just one of the many reasons I respected the man.

I stared at my unopened Bible, the one I kept at work. I'd been so angry with God the past couple of weeks, I hadn't even looked at the thing. Filled with conviction, I began reading where I had left off.

Lost completely in the story of Joseph, I almost didn't hear Bruce's door opening. "My eight o'clock just canceled."

I glanced quickly at the computer screen. "What? When?" Looking closer, I noticed that I didn't recognize the name. In fact, I hadn't made the appointment at all.

"Looks like I've got an hour, so come on. It's been a while since we had a chance to talk."

I shook my head, realizing I'd been duped. "You're getting sneaky, old man." Bruce had been on me to schedule myself an appointment. My last excuse was that he didn't have any open slots. I guess he took care of that problem.

Settled into his favorite chair and watching my mannerisms the entire time, Bruce looked thoughtful as I sat opposite him.

"You're better today," he stated, still watching me.

"Glad to hear it." I wasn't trying to be disrespectful, but his skillful scrutiny was making me uncomfortable.

"But it doesn't change the fact that you've been moody, short, and an all-around unpleasant person to be around. Not to mention, you almost lost your cool with Rex the other day, and you know that can't happen. So what's going on? No deflecting this time."

I sighed, falling back lazily in the chair. I owed Bruce an explanation. He'd been more than patient with me. Finally I smiled. "I met a girl."

The look on his face morphed from surprise to understanding. "Well, I guess that would do it. Who is she?"

"The new director at Hartsford."

Bruce's eyebrow shot up, and I didn't like the look on his face. It was a look of recognition.

"You know her?" I didn't know why, but that bothered me. It seemed like anytime I mentioned Grace to someone, whoever it was had either met her or heard of her. I knew she was striking, an unforgettable presence, but her growing status in the community made our pairing that much more unlikely.

"The city is kind of in a buzz about the banquet this weekend. She has Carter Fields coming, you know. The dinner sold out the first day tickets became available. A dinner that costs fifteen thousand dollars a plate, mind you."

I knew Grace was from the elite, but she lived so simply, was so unassuming, that I found myself forgetting our class difference. Insecurity gripped me. How long could I pretend I wasn't an ex-con and she wasn't a New York princess?

"What else have you heard?" Bruce immediately noticed my change in tone and looked sympathetic, like a father letting his son down easy.

"Just that you aren't the only one smitten with her. She's charmed more than a few businesses into supporting that center, which is great. It's about time the city rallied around something worthwhile." He paused, choosing his words carefully. "Considering she's the first girl to even turn your head in a long, long time, do you think that maybe you are choosing to pursue something you know will have no chance of materializing?"

The shot to my pride hurt almost as much as realizing he thought I wasn't good enough for her. "I don't have a crush, Bruce. We're in a relationship. A mutual, exclusive relationship." The surprise on his face only fanned the flame burning inside me. "And for the record, she pursued me."

Bruce's office suddenly felt stuffy and I was done with the informal chat.

"Matt, I'm sorry. I didn't mean—"

"No, I know exactly what you mean. And I'm fully aware that we are from different worlds, that our chances of making it are slim at best. That edginess you mentioned, that short fuse you are so concerned about? Well, that was me trying to stay away from her, and I just can't, okay?"

Bruce watched as I took several deep breaths to calm down. Once I was under control, he leaned back and changed the subject.

"How are you sleeping?"

"Just fine. No nightmares for a couple weeks now." I didn't mention that I was still waking up every two hours to prevent them, but my interest in this little heart-to-heart had ended.

Bruce was no dummy. He could tell by my defensive posture and terse answers that he wasn't getting behind my defenses.

Sighing, he crossed his arms. "So I guess you're going to the banquet, then. I don't envy the pretentious dress-up part, but I must admit I'd love to meet Carter Fields."

My stomach burned. Grace hadn't invited me. Granted, this thing between us was new, but still, after last night shouldn't she have at least mentioned the possibility of my going?

Feigning a smile, I stood. "You know me, Bruce. Knocking elbows with the rich and famous isn't really my thing. Anyway, this has been fun, but you actually pay me to work."

Before he could protest, I was out of his office and back at my desk. I doubted if my mood could get worse, until I saw Grace had texted me again.

Grace: Sam wants to go to the hotel tonight and sample all the food they are serving, so I'll probably miss you when you come by to see Marcus. :(

I squeezed my eyes shut until I stopped seeing red.

Me: That's fine.

Grace: You ok?

Me: Peachy.

Grace: Do you want to come over after I get back? It may be late.

Me: Do you want me to?

Grace: Yes, of course.

Me: Then I'll be there.

I stared at our conversation while trying to get my warring emotions under control. If Grace and I could exist in a vacuum, then there'd be no issue. We were a perfect fit. But we couldn't, and each day I was reminded that our very new, budding relationship was just one step away from being completely torn apart.

CHAPTER 22

GRACE

Glancing at my watch again, I tried not to look agitated. "You about ready?"

We were still seated in the restaurant at the Hotel Mayan, even though they'd shut down the kitchen thirty minutes ago. Sam looked up from his furious scribbling and smirked. "What's the rush? You have a hot date tonight or something?"

His comment was meant to be a joke, but when I didn't respond he scowled. "It's awful late to be meeting up with someone, don't you think?"

"Sam, I'm twenty-five years old. I think I'm well past the age when I need a curfew."

"Does your dad know you're seeing someone?" His voice was clipped, as if he was responsible for me in some way.

I was beginning to wonder if that wasn't the case. If maybe this entire job thing had been my father's way of keeping tabs on me after I told him I was moving out. I pushed the ugly thought aside. I knew better. My parents weren't controlling or manipulative, but they were protective. At first I had no doubt that Sam's visit was at their prompting, but now I wasn't so sure. He'd been acting strange ever since that first day. Our normally playful banter felt strained and even uncomfortable at times.

"Sam, I'm ready to go home. It's ten o'clock, and I've been in these shoes since six this morning." I glanced around the sparse dining room, taking in the soft music coming from the hidden speakers.

I wanted to see Matt, and every minute that ticked by jeopardized his coming over. I had already sensed that something was off with him today. His texts were short, snappish even. The old Matt, the guarded one, was trying to resurface.

Sam sighed, realizing that I was done working for the evening. "Gracie, you don't know anything about this guy. You're vulnerable right now and you're nursing a broken heart. I just don't want you jumping into something you're going to regret. I can understand your wanting to forget, but this isn't the way."

Sam's blue eyes pleaded and I realized the entire day had been a lame attempt to keep me away from Matt. I wanted to be angry with him, but knew he was only trying to intervene because he cared. He didn't know Matt the way I did. He didn't know that I wasn't using him to forget Stewart. I had healed before Matt ever entered the picture.

"Sam, I don't love Stewart anymore. Sometimes I wonder if I ever did, or if he was just what I always thought my next step was. Did he hurt me? Yes, of course he did. But I'm not hurting right now. I'm happy."

Sam's brown hair fell over one eye when he leaned in and rested his hand on mine. "I'm glad you're happy, Gracie. That's what I wanted when I sent you out here. I never liked Stewart anyway. He's pretentious."

I laughed at the way he scrunched his nose. "And you're not, Mister 'I'll buy an island just to get some peace and quiet'?"

"Hey, I told you that in confidence." He tried to pout, but doing so was impossible through our laughter.

His eyes fixed on me and suddenly that uncomfortable feeling took over again. "You really have blossomed, Gracie. You're self-assured and witty. You took a situation that would have broken most people and turned it into something special. Any guy would be lucky to have your attention, even if he is just a rebound."

Of course he had to get one last slam in. "Matt's not a rebound."

He let go of my hand and raised his own hands in surrender. "Whatever you say. Just promise me you'll be careful."

"I will. Now please, slave driver, let me go home or I will be a walking zombie tomorrow."

He packed up and stopped by the hotel concierge, giving me just enough time to text Matt that I was on my way and would be there in fifteen minutes. I was grateful we had taken two cars to the hotel. I had strategically avoided letting Sam see where I lived, knowing full well he'd have me relocated in less than an hour. My complex was even scarier at night, especially when groups were hanging out around the parking lot, drinking and cutting up.

Matt was waiting by my door when I pulled in. He looked incredible. A snug black T-shirt stopped just below the waistband of faded denim. His thumbs were hooked in his jeans pockets, while a foot rested casually against the wall behind him. I suddenly felt nervous, or maybe just eager. My emotions jumbled when I saw him.

Matt glanced up, and when our eyes locked, a ball of heat exploded in my gut. "Hi," I said as I shut my car door.

He pushed off from the wall, his voice matching the scowl on his face. "You didn't loop the parking lot before pulling in."

Immediately the heat dissipated with his cold stare. "I saw you, Matt. I wasn't worried."

"So when I'm not here, you do it?"

Busted. Okay, now what was I supposed to do? Lie? No. I couldn't lie to him even if I wanted to, which I didn't. He was far too perceptive.

"Okay, no, I don't, but I'll start. I promise."

He smiled and closed the distance between us. My heart picked up speed, anticipating his kiss. The kiss I'd missed all day. But he didn't kiss me, just took my face in his hands, softly caressing my cheeks. "Your safety is important to me."

Breathless and so ready for contact, I whispered, "I know."

He stepped back so I could unlock the door to my apartment. I had to remind my feet to move. Just when I got the key in the lock, Matt was on me. The keys were gone from my fingers, and I was completely immobile against the door. His hand over my mouth muffled my shocked scream.

"Do you see how quick that was, Grace?" his harsh voice whispered in my ear. "Seconds are all it takes for someone to overpower you. Never turn your back like that."

He let go of me and opened the door. I was shaking when he pulled me inside, slamming the door behind us.

Angry now, I glared at him. "You didn't have to scare me like that."

"Yes, I did." His voice was full of exasperation. "Because telling you over and over isn't working. I may not always be here and you have got to learn to protect yourself."

He was doing it again. Talking as if he was about to walk away. "What do mean by you may not always be here? Are you breaking up with me already?"

He sat on the couch, head suddenly in his hands. "Grace, at some point we're going to have to accept that we are different. A fish and a bird are separated for a reason. They can't breathe in each other's world."

I took off my heels and dropped next to him, carefully tucking my feet under me. "Last I checked, we weren't either of those things." I ran my fingers over the short hairs above his temple. "Where is this coming from?"

He met my eyes, still defensive, but at least his hand had found mine. "Why didn't you invite me to the banquet?"

Startled by his question, I answered honestly. "I didn't think you'd want to go. You've made no secret of your dislike for the people who tour the center. The banquet will be full of those and worse . . . their spouses."

The distaste in my voice made Matt chuckle. "Grace, if it's important to you, then it's important to me, even if I have to dress up in some monkey suit and play nice for a night."

Smiling, I held his face, forcing him to look at me. "Matt Holloway, will you be my plus-one on Saturday?"

His humor turned to frustration as he stood. "Don't patronize me."

"I'm not," I assured him with a laugh. Man, he was testy. "I would be thrilled to have you escort me to this thing." I wrapped my arms around his waist, smiling up at his hardened face. "I'll enjoy having the sexiest date there."

Those words finally broke through his armor, and quickly his arms wrapped around me. "Sexy, huh?" He grinned, making no attempt to hide that he liked those words.

I blushed, a little embarrassed by my boldness. "You know you are. Don't even try to act humble."

He responded by leaning down to kiss me, embracing me tightly. Still dazed, he pulled me over to the couch and propped my aching feet on his lap, gently massaging them.

"Now tell me about your day," he said.

I leaned back, taking in the handsome face of my new boyfriend, and did just that.

CHAPTER 23

MATT

I tugged at the collar of my rented tux while Naomi stood in the corner trying to hold in a laugh. It was bad enough that I had to stop by just to get the bowtie tied, but Naomi's muffled amusement was just making the moment worse.

"I'm sorry," she giggled when I looked at her with annoyance.

Jake wasn't much better, enjoying my discomfort far too much. Worse, I was borrowing his car, since my bike was no chariot. Dealing with the logistics made me feel like a teenage kid getting ready for prom. A cold chill descended . . . I never went to prom. No, I was incarcerated my senior year, studying for the GED.

"What am I doing?" My strained voice was just loud enough for Jake to hear. He saw the unease in my eyes and offered a reassuring smile.

"You're taking your very beautiful girlfriend to dinner. The rest of this stuff doesn't matter."

Taking a deep breath, I stopped messing with the jacket, even though I could swear the thing was going to choke me to death.

Jake stepped aside and I presented myself to Naomi, waiting for her verdict.

Her smile was encouraging as she came forward and brushed some lint off the jacket. "What can I say? You're an all-around Prince Charming." She stood next to Jake, his arm automatically wrapping around her.

"More like the Frog Prince." I sighed, putting my hand out for Jake's keys.

He dropped them in my palm, but not without a few jokes at my expense.

"Oh, don't pretend you aren't giddy to have my Harley for the night," I retorted over his laughter. "And if there is so much as a scratch, I swear . . ."

"Simmer down. Naomi's driving." Jake laughed louder when my mouth dropped open. He was enjoying my anxiety far more than he should have been. "Just kidding. We'll be gentle. Now, get out of here before Grace starts to think she's getting stood up."

With one more quick hug from Naomi, I was out the door and on my way to Grace's apartment. A sixteen-year-old kid on his first date would have been less nervous than I was when my knuckles rapped on her door. Waiting, I wiped my clammy palms on my heavily pressed tux.

The door swung open to reveal Grace, looking like an angel against the soft light of her living room. My eyes wandered, drinking in every inch. The material flowed over her flawless body in an easy, seductive way. The dress was all white, except for the shiny silver strip around her slim waist.

My mouth was still open when I met her sparkling eyes, the blue a remarkable contrast to her dress. I had to work to get my breath back. "That dress is . . ."

"A little much, I know, but my mother insisted and, well, I'm a sucker for beautiful clothes." She smiled shyly as she often did when acknowledging her family's wealth.

I approached, careful to only lightly touch her hair. She looked too perfect to be real. "Your mother has great taste. You look unbelievable."

Her hands found the lapels of my dark tux, tugging me closer. "You look pretty amazing yourself." Her soft lips touched mine, but I hardly moved, not wanting to ruin perfection.

I may be dressed the part tonight, but Grace was in her element. She belonged in fancy gowns, going to dinners that cost half a year's salary. I looked around her run-down apartment complex and realized that the meager accommodations were her "tux." She was dressing the part for her job, but in reality Grace didn't belong in this world . . . my world.

The awareness saddened me, but I pushed the feeling aside, determined to give Grace a night she would always remember. She'd put her heart and soul into the banquet.

I offered my arm the way I'd seen tuxedoed men do in movies. "Your chariot awaits, my lady."

The door shut and locked behind us as we walked toward Jake's fancy sports car. I glanced down at Grace's bare shoulders and caught the slight sparkle of glitter on her skin. So subtle, one would have to be very close to notice. Smiling, I pressed my mouth to the very spot I'd seen shimmering and then opened the passenger door.

She turned with the playful look in her eye that drove me crazy. "Matt Holloway, I must say you can be very charming when you want to be."

Serious now, I wrapped my arm around her waist, tucking her close to me. The beads on her waistband felt as delicate as she did. I kissed under her ear ever so carefully. "I want tonight to be perfect, Grace."

Fingertips, soft as feathers, touched my cheek. "It already is. You're here."

Forget it, I thought, and my mouth crushed hers. She could deal with the makeup later. I needed to touch, needed to forget what a slippery slope we were on. Needed reassurance that I wasn't crazy for traveling this path with her.

She swayed when I pulled away, boosting my ego a little. I loved that I had such an effect on her, that I was the only one who could rock her regal poise.

Grace explained the order of events while we drove. Cocktails and hors d'oeuvres, dinner, then Carter Fields would take the stage, followed by a strict thirty-minute book signing. The silent auction would be going on during the entire banquet, and winners would be announced at the end of the night. She apologized in advance if she ended up disappearing throughout the evening.

Reassuring her, I lightly touched her cheek. "Don't worry about me at all tonight, Grace. I'm here for you, in whatever way you need."

She let out a long, grateful sigh. "I've never done this without my mother before. My stomach feels like someone just released a thousand butterflies."

"You'll be great. I've seen you charm everyone who comes for a tour of the center. I have no doubt they will all be handing you their wallets before the night is over."

Grace glanced at me playfully again. "That's the plan. I can't wait to show the kids what we are going to do to the building."

"How many people are expected?"

"Two hundred," she said proudly.

Two hundred people at fifteen thousand dollars a plate. It didn't take a math genius to know she was raising some serious cash.

"Grace, that's . . ."

Her eyes sparkled. "I know."

Once again she amazed me. I had doubted her ability to fill Liz's shoes, but as always she took my expectations and shredded them. I was beginning to realize that no task was too big for her determined spirit.

We were the first to arrive at the hotel, but the valets were already in place and ready to take our keys. A wide red carpet started at the curb and continued to the threshold of a grand entryway.

I watched in awe as Grace examined every inch of the entrance, talking protocol with the valets. She was efficient but gentle, and never once came across as snobby. She followed the same pattern with the various servers in the ballroom, adjusting the settings and flowers as needed on each table.

I hung back in the shadows, glancing around the ornate room that screamed elegance and wealth. Enormous chandeliers hung from the ceiling, which had elaborate murals painted on it. The room was filled with flickering candles and vases of flowers. Every table looked like a masterpiece.

To say I was out of my element was an understatement. I didn't know where to go or how to help, or even what was acceptable to touch. Several servers stopped by to offer me food, but everything on the tray was unrecognizable to me, except the caviar, which I refused to eat just on principle.

I was so caught up in watching the grand spectacle that I didn't notice Sam approaching until he was right next to me.

"You look lost." His words weren't said out of concern for my welfare but more as an accusation.

"Just giving Grace the space she needs before guests start to arrive." My voice was as short and clipped as his. I turned my head to acknowledge him, the standoff beginning.

"I checked you out."

"I'm sure you did." I watched him closely, never exposing that his words had gotten to me. My stony stare and lack of interest was having the effect I wanted, and I could see Sam's jaw tighten.

"You're not good enough for her."

"I think that's Grace's decision to make. Not yours." My words may have sounded apathetic, but the spark crawling up my spine was anything but.

"Gracie is finding herself, and she's pushing boundaries just to see if she can. But rest assured, you are just part of the growing pains . . . nothing more." He walked away when he'd finished, leaving me to stew not only on his words but also on his calling her Gracie, a vast reminder of this guy's closeness to her family.

The room suddenly felt hot, and I tugged at the stiff, constricting shirt collar. Grace appeared while I was still fidgeting, sending me a reassuring smile.

"I'm so sorry. I'm finished now, though, unless there's a fire to put out." She slipped her hand in mine, slightly tugging. "Come on, it's mingle time. I need more of that Holloway charm." She finished with a quick kiss to my cheek, finally noticing how rigidly I was standing. "You okay?"

Taking in her worried expression, I forced a smile and gave her hand a squeeze. "Just enjoying the view." She blushed as I made a point to look at her from head to toe, distracting both of us from my obvious discomfort. Satisfied that I was okay, she led us over to a group of people who had just come in the door.

Grace managed each conversation masterfully, balancing interest in each person with subtle pushes for funding the center. I tried to say as little as possible, knowing I was more likely to put my foot in my mouth than to contribute. When the men got a little too charmed by Grace, I would subtly slip my hand around her waist, protecting her from their glances or fleeting touches.

After a long twenty minutes, the crowd was shuffled into the dining area just as a live band began playing soft dinner music. Each table was marked, and I tried to hide my annoyance at the sight of Sam's name card next to Grace's. Luckily, five others joined our group, so Sam kept his threatening stares to a minimum. However, the conversation at the table revolved mostly around the stock market, profit margins, and subtle hints of one's bank account.

At least the entrée was recognizable—filet mignon. Even in my tense state, I had to admit it was the most tender piece of meat I'd ever put in my mouth. The food was almost enough to improve my steadily declining mood until one of the ladies at the table smiled weakly in my direction.

"So, Mr. Holloway, what do you do?" The many diamonds on her neck and wrist could have funded a small country.

Returning her fake smile, I casually answered, "I'm the manager at a counseling office downtown. We work mostly with troubled teens."

"A manager. That's nice." I let her dismissive words roll off my back. I couldn't care less what she thought of my position.

Grace jumped in. "Matt also works with the kids at the center. He has a remarkable way of getting through their defenses. It's our greatest goal to show these kids consistency and trust." She squeezed my leg under the table.

"Oh, that's lovely, dear." The lady turned back to other conversations, eager to avoid any talk of the center.

Grace leaned in, her breath light on my collar. "I warned you about the spouses." Her voice was apologetic, and for some reason her concern irked me. I wasn't embarrassed about my job or my position. I believed in what I did every day, and some overpampered socialite wasn't going to change that.

I stuffed another piece of meat into my mouth to avoid saying what I wanted to. I was eager for Carter Fields to take the stage, but for completely different reasons from the others'. His speaking meant this night was that much closer to being over.

I stood by Grace as she said good-bye to the last couple leaving. The rest of the night had gone off without a hitch, and even I was inspired by the message Carter Fields delivered about sacrifice and helping the next generation. His words were so wrought with emotion and passion that one would have to have been dead not to write a check. As promised, Grace held the signing to only thirty minutes and then escorted Carter Fields to his car while the guests continued to mingle.

By then I felt ready to collapse. I'd grown up in a terrible neighborhood and spent two years in juvie, and yet I had been more on guard the past three hours than ever in my life. Dress it up with diamonds and pearls, but a snake is still a snake, and I'd met more than my share that evening. Of course, they weren't all bad. Some were genuine in their desire to help the center, and I noticed Grace spent the most time with those folks. She had an uncanny ability to spot a fake—one more thing I admired.

The night did bring about a clarity I hadn't expected. Grace was by far the most beautiful, intriguing, and special woman I'd ever known. If I thought she had me on my knees before, I was completely lost now.

The door closed behind the lagging guests and Grace immediately kicked off her shoes, hanging her head in exhaustion. Before I could move, Sam swept her up in a huge embrace.

"Gracie Belle, you blew me away. I think you outdid your mother tonight." She couldn't see his face while he held her, but I could, and I didn't like it. A man didn't shut his eyes when he held "family."

Completely oblivious, Grace hugged him back. "Not possible, but thank you. I can't wait to see the final numbers."

Sam released her, looking mischievous and far too smug for my liking. "Nope. It's going to be a surprise. I'll give you the final total after all the bills are paid. Then we'll start renovations. I hope you aren't sick of me yet, 'cause I'm going to be around a lot more."

I didn't miss the way Sam's eyes rested on me when he uttered those last words. A promise or a warning. I wasn't sure. Well, he wasn't the only one with something to say. If the fund-raiser was an attempt to scare me off, the man obviously didn't know whom he was dealing with.

Walking up behind her, I slipped my hands around Grace's waist and pulled her tightly against me. Her reaction to my touch was the only message I needed as I lightly kissed her jawline.

She rested her head against my chest and closed her eyes for a second. "I'm so ready to go home." Our familiarity and comfort with each other was unmistakable, even to the hardheaded Sam Hartsford.

For the first time in hours, I felt a grin spread. "Let's go, then."

I released her and she slipped her shoes back on before saying good-bye to Sam, taking a few minutes to finalize follow-up details. I could tell he was trying to come up with some reason for her to stay, but he gave in when he saw the exhaustion on her face.

"Sam, it was good to see you again," I lied before wrapping my arm possessively around Grace and leading her out the door. My parting look told him exactly where he could put his "growing pains."

CHAPTER 24

GRACE

Now that the banquet was over and Sam had finally returned to New York, things felt like they were getting back to normal. I spent the next two days familiarizing myself with all the changes Darius made while I was overwhelmed with banquet planning.

Calling the new approach strict was an understatement, as Darius pretty much cleaned house. Twenty kids were now on our banned-indefinitely list. In addition, all the kids were getting scanned on entry for guns and knives. I knew the changes were necessary after the incident with Eric, but they still saddened me. The facility was supposed to feel like a home, not a detention center.

Matt was the happiest with all the changes, assuring me that safety is a gift most of the kids aren't afforded. Sighing at a name I recognized on the banned list, I wondered how he had gotten into such a bad crowd. Trey had been one of my favorites. Sure, he had a little crush on me, irritating Matt with his hugs, but the kid was witty and charming. His future had so much promise, and now my ability to influence it was completely gone. I wanted to call and ask

Liz how she did it. How did she survive watching kid after kid slip through her fingers?

Eager for a distraction, I picked up my cell and dialed my father. He'd left me two messages already today. I wasn't consciously avoiding him, but deep down I knew that Sam had likely given a full report on my welfare . . . one that included Matt, no doubt. It wasn't that I was keeping him a secret or anything. I just wanted my father to meet him before he let some old files and Sam's opinions cloud his judgment.

"Hey, Gracie Belle, give me one second, baby," my father said. I heard his muffled voice as he politely dismissed whoever was in the room. I smiled to myself, loving that my father made me feel important in that way. I could call or stop by the office anytime, and he always made time for me.

"Sorry about that. So I heard you were quite the vision on Saturday. Sam just went on and on." The pride in his voice was unmistakable.

"The banquet was pretty amazing. I'm dying to hear the final numbers, though. Has he given any hint?"

My father laughed. "Sorry, baby, I'm not even touching that one. Sam made me promise, and you know how he is about surprises."

I folded my arms and pouted, feeling like I was back in high school. Sam had made a big point to tease me for months about my eighteenth-birthday present, swearing my father to secrecy. He had so much fun torturing me about the secret that when the present finally came, I was too mad to even enjoy it. Well, until Lacey and I were on the plane to Fiji, and then I decided to stop hating him.

Daddy's voice broke through my reverie. "So was Carter Fields as epic as they say he is?"

I laughed at my dad's attempt at modern lingo. "Yes, he really is." I went on to tell him all about the banquet and how inspiring Carter's message had been.

We talked for at least fifteen minutes before my father addressed the elephant in the room. "So, Gracie, that's it? Nothing else going on in your life that's big right now?"

I stifled a laugh. "Is there something you want to ask me, Daddy?"

He let out a heavy sigh. "Sweetheart, you have no idea what it's like to watch your daughter hurting and not be able to help her. Seeing your sadness after you and Stewart called off the wedding broke my heart. I just want you to be happy."

"Matt makes me happy," I assured him, knowing Sam had filled him in on my new boyfriend.

"It seems awfully soon, baby." The concern in his tone brought tears to my eyes.

"This isn't a rebound, Daddy. Matt is a wonderful person, warm and compassionate. I know if you met him and took the time to get to know him, you'd like him as much as I do."

Silence answered my pleading voice, and I internally cursed Sam for attempting to poison my father against Matt.

"You're a grown woman, Gracie, so I'm not going to tell you what to do. But, your loving, experienced, and protective father strongly feels that you need to spend time on yourself. Figure out what you want to do without the distraction of another relationship. If Stewart's not the guy, then so be it. But don't settle for less than you deserve. Be patient and make sure you find someone who has long-term potential."

I bit my lip and squeezed my eyes shut, with the words I wanted to say lodged in my throat. First Sam and now my dad. If one more person implied that Matt wasn't good enough for me, I was going to scream. "I've got to run, Daddy, but love you. I'll think about what you said."

"That's all I want. Love you, too, Gracie. I'm so proud of you."

I hung up feeling oddly conflicted. My time in Asheville had been short, only a couple of months, but I'd grown so much in that time that it felt like years. My family still saw me as the naive girl who was nursing a bitter breakup and searching for answers. I'd changed, though, grown. New York had been my cocoon, but in Asheville I was finally a butterfly.

Walking toward the door to my office, I looked out onto the court where Matt and Marcus were getting in a few last-minute baskets before closing. Matt caught me watching and smiled before charging the net for a layup. My insides went liquid the minute his eyes were on mine, and I knew without question that our relationship had nothing to do with Stewart or my quest to find myself. Matt and I connected in every way—our interests, our passions, and our beliefs all melded into one brilliant medley. In time my family would understand.

When Marcus saw me approach, he shook his head and snarled at Matt, "Show-off."

"Oh, I don't know, you were putting up some pretty sweet moves yourself," I assured him with a smile. "Why don't we make it interesting? If you get the next point, Matt owes us both dinner at Pizza Kitchen. What do you say, Matt?"

He winked at me before tossing Marcus the ball. "I'll take that wager."

I knew without looking that Marcus would score, but cheered all the same when he sunk a perfect free-throw shot. I loved seeing Marcus smile; it was a rare occurrence, but when he did, joy radiated from his face like a ray of sunshine. The thin, hard shell he'd kept tightly around himself, the shell no one before had been able to penetrate, was melting.

I locked up my office and met the guys at the front doors. The minute we exited, Matt wrapped his arms around me and pulled me close so he could kiss my temple. "You think you're pretty sly, don't you, Ms. Covington?"

Matching his teasing grin, I shrugged. "I was in the mood for pizza. You were just a means to an end."

Marcus made a puking face when Matt retaliated by locking me tightly against him and tickling me until I screamed.

"Come on, I'm hungry!" Marcus whined, standing by my car.

Matt let me go and gave Marcus a fake scowl. "You're always hungry."

Handing Matt my keys, I slid in the passenger seat and listened as the two of them bantered all the way to the restaurant. They sounded like siblings and I had a glimpse, just for a moment, of what my future could look like. Matt caught me staring and responded with a wink before turning his attention back to the road. My stomach fluttered, but not from Matt's sexy wink. It fluttered because I knew in that moment I was in love with him.

Marcus ate an entire pizza by himself and was on his second roll of quarters in the arcade. I knew we should cut him off soon, but I had no defense against his big brown pleading eyes.

Finally Matt called that it was the last game, despite Marcus's protests.

"Come on, man, just a little longer."

"It's late, Marcus. Last game. Grace's choice." The tone of Matt's voice stopped Marcus's arguing, and I picked foosball since I knew we could all play.

"Marcus and me against you, Matt." I smiled, pointing to the game table. Marcus hooted and ran over to spend his last quarter.

Matt and I walked over together, but he looked pensive. "You okay?"

"Yeah. It's just the way Marcus was playing basketball tonight. He's favoring his right side. I noticed it when he was playing Buck Shot, too. He couldn't lift his right arm high enough for the shot."

I jerked my head toward the impatient kid hollering for us to hurry up. He seemed fine to me, just like any other ten-year-old at an arcade.

Matt noticed my concerned face and kissed my cheek. "I'm sure it's fine, Grace. Don't worry so much." I forced a smile, trying not to overthink things. If Marcus was being hurt, surely he would say something.

I stood next to Marcus and prepared for an intense battle of table soccer. We beat Matt handily, and after high-fiving Marcus, I wrapped my arms around him, forgetting Matt's comments completely until Marcus flinched in my tight embrace.

I drew back sharply. "Did I hurt you?" I went to examine his side, but he backed away so quickly, I missed my chance.

Marcus scrunched up his nose and looked around the crowded restaurant. "Girl cooties, Ms. Covington. You want me to get teased for the rest of my life?" His voice was full of mirth, but his eyes told a completely different story.

Matt and I exchanged a quick glance, but instead of calling him out, Matt just rubbed Marcus's head. "One day you'll like those girl cooties," he promised. "Let's finish up. It's almost time to go."

Marcus ran ahead to our table for one last piece of pizza, and I tugged on Matt's arm, trying to get some explanation.

"Not here, Grace. When Marcus trusts me enough, he'll tell me what's going on."

"But—"

"Grace." His voice was dismissive and sharp. "I know what I'm talking about."

There were emotions storming in his eyes that sent a fierce pain to my heart. They weren't the eyes of a man trying to figure out the best way to counsel an abused child. They were the eyes of a man who had *been* that abused child.

CHAPTER 25

MATT

Grace was uncharacteristically quiet. She barely said more than good-bye to Marcus after we left Pizza Kitchen, and she wrung her hands in her lap most of the way back to the center. I knew she was worried about him, and I was, too, but cornering Marcus would only cause him to retreat or fight back. Neither of which I wanted.

I pulled into the parking lot at the center to get my bike, waiting for Grace to say something. She finally looked up when I put her Mercedes in park.

"Will you come over for a while?" Her voice was soft and careful, like she was dealing with some wounded animal.

"Of course." I reached out to touch her cheek, trying to reassure her. "Hey, Marcus is tough, but I'm close, Grace. Just give me a few more weeks to find out what's going on. For all we know he got into a fight in the neighborhood."

"Was that the excuse you would use?" Her eyes teared up as they met mine, and I drew my hand back sharply.

My shock at her bold question left me speechless and she nodded in response, determining the answer for herself. Suddenly the car felt hot, blazing hot, and I wanted to escape, get away from that expression of pity on her face.

"I'll meet you there," I muttered, jumping out of the car for air. I watched as she moved to the driver's seat and caught her swiping at her tears. The small gesture should have touched me, but I only felt fury and embarrassment. I didn't want her to see me as some weak victim. I'd overcome my past, redefined my future.

My hands shook the entire way to Grace's apartment as I tried to find any possible way to avoid the conversation ahead without actually lying to her. Because I wouldn't do that. I learned the hard way that lies in a relationship only lead to anger and angst. Maggie's face filled my mind, a haunting reminder of my failures. It was as if Grace's words opened the floodgates of hell and all the demons that were buried in my dreams suddenly resurfaced. Memories, horrible memories of the fear and helplessness, flooded me. Memories of my father's raised hand, and of knowing that pain was coming while also wondering how bad it would be this time.

I yelled, my voice reverberating in my helmet, then released in the wind. I realized I couldn't be around Grace tonight. My control was slipping inch by inch and I couldn't let her see me this way.

She had beaten me to the apartment and was waiting patiently by her door. I removed my helmet and shut off the engine, but made no attempt to step away from my bike. "Listen, it's late. I'm just going to head home."

I knew Grace could see right through me, especially when she moved closer, but I didn't care. My breathing was coming in short, hot waves. I expected her to yell at me, to demand answers I wasn't ready to give. Instead, she slipped onto the bike behind me and just held on, squeezing me tightly while she kissed my back and neck. They weren't kisses for seduction but for comfort.

"Grace." I tried to pry her fingers from my waist, but she just tightened her grip, getting closer to me.

"Please don't go," she begged. "You don't have to talk about it, and I won't ask again. Just please don't put those walls back up, not after we've come so far."

I hung my head, my heart and my mind telling me to do opposite things. My heart finally won out and I moved closer so I could see her face, pulling her in for a kiss that seemed to calm my racing pulse. "Okay, I'll stay."

Grace grabbed my hand and led me into her apartment, not saying a word. Awkwardness and unanswered questions hung in the air as she moved across the kitchen to get us some water. I found a spot on the sagging couch, reminded once again how much I hated her living this way. She'd done a lot with the dingy space, including refinishing, recovering, or repainting practically every piece of furniture in the apartment. No amount of touch-up, though, could change the fact that her place was a vivid reminder of everything I had despised about my life growing up.

She was suddenly next to me, curling up her bare feet beneath her as she always did when she cuddled. "Do you want to watch a movie or something?"

She was willing to let it all go, to pretend she hadn't just discovered something about my past that explained almost every reason I was afraid to be with her. Suddenly I was hot again, my thin T-shirt sticking to the sweat now prickling my back.

"My father was a drunk." The words flew into the silence, shifting the tension from uncomfortable to downright stifling. I hated remembering it, hated being in the same type of apartment that had been my prison for so long. I stood, then began to pace short, furious steps across Grace's dim living room. I needed to create some space between me and the girl who deserved so much more than what I could offer as her boyfriend.

Grace was thoughtful as her blue eyes watched me, though she didn't say a word. I knew she wanted to know more, but she was keeping her promise not to ask. As always with me, denying her was impossible.

I continued, "I don't know if he was always that way, or just later in life, because my mother was completely devoted to him despite everything. He didn't start off hitting me. As a young kid, my memories are all of my mom, like she kept me hidden or safe somehow from his wrath. But then I started noticing bruises on her, and sometimes she'd have a wrap around her arm. She always gave excuses or called herself clumsy, but deep down I knew better. One night I snuck out of my room—I was probably six or seven—and heard them fighting. He was screaming at her, accusing her of lying to him, and then I heard a crash."

Stopping for a second to get my beating heart under control, I looked back toward Grace, who was clutching a pillow in horror. Her face said it all. She'd never known that kind of life or abuse—a fact I was grateful for. But I also knew that it meant I was bringing in a darkness she could never fathom. Maybe it was better this way, to let her hear all about the violence so she could walk away somewhat untouched by it all.

"I, of course, barged into the room terrified. My mother was on the floor, bleeding, and my father was standing over her with a belt in his hand. She screamed when she saw me, got up, and ran to protect me, but she wasn't fast enough." I had to stop the tears that threatened. Missing my mom could still creep up and cut me off at the knees.

"That was the first night I understood pain, real pain. I understood helplessness and fear. She kept me home from school that week, claiming I had the flu, and begged me not to tell anyone. She said they would take me away from her. She promised to protect me, that it would never happen again. But that night opened the floodgates for my father. He'd always start with her, but if he didn't get enough, he'd come after me, too."

My voice was calm, my words matter-of-fact, but Grace's hand flew to her mouth and tears trailed down her cheeks as she watched me. "Matt . . ." She stopped, not knowing what to say.

Taking a deep breath, I continued to pace. "When I got to be about fifteen or so, I shot up and bulked out. I learned how to fight back. After one night when I overpowered him, he stopped coming near me. He also stopped hitting my mom when I was around."

Calmer now, I walked back to the couch and pulled her close to me. She fell easily, holding on for comfort. "Grace, this is why I'm so insistent about you learning to protect yourself. It's why, despite having a wait list of seasoned athletes, I choose to work with the underdogs at the gym. The small guys who get bullied, or the heavy-set kids with low self-esteem. I never want anyone to feel that kind of helplessness. You don't have to pity me. I'm a survivor."

Her head shot up, tears still shimmering in her eyes. "I don't pity you, Matt. I admire you. I'm in awe of you, actually, and have been since the first night you growled at me." She smiled as she recalled our first meeting. "You have it so together despite your past."

I closed my eyes, lying back and pulling her next to me. I didn't tell her about the nightmares or about my mom's death. I'd let her believe for a little while longer that I was no longer scarred by my past. I'd overcome the nightmares before. I would again. I just needed to fight harder.

Feeling emotionally and physically exhausted, we just lay there together. Grace turned on the TV, but I didn't hear a thing except the soft beating of Grace's heart next to mine. I squeezed tighter and told myself I'd only close my eyes for a second.

I stared, my heart racing in my chest, at the woman I loved in the arms of another man. I would do anything for her—kill for her if I had to. He stood quickly, and she attempted to cover herself back up.

Raising his hands, he backed away from my murderous glare. "I don't want any trouble."

Well, trouble wanted him. I rushed him, knocking him to the floor with one blow. Adrenaline surged and the punches kept coming until I heard Maggie scream, "You're going to kill him!"

Finally able to breathe, I forced myself off him, but was still shaking from the rage. He could hardly move, so I picked him up by his shirt and threw him out of the apartment. Slamming the door with outrage, I turned my stony stare back to the woman who had betrayed me.

"What do you expect when you leave me home all day?" Her words were harsh, aggressive, and full of hate. She eyed me with suspicion, as if waiting for me to come after her.

I yelled back, accused her of giving herself away, and reminded her who paid the bills. I was so conflicted and furious, yet still wanted to protect the girl who was shaking with emotion. Her emotion soon turned to rage and she came at me, crazed.

Her green eyes blazed with fire as her hand slapped my face. Then she started clawing and screaming. I grabbed her hands, my stomach already on fire and my heart racing out of control at this point. I wanted to shake her and demand that she love me the way I loved her. But her screams and slaps kept coming until the edges of my vision turned red. Fury and frustration hissed through me like a snake before the strike and I snapped.

I knew the minute my hand made contact with her face that I was cursed. She fell immediately from the slap, huddling in the fetal position as if ready for more blows. I stared at the hand that had just done the one thing I swore I never would, and almost retched on the spot.

"I'm so sorry," she cried, looking up at me. "It's my fault. I shouldn't have provoked you."

Her words ripped through my gut, tearing apart the very fabric of who I was. They were my mother's words . . . only now I was the monster.

"*Get out,*" *I whispered, barely able to keep down the bile in my stomach.*

"*No, Matt, please!*" *She stood, grabbed ahold of me, kissing the very hand that just hit her. "I'll be better, I promise."*

I couldn't look at her, couldn't breathe. Pushing her through the door, I then slammed it hard despite her cries. I barely made it to the bathroom before the disgust and self-loathing came up with everything I had eaten that day.

Grace's voice pushed through the haze, and suddenly I was awake and aware of the fear on her face. Jumping off the couch, I stared at her wide, terror-filled eyes, and felt the bile in my throat all over again. "Oh, Grace, no!"

CHAPTER 26

GRACE

I didn't know how to respond. Matt was shaking uncontrollably, staring at me as if he'd just seen a ghost. I tried to approach him, but he backed away from me, terrified of my touch.

"Where did I hurt you?" His raspy voice was full of remorse as he tried to control his erratic breathing.

I knew he was having a nightmare the minute his body started jerking around next to mine. At first, I thought I'd let him sleep it out, but he looked like he was in pain, so I woke him. Now I wondered if that was a bad idea.

"Matt, it's okay. You were having a nightmare, that's all." I tried to approach again and this time he let me come close. Suddenly his hands were everywhere, examining my arms, face, neck, everything for some kind of evidence that I wasn't hurt.

"I didn't hurt you?" He seemed desperately relieved when I shook my head, and he pulled me against him so tightly I thought he might break me in two. "Grace, baby, I'll never hurt you, I promise. I'm so sorry."

Matt was still shaking. Completely gone was the steady, calm man I knew. I embraced him back, rubbing along his spine to reassure him. "I know you won't. It was just a dream."

He suddenly pushed me away, moving across the room. His face hardened, the distance and wall between us reappearing so quickly it startled me. "It wasn't, Grace. That's the problem. I shouldn't be here, doing this with you. I'm a monster . . . just like my father."

"No, you're not," I argued, getting worried. "You're kind, affectionate, and the most gentle person I know."

"Stop it! You don't know me. I'm my father's son. I'm doomed to repeat his mistakes. He loved my mother, but it didn't stop him from hurting her over and over again. It didn't stop him from taking a gun and shooting her because he'd rather die than lose her. And despite everything, despite hating him and swearing I'd never do it, I still became him!"

The sheer volume of his voice scared me almost as much as his words did. But I wasn't scared of him—I was scared *for* him. Awareness hit me as I remembered him telling me that his parents were dead.

"He killed her?"

Matt just nodded. His eyes remained distant, but the hardness was gone. He looked lost, broken. The helplessness that he said he never wanted to feel radiated off him as he stared at me.

My heart broke for him. He'd been beaten, abused, neglected, and then abandoned. "I'm sorry, Matt." I tried once again to touch him, but he wouldn't let me near. Frustration gripped me. "Why are you pushing me away? Why won't you let me comfort you?"

His gaze pierced me, dared me to respond. "I hit her, Grace. The last girlfriend I had. She cheated on me and I . . . I. HIT. HER."

My mouth fell open. Everything made sense. His distance, his resistance to our relationship, his incessant need to keep me safe. I searched my heart for fear but didn't find any. Somehow I knew he would never hurt me. I walked toward him despite his protests and took his head in my hands, forcing him to look at me. "I'm not afraid of you. I know you would never do that to me."

"How can you know that when I don't?" The hurt and fear in his eyes said it all. Here was a man who feared no one, who would stare a dragon in the face to protect the ones he loved, and yet wouldn't let himself be free from his own mistakes.

Very softly, I pulled him closer and touched my lips to his, then to both of his eyes and cheeks. With every feathery touch, I felt him relax and pull me tighter.

He buried his head in the crook of my neck. "I don't know how to walk away from you."

"Then don't. Instead, tell me. Trust me. And I promise, if I'm worried at all, I'll walk away from you."

He didn't move, just continued to hold me. Eventually he nodded and we sat, hand in hand, while he told me everything. The horrors of his childhood were many, as was the confusion he faced after his parents' deaths. He told me how he met Maggie, and that she, too, had been abused. He told me about the night he lost it and how he'd never let himself care for another woman since. Not until me.

He told me about the chaos after that night, how he picked fights, looked for trouble and often found it. He became lost in a world of robbery, underage drinking, assault, vandalism, and anything else that would dull the pain. He told me about getting arrested and being put in a juvenile detention center.

"I truly thought my life was over that day," he admitted. "But then I met Bruce, and everything changed."

"How so?"

"Bruce ran a prison ministry at juvie. He'd come down once a week on Sundays to do a Bible study. We didn't have to go, but we got out of work detail if we did. Some buddies and I went for that reason alone. The minute I saw Bruce, I wanted to run. The guy was built like a brick wall and completely intimidating. We listened out of fear, but soon, I don't know, I started going because I wanted to know more. I wanted to understand who Jesus was and how He could fix all that was broken in me. In that small room I gave my life to Christ, and a year later Bruce sat waiting when I walked out the doors of my prison. I owe him my life."

The admiration and respect that Matt had for Bruce was unmistakable. All I could think of was how badly I wanted to meet him and thank him for being there for Matt. "He sounds like an amazing man."

"He's the only real father I've ever had." Matt stood, looking restless again. "I don't understand why all of a sudden I'm struggling again. It's not supposed to be this way."

"Why do you say that?"

He turned, confused. "Because I overcame this! I haven't had nightmares in years, Grace. Years. Now they're every night. How is that possible when I'm still following Christ and serving Him? I'm supposed to be free." He shook his head. "Maybe it's us. Maybe this is God's way of telling me that I need to stay away from you."

Suddenly I was standing, too, ready to fight if I had to. "I don't believe that, and neither do you or you wouldn't be here. Matt, I truly believe that Christ overcame your past, and when He did, you were given a new and glorious life. But for some reason, He wants you to let Him overcome this again. Faith is a journey."

He sighed and clasped his hands behind his head. "I feel like a failure."

I saw the defeat in his face and understood. I felt the same way when Stewart and I broke up. That I had somehow failed God and myself. That all my convictions and choices had been for nothing. It was the worst time of my life.

185

Stepping near him, but giving him the space he seemed to need, I repeated the words my father told me when I lay on my bed, brokenhearted: "It's when we're weak that Christ is strong. Our failures are our eventual triumphs when we step back and let *Him* take control."

Matt let out a surprised laugh and gently placed his hands on my face. "How did I ever find you?"

Smiling back with a gleam in my eye, I gripped his shirt. "You didn't. I found you, if you recall."

"Then I'm the luckiest man in the world."

My pulse hammered everywhere at once. The way he looked at me, just that one long, lingering stare, had my body yearning. Capturing me in a mind-blowing, emotional, and completely vulnerable kiss, he destroyed all that was left of my defenses. The openness we shared translated into a closeness that had me near tears, and I wanted more. Wanted to experience every part of him.

As if Matt could sense the danger of being alone with me after having such an emotional night, he pulled back, looking physically tormented in doing so. "I have to go," he rasped, his forehead still on mine.

I let him leave, not trusting my own desire. He kissed me once more before I shut the door behind him. I put my forehead to the smooth wood, thinking how profound my father's words had been in my life. The path was rocky getting here, but in the end I'd found more. So much more.

CHAPTER 27

MATT

Grace's words haunted me all the way home. "Our failures are our eventual triumphs." Maybe it was time to talk with Bruce again about the nightmares, figure out how to move past them. One certainty existed: Grace was my future. She deserved a man who could love her in a healthy way. A man who would be able to lie next to her one day without fear of lashing out in his sleep.

I texted Bruce before going to bed, being sure to set my alarm. The memory of Maggie had shaken me up, and I didn't think I could stand seeing my mother die again in my mind tonight. Why couldn't I dream about the good stuff? Why was I always haunted by the one day I would do anything to change?

Sighing, I closed my eyes, and tried to get at least a few hours of sleep.

The alarm chirped for the third time and I slowly rolled over, slamming the snooze button. My body did not want to move and my eyes were certainly unhappy about the light pouring through my bedroom window. Between my restlessness and the two-hour wake-up calls, I wasn't sure if I got even three hours of sleep. Groggy, cranky, and in desperate need of coffee, I knew my body and mind couldn't sustain this routine much longer. I could already tell the difference in my workouts, from having less and less strength when lifting weights.

Glancing quickly at my phone, I read the text from Bruce. He could meet in an hour. Fighting through exhaustion and irritation, I readied for the day and drove to the office, carefully preparing myself for the conversation I'd been avoiding for months.

Bruce looked as worn out, with dark circles under his eyes, as I was when I strolled into his office. "Rough night?" I asked as he looked up.

"You could say that."

He didn't offer more, but handed me a cup of coffee as he sat down across from me. Warmth spread through my body as I sipped, easing some of the tension. Toasting him with my cup, I smiled. "I knew I liked you for a reason."

"How was the banquet?"

"Pretentious and stuffy, but totally worth my overpriced tux to see Grace in her dress." I smirked as Bruce laughed. "Carter Fields wasn't so bad, either."

"Yeah, yeah. Don't rub it in. So what's with the early-morning wake-up call?"

I picked up the journal I had set on the floor. "I'm ready to talk about these," I said, handing off the journal to Bruce's waiting hands.

He sat back and slowly read through my handwritten notes, nodding periodically. I waited patiently, knowing Bruce never rushed through research. After several minutes, he closed the book and crossed his massive arms.

"Matt, what do you remember about that night?"

We'd talked about my mother's death before, but it had been a while. "I'd been out with some buddies, watching a game at Shakey's Sports Pub. I drank, but planned to keep it only to two beers since I was driving. I didn't stick to that plan, but I still don't remember overdoing it. This is where my memory gets foggy. I remember driving home, but that's it until the next morning. My only guess is I was way drunker than I suspected. I'm lucky I didn't hurt anyone that night."

"And the next morning?"

"I woke up completely undressed, which didn't surprise me at the time, but I couldn't find where I put my clothes, and I had a massive headache. That's when I heard the message. I didn't have a cell phone. If only they'd let me get a stupid cell phone!" I stopped for a moment to keep from getting too worked up and continued with the story, the familiar shame gnawing at my insides. "I stumbled to the kitchen to get some aspirin when I saw the light flashing on my answering machine. Mom's voice was panicked. She sounded terrified and begged me to come get her. I threw on some clothes and went straight over, but it was too late. The apartment was already roped off as a crime scene, and my mom was dead."

Bruce nodded and then seemed to be concentrating on a conversation going on in his head. I hated when he did that.

"So, Doc, what's the diagnosis? How do I make them stop so I can get on with my life?"

He rubbed his chin. "I'm not sure you need them to stop." He smiled, offering me no further information. "Matt, I have a theory, but I need more evidence before I'm sure."

"Well, please tell me what it is because setting my alarm in two-hour intervals is getting old. I just want all this to go away."

"You've been waking up every two hours? No wonder you've been such a pain in the butt these last few weeks." Bruce's candor made me smile despite my irritation. "Tonight, no alarm at all.

Wear yourself out, get nice and comfortable, and then let yourself fall into a deep sleep."

Irritation soon turned to panic. "You have no idea what you're asking me to do," I whispered. To intentionally live through that nightmare seemed like a brutal experiment, especially when it was just to test his "theory."

Bruce's large hand was suddenly on my shoulder, reassuring me with a squeeze. "You can do this, Matt. You're strong enough, and you have a whole new motivation to get healed again."

I knew he was referring to Grace, and I simply nodded, trying to accept his solution to the problem. As if he sensed my need to change the subject, Bruce sat back. "How's Marcus doing?"

Feeling steady once again, I relaxed. I definitely preferred talking about someone else's problems. "I think someone is hurting him. He's making excuses and favoring his right side. Grace hugged him last night and he almost cried out in pain."

Bruce's jaw stiffened. He was a fairly calm guy, considering his background, but when it came to kids, Bruce would fire off like a rocket. More than once I'd had to cancel appointments because he needed to pull himself together after counseling abused children.

"You think it's at home?"

I shook my head, still thoughtful. "Nope. He lives with his aunt, and the way he talks about her, I just know it can't be her. He's intensely protective of her. She rescued him from foster care and her love is the only sure thing he's got. I considered maybe she has a boyfriend or something, but he never hesitates when I drop him off at his house, just bounces right in."

"When he's not at the center, where does he go?"

I smiled because I'd asked myself that same question. Maybe I was picking up more from Bruce than I realized. "That's what I'm trying to find out. I saw him outside the center the other day talking to someone, but I couldn't see whom. Everything in Marcus's posture told me the conversation was hostile, but when I tried to get him to tell me who it was, he completely shut down. It took a week before he started speaking to me again. My normal tactics don't work with this kid, so I'm trying to be careful and not corner him."

"That's smart, but don't wait too long, Matt. These things tend to escalate. If your instinct says push, then push. Okay?"

I nodded, feeling the weight of the responsibility on my shoulders. Grace certainly would rather I push, use the system even, but I wasn't ready for that extreme yet.

The door buzzed, letting us know Bruce's eight o'clock had arrived. He jumped up and peeked out the door to say he'd be right out. I stood to leave, but he stopped me and rested that fatherly hand on my shoulder again.

"Let me pray for you?" It was a question that I knew demanded vulnerability. Despite my panic, I nodded, knowing I trusted him more than any person on this earth.

"Dear Lord, Your ways are not our ways, and our wisdom is foolishness to You. Lord, please lead us down Your path. Your Word promises peace and comfort. Grant that to Matt today. Give him the answers he seeks, and the humility he needs to let go. You are the Father neither of us ever got to have on this earth, but Your love meets all our needs. Thank You, Lord, for Your faithfulness and Your promise to never leave us or forsake us. We anxiously await Your provision in Matt's life and in Marcus's. In Your precious name, amen."

Tears stung at my eyes, tears I had refused to shed for so long. But somehow in that office, with Bruce's hand on my shoulder, I felt broken. Broken from my lack of trust and faith, broken over my inability to love without restraint, and broken that instead of going to the Father for help, I shut Him out in anger because I was hurting.

Giving me a second to pull myself together, Bruce left me alone in his office and made small talk with his next patient in the reception area. I said my own silent prayer, the first in a while that didn't come with bitterness. I prayed for strength. I knew in my heart that tonight would change everything.

CHAPTER 28

GRACE

I woke up thinking of Matt, missing him, even though he'd left only hours earlier. He was consuming more and more of my thoughts every day. Not a bad thing necessarily, but certainly distracting.

Reaching over to grab my morning devotional, I read the wisdom of others and said a prayer to start my day. My prayers for the kids at the center were the norm for me, but today felt more urgent in light of yesterday. I prayed for Marcus, for him to open up and trust Matt. I prayed for Matt himself—that today would bring some level of healing instead of more fear that we were getting too close. As I prayed, the heaviness of both situations lightened a little, but I still felt burdened.

Glancing toward heaven, I shook my head. "Okay, I know I'm supposed let go and let You, and all that stuff, but I'm having a really hard time doing it." I waited, as if I would hear an audible answer, and then chuckled. I knew the answer already. The Bible clearly says that we are not to worry about tomorrow and we are to cast all our anxieties on Him. But, man, if that wasn't hard!

Letting myself accept that I was a work in progress, I slipped into the shower and finished my morning routine. When I first started at the center, I hated the 6:00 a.m. wake-up, but now I found I enjoyed the early mornings. I loved the two hours of quiet at the center before it became swarmed with eager children. I loved that each day felt hopeful and fresh, and that I wondered whom God would put in my path to influence.

Still smiling as I reached the front doors of Hartsford, I eagerly unlocked the building and let myself in. I was the first to arrive, a usual occurrence, although Darius had been arriving earlier since Sam's visit. Thoughts of Sam made me scowl. I wanted the final numbers from the banquet, wanted to start to see my visions and plans for this place begin.

So lost in thought as I stepped into my office, I didn't notice the mess until glass crunched underneath my foot. Startled, I flipped on the light and took in the scene. Three high windows had been completely smashed by bricks that had landed in various places throughout my office. A message was scrawled on each brick: *Go Home. Death. Fear Us.*

If there hadn't been thick steel bars, which remained steadfast, protecting the shattered windows, I would have immediately questioned my safety. Someone was trying to scare me, bully me even.

The front doors slammed shut and footsteps echoed across the gym floor. I met Darius in the center of it, holding the three offensive bricks in my hands.

"Someone doesn't like the new rules," I said, handing off the *Fear Us* brick.

Darius's dark eyes went hard as he took each of the bricks from my hands, examining the painted words. "Where did you find these?"

"In my office, along with a million pieces of shattered glass. You may want to check yours, too."

Sure enough, each of the offices had their windows smashed by bricks with messages demanding that we back down. We headed to my office, since it had the most damage, and started tossing the larger shards of glass into a big plastic container.

Darius shook his head. "That's it. Sam's going to shut us down."

The crash of glass being tossed into the container almost wiped out his words. I touched his arm to reassure him. "No, he's not. This just comes with the neighborhood."

Darius stood, turning his back to me. "You don't get it, Grace. Nothing's the same as it used to be. After the last incident, Sam made it clear that if he felt you were in any danger whatsoever, he was closing us down. It's a miracle we made it past the first of the year as it is."

Shock and frustration coursed through me as I stood. "Darius, what are you talking about?"

He turned, his eyes ablaze with exasperation. "Why do you think Liz left? Sam told her she had to have the center self-sustaining in three years. It's been five, and Liz wasn't able to get us any outside support. Sure, everyone supported us verbally, but no one would commit funds. Not until you came. Sam told us that you were our last hope, that if you could get us funding, then he'd let us stay open. No one believed you could do it."

"Then what's the problem? We did do it."

He ran both hands down his face, stretching the skin. "Yes, we did, but at what cost? Sam pulled me aside last week and told me that your safety was not worth the risk, funds or no funds. He was furious I let things get out of control like they did. He said that if he had any idea the neighborhood had gotten so bad, he never would have let you come here. As soon as he hears of this, he's going to take you away. And when he does, those businesses will never keep their commitments."

I felt the sting of betrayal. Despite all his talk about me growing and blossoming, Sam was still sheltering me.

"Then we won't tell him." My words surprised even me.

Darius cocked his head. "Grace, deceit is not exactly your forte."

"I'm not going to lie to him. I'm just not going to offer information that he doesn't need."

Darius let out a snort. "Sounds like the same thing to me. But okay, I'll play along—only because my heart would break if we walked away from these kids. But this has to stay between you and me."

I could tell by the look in his eyes that he was referring to Matt. I understood. Matt was almost as bad as Sam when it came to my safety. But somehow I didn't feel the same contempt for it. Matt's concern came from an honest place. He wanted to shield me from the horrors he'd experienced as a child. Sam's came from a lack of faith in me. And it hurt more than I cared to admit.

Darius collected all the bricks and threw them into the back of his car. Our goal was to make it look like a random act, not a targeted threat. The plan seemed to work, as neither Jeff nor Steven questioned us, just pitched in to help clean up the glass. By three o'clock all the windows had been replaced by Glass Solutions, their quick response a favor to Jeff, who knew the owner.

When Matt strolled in two hours later, I'd almost convinced myself that the incident never happened. Marcus had a ball in his hand before I could even say hello, and although Matt seemed distant and lost in thought, he played with Marcus for over an hour.

I watched them both from the bleachers, noticing Marcus hit half the shots he usually did because he couldn't push off with his right arm very well. Matt noticed, too, but still managed to stay nonchalant. I didn't know how. I wanted to shake Marcus, insist he let us help him.

I thought of the bricks that demanded retreat. *No way.* God put me at Hartsford to make a difference, one that exceeded whether the center was in the red or black financially. Helping these kids was my mission, and I wasn't going anywhere.

Lost in my newfound conviction, I didn't even hear Matt approach. "Hey, you look ready to kill someone. Everything okay?" He lightly grazed my hair, slipping the strands through his gentle fingers.

The touch surprised me. Since our agreement about boundaries, he'd kept a good distance from me when we were at the center, embracing me only after the doors shut behind us when we left for the night.

Standing up, I took in his face. Wet with sweat from taking on a demanding ten-year-old, but full of concern.

"I'm good." I smiled to reassure him and then glanced at Marcus, who stood with his hands on his hips, waiting. "How's that going?"

Matt looked behind him and shrugged. "Like banging my head against a brick wall, to be honest."

His voice was strained, distant. There were so many questions I wanted to ask him, so many things I still wanted to learn about him, but it was neither the time nor the place.

"Are you coming over tonight?" I asked, still watching him.

"No, not tonight. I'm going to get in an exhausting workout and then take care of some unfinished business." His eyes turned hard before they closed. When they opened again to meet mine, his calm facade was back in place.

"Should I be worried?"

He forced a smile—one that could be called weak at best. "Nah. I'll tell you about it tomorrow, if there's even anything to tell."

Marcus demanded from across the court, "Come on, Matt, you gonna flirt with your girlfriend all day or play some ball? We only got a few more minutes till the games start!"

He rolled his eyes. "Duty calls. I'll come say good-bye before I leave."

With that he jogged back to Marcus, did a quick juke, and then dunked the ball. Marcus seethed and yelled expletives, which made Matt laugh hard even as he scolded him for his mouth. My heart pinched and I wondered how I ever thought I knew love before him.

CHAPTER 29

MATT

"I'm gone," I stated, setting a few bills on the bar. We were in the eighth inning and there was no way my team was going to come back.

"Ah, come on, Matt, don't be a sore loser," Chris hollered. Of course he would say that because he was the most obnoxious winner on the planet and I had stupidly bet twenty bucks on the Braves tonight.

I slid the twenty over to him before making my exit. The sight of my money without even a final score shut him up real quick, and I made it out of the dark, smoke-filled bar without another word. The clunker I called my car sat just outside the door. It whined and hissed, but eventually sprang to life with a grinding sound. I'd need to get under the hood soon and see what was going on, although I already suspected the engine was going.

My apartment was only two blocks away, thankfully, since I'd exceeded my two-beer limit tonight. The thought bothered me more than I wanted to admit. The fact that I didn't stop when I said I was going to reminded me too much of my piece of crap father.

The car stuttered and knocked as I turned into the dark parking lot of my run-down complex. This place was by far the nastiest apartment in town, but my mom had very little money and few options when we rented the one-bedroom dump. To me, it represented freedom, so I could deal with the stained carpet and peeling walls. Anything to be away from him.

The air was thick and stuffy when I pushed the door open, and I quickly turned on the window AC when I entered. I'd let myself have it on for ten minutes, I decided. Last month's bill was more than I could afford, and I had to sell some lifted CDs to pay it. Guilt tugged at me a little, but I pushed the feeling aside. Theft wasn't my ideal choice, but I would do anything to not go home . . . even that.

The smoke odor from the bar lingered on my clothes, turning my stomach. I had my shirt halfway up when I heard the phone ring from the kitchen. Sure it was Chris calling to gloat, I ignored the call and just let the machine pick up.

The sheer terror in my mom's voice had me frozen in place. "Matthew, honey, it's me. I need you to come get me, right now. He's gone crazy, I think. I don't know. Just please, come . . ." She started crying and may have said more, but I was already out of the apartment and sprinting to my car. She lived ten minutes away, but I got there in five, running lights, exceeding speed limits, whatever I had to do.

Finally I pulled into the drive and bolted for the door. The adrenaline must have sped up the effects of the alcohol, because I suddenly felt light-headed, stumbling down the hallway to find her.

She was staring out the window in the small, ugly bedroom, the one that held so many horrible memories for me that I shivered upon entering.

"You were right." She kept her back to me. "I should never have come home." She started crying harder, shoulders shaking. I walked toward her and wrapped her fragile body in a hug.

She cried out in pain and I immediately let go. Gently turning her, rage washed over me. Her left eye was swollen shut and there were bruises around her neck and down her shoulder.

"He hit you again." I grabbed her suitcase and flew around the room stuffing blouses and pants into the bag. "He's lucky he's not here." Shoes. Socks. "Next time he touches you, I will kill him."

Mom rushed over to me and took my face in her hands. "Matthew, no. You're better than this. Better than him. One day I want you to let go of this anger and make a life for yourself."

Balling my fists, I made her a promise. "We will make a life. You and me, Mom. He will never hurt you again. I won't let him."

We made it as far as the hallway before he came home. Blocking our escape, I saw him lift a nine-millimeter pistol and point it right at us. "You're not going anywhere."

Acting on instinct, I pushed my mother behind me and stared into the vicious eyes of my father.

His lips curled upward. "You always were an obstinate little brat."

I now understood my mother's fear. He had snapped. His eyes were too wild, his voice too calm. I pushed her and we slowly backed into the bedroom. I needed to find a weapon, something that could defend us from him.

My father followed slowly, never lowering his weapon until he was standing in the doorway and we were trapped inside.

"Marcie, come here," my father demanded.

My mother started to move around me, but I blocked her. My father hurled more insults at me, but I didn't care. I needed to get us out of there. Panic rose up each time he screamed at my mother, but I refused to let her pass.

Then he racked his pistol. "Marcie, I'm losing my patience. I'll shoot him. I swear I will, and society will thank me for it!"

The shaking stopped and my mom pushed off me, getting around my body so she could face him. "No, stop!" I yelled, gripping her tighter.

"Marcie, this is your last warning . . . Get over here!"

She lunged in front of me right as the gun went off. Her screams mixed with the deafening shot left me stunned until the momentum of the bullet slammed my mother's body into mine, sending us both to the floor. The wind left me the moment of impact, and the pain in my chest was so extreme, I was sure I would look down and see my own blood flowing. But it wasn't mine . . . it was hers.

I turned my body, letting her down gently on the brown, stained carpet. Blood was everywhere, on my clothes, her clothes. I grabbed the first garment I could find and pressed it against her, trying to stop the thick crimson pouring from her chest.

Her eyes were weary and she was barely hanging on. I couldn't find words as I watched her with terror, pure terror.

Then she smiled. "You are my greatest joy, Matthew. I love you." Eyes closed, head turned, she died right there in my arms. I didn't know whose screams were louder, mine or my father's.

I turned to face the man who was kneeling with his head in his hands, screaming her name over and over. Before I could register my actions, the gun was in my hand, pointing at the monster who had just ripped my life apart.

His eyes met mine; those dark, evil pools were now swimming in tears. "Do it," he demanded.

My finger hovered over the trigger, every ounce of my body wanting to pull. But her words replayed in my mind, "You're better than this. Better than him." Somehow I found the strength to lower the gun and, with shaky hands, set it back on the floor.

His eyes narrowed. "I knew you couldn't do it. You're not a man; you're a coward!"

He was right. I was a coward. Fear and shame pushed me forward as I walked from that room, leaving my mother's dead body in the hands of the man who killed her. I heard the gun go off before I reached the front door, but never once looked back.

Suddenly the door flew open and Mom's neighbor, Ms. Andrews, stood in front of me, her eyes wide. I could feel myself swaying and *thought of the cookies she baked for me sometimes when I got home from school.*

"He shot her," I whispered, wondering where the sound came from. The room was starting to spin and Ms. Andrews suddenly had a twin sister.

"Come here, sweetheart. Don't you worry, I'll take care of everything."

Soon we were in my car. I was warm and noticed a blanket around my shoulders. Then I was cold because somehow we were in my apartment and my clothes were gone. Ms. Andrews ushered me into bed, promising that she would tell the cops everything.

"You were never there, Matthew. This was all a dream. It's time for this horror in your life to be over. Just sleep, sweet boy."

Her words sounded glorious, so I did as she said. I closed my eyes and pretended nothing happened.

I jolted out of bed, the sheets stained with sweat and balled up from my thrashing around. My breathing settled quicker than normal and the panic I usually felt was absent. In its place, though, was pure, raging anger. *How could I have forgotten?*

Tearing from the room, I reached the toilet just in time to retch all the emotion and fear of the dream. It was as if her blood still covered me, warm and thick.

I splashed water on my face, gripping the sink as I tried to calm down. Looking up I saw a coward in the mirror. I had been too weak to face that night, so I buried the pain and agony for nine years. *Nine years!*

Stumbling back to my room, I fell onto my knees in front of the bed and screamed out to God. How dare He leave me in darkness? How dare He let the shadows of my past life overtake my future? He was supposed to erase my past, not leave it to haunt me. I had given Him everything!

"How could you?" I screamed, thinking of how hard I had fought to become the man He wanted me to be.

Gripping my Bible, the book that held all the promises that God didn't keep to me, I threw it hard against the wall. Pages fluttered as it hit the ground. Pages of notes I had taken during sermons. Sermons that also promised me things that weren't delivered.

My heart heavy, I crawled over to the book that had been my guiding light and picked up a lone page. The verse stood out in big letters, ripping my heart in two.

My grace is sufficient for you, for my power is made perfect in weakness.

The words hung in the air as tears poured from my eyes. Crumpling the page to my chest, my head hit the ground in agony.

There was no fight left in me.

I reached out and grabbed my phone, my hands still shaking as I pressed the buttons.

Bruce's groggy voice answered.

"It was real," I whispered. "It was all real."

Calm and caring, Bruce's tone felt like an embrace through the phone. "I know, Matt. I'll be right over."

I was sitting on the porch, still trying to calm down, when Bruce let himself in. He didn't say a word, just took a seat in the patio chair next to mine.

"So you knew," I said, trying to keep the accusation out of my voice. This wasn't his fault. He wasn't the coward, I was.

"After I read your journal, I felt pretty sure they were repressed memories, yes. You seem angry."

"I am angry!" I yelled, balling my hands into fists as I sat up. "My mind has been blank for nine years because I wasn't strong enough to handle my mom getting shot. Instead, I got to watch it over and over in my head every night. How does any of that make sense?"

"The mind is a tricky thing, Matt. When it's overloaded with trauma, a defense mechanism kicks in to protect it. And what happened that day was traumatic. You shouldn't feel weak just because you didn't remember. Maybe you weren't mentally or spiritually ready to until now."

I shook my head. "Or maybe God knew that if I knew the truth, knew how close I had been to saving her, I would demand to know why. Why He allowed that night to happen."

Bruce sat back, looking thoughtful, then turned to me. "You don't think God wants you to ask why?"

I shook my head.

"Well, I think you're wrong. Time and time again in the Bible, God's people ask Him why. Gideon, Habakkuk, Job, and even David. A typical human response is to be angry. It's okay that you're angry, Matt. It's okay that you're hurting. Scream out, do what you have to, but then you are going to have to let go and trust that God will do a mighty work with your past."

For some reason his words were like a lever releasing the floodgates of my emotions. Tears came slowly at first, but then in deep sobs. Yes, I had been angry with God, but mostly I was angry with myself. Terrified of who I might become. I wanted to pull that trigger. I wanted to kill my father that night. Bruce scooted closer and put his hand on my back, comforting me.

"I don't want to be like him. I'm so scared I'm going to be like him," I admitted through my tears.

"Matt, as a child, you were a victim of your environment. You didn't have control over your circumstances, but you do have control now. You do not have to repeat your father's mistakes. Yes, bad things happen in this evil world, but God always does something redeemable through them. Sometimes we see it, sometimes we don't. God has done an amazing work in you."

I lifted the hem of my T-shirt and wiped my face, tired of how weak I'd become.

Bruce continued, "Just look at all the people you have poured into because of your testimony. You've helped lost and broken boys find confidence and strength of mind. You've given them a purpose. Just think of Marcus. Do you really think you could have understood him if you hadn't lived the life you did? You've chosen to live victoriously despite being a victim."

The words of 2 Corinthians filled my mind again. *My grace is sufficient for you, for my power is made perfect in weakness.*

Then, as if God Himself was comforting me, I felt a peace wash over my broken spirit. Suddenly I understood the promises. God never said He would erase our shortfalls, but would use them for His glory. The magnitude of His mercy rocked me to the core. He wanted all of me, had great plans to use me for His purpose, mistakes and all.

I spent the rest of the day in a haze of freedom. The guilt and shame were finally gone.

Moving around my house in a blaze, I cleaned up and set the marinating meat in the fridge. I had asked Grace to come over tonight and let me cook for her. She would be the first houseguest I ever had besides Bruce. My home was my sanctuary, and I never wanted anyone there who could one day represent a bad memory. Tonight was different. I wanted Grace to be in my home, experience this part of who I was.

I had asked her to come straight over from the center, and she knocked right on time. I still didn't like her driving to her apartment after dark without me following her. I knew it was too soon, but I could picture her here, in this house with me, forever.

A smile lit up her beautiful face when I pulled open the door. My greeting consisted of taking Grace in my arms and kissing her until I had to help support her weight. I wanted to laugh as joy pulsed through me. I had everything I wanted. Everything my mother had hoped and dreamed for me. I'd done exactly what she begged me to do. I'd made a wonderful life for myself.

"Wow. Hello to you, too." She gripped my shirt until she regained her footing. "I take it you had a good day?"

Staring down at Grace, I couldn't help but smile. "I've had a good month, thanks to you."

"Well, it's been more than a month, but who's counting?" Her teasing words were followed by feigned hurt, as if I'd forgotten our time together.

Leaning in to whisper in her ear, I felt her shiver at my touch. "Sweetheart, I remember every second from the first moment I laid eyes on you, and I've been trying to get my world upright ever since."

Grace punched my arm, which wasn't exactly the reaction I expected. "No, you don't. You didn't even like me the first few weeks you knew me. I had to practically throw myself at you to get your attention."

I backed her to the wall, pressing my hands against it on both sides of her face. Her eyes flashed with heat, sending my pulse up another notch.

I moved closer and said in a low, seductive tone, "A man does not go mattress shopping for just anyone. From the moment you popped into my gym looking terrified, I have wanted you."

Her cheeks flushed a beautiful pink. "That was you? I thought my dad bought the mattress."

"No woman of mine is sleeping on the floor or some ratty secondhand couch."

Her eyes darkened, warning me that there'd be trouble if I didn't put some space between us soon. "So I'm your woman now?"

"Don't you forget it." I took her mouth in mine before she could respond, and showed her exactly how much she meant to me. We probably lost hours in that kiss, but I had no strength to tear myself away. Finally she stopped us, her breath and resolve as strangled as mine were, and we pulled ourselves together.

Grace wanted the grand tour, so I took her around the place, showing off every corner. My house wasn't much when it came to size and decor, but every inch of it represented who I was, from the lush leather couch in the living room to the punching bag that hung from the ceiling in the second bedroom. Three wide, curtainless windows in the living room afforded a view of the backyard, and I couldn't wait to show her my oasis.

Taking her hand, I led her through the back door and smiled when she gasped.

"Oh, Matt, it's beautiful, like a Japanese garden."

"Why do I get the feeling you know that firsthand?"

She smiled shyly and then shrugged. Of course she had been to Japan, because that's what rich people do. They travel, experience life all over the globe. I pushed the uneasy thought out of my mind and instead pulled her in front of me, wrapping my arms around her tiny waist. Just feeling how perfectly she fit in my arms calmed me. I wouldn't be able to give her trips around the world, but I could give her every part of me—mind, body, and soul. Somehow with Grace, I knew that would be enough.

"Are you hungry?"

She shook her head no and leaned back against my chest, closing her eyes and enjoying the quiet of my yard. I imagined it was a nice change from the center's constant noise and the obnoxious sirens and thumping music that often throbbed at the Raintree Apartments.

The gentle gurgle of water gliding over a rock and into the fishpond was soothing. I glanced at the hammock and pulled her along with me.

"This is my favorite spot in the entire world. Will you join me?" I couldn't figure out why I was nervous asking that question. Probably because I felt that in doing so I was handing her a piece of my heart.

She smiled, beautifully. "I'd love to."

I held the hammock steady so she could get in, and then did my best to join her. The woven material rocked and moved every time I tried to get in. Several attempts and lots of laughter later, we were finally settled and looking up toward the darkening sky.

"I'm usually more skilled than that," I assured her. She giggled and ran a finger along my chest, her body halfway on the hammock and halfway on me.

"I like that you've never been on here with anyone else. It makes me feel special."

I looked down at her, soaking in the way the setting sun cast a soft light across her face, the way her eyes stayed warm on mine. I prayed she could feel the truth of my words. "You are special, Grace. Nobody has ever meant more to me than you do."

She leaned up to kiss me and then snuggled in close, letting me inhale the wonderful mix of her perfume with the citrus scent of her hair. We lay in comfortable silence until Grace spoke.

"So did you take care of the unfinished business yesterday?"

I held her tighter and then told her all about the dream and my talk with Bruce.

"At first I was so angry, felt so betrayed. But now I realize that my forgetting was just another part of God's great mercy. I wasn't ready to face that night. I wasn't ready to face my past and let it go. I think I am now."

Grace sighed as a lone tear trailed down her face. "I don't know how you do it. How you came from such horror to be the amazing man you are."

Reaching down to kiss away her tear, I pulled her closer. "I didn't. God took something evil and ugly, and totally transformed it. My life has always been a gift."

I watched her as she closed her eyes, snuggling closer. I felt I knew her better than I'd ever known anyone. Yet I knew nothing about her life before we met. Sadly I realized that part of me didn't want to know, didn't want to be faced with how different we were, but now it mattered.

"Grace?"

"Hmm?"

"Tell me about New York. Your life. Your friends. All of it. You know every piece of me—even the stuff I'd rather you didn't—and I know nothing about your life before North Carolina except that all the people you love call you Gracie Belle." I couldn't help but say the name with a little disgust, thinking of Sam's face.

She stiffened, making me even more curious. "I mean, you talk about your family a lot, but never about friends. Don't you keep in touch with anyone from home?"

Grace looked up at the night sky. "My best friend and I had a falling out before I left, and most of the others were never close enough to worry about. They don't understand why I wanted to leave. That world sucks you in, and it's very hard to walk away from it."

"But you did. Any regrets?" I held my breath, almost hoping she wouldn't answer.

She turned so she was on top of me and whispered, "Not one," then kissed me. Fire erupted everywhere within me as her hands moved over my chest and into my hair. I'd need to stop us soon, before my body trumped my mind. Grace had drawn a line for me and I respected her enough not to cross it.

CHAPTER 30

GRACE

Guilt consumed me. I should have told Matt about Stewart, but I just couldn't form the words. I decided that if he asked for more details about Lacey, I would tell him, but he never did. Instead, we talked about my childhood and college, and a lot about the work I did with my mother. Never once did the word *boyfriend* come up, and certainly not *fiancé*.

My head drooped in my hands. I would tell him. I would. I just had to figure out how to do it without him thinking the same thing everyone else did—that our relationship was a rebound. Oh, if they only understood. If I'd known what love and passion were supposed to feel like, I would have broken it off with Stewart years sooner. I never knew what I was missing.

"Now that does not look like the face of the woman who just weeks ago took the Asheville elite by storm." Sam rested casually against the doorjamb with his signature smirk.

Scowling, I turned my head away. "I'm not speaking to you."

His laugher filled the room as he strolled to my desk. Placing his heavy, manicured hands on my shoulders, he leaned in. "And here I was going to hand this envelope off to you without delay. Too bad."

He made a *tsk* sound and jumped around my desk before I could grab the envelope in his hand. I went after him, jumping for the cursed thing he held high above his head. His laughter as he evaded my pursuit only made me madder.

"Dang it, Sam. Just give it to me!" My words came out like those of a spoiled brat and seemed to only incite more laughter from him. Finally he lowered the envelope enough so I could snatch it away, and I tore it open to see the number I had been waiting for.

The number was printed in bold black. "Oh my—$4,284,500." I dropped onto the couch in shock, my mouth hanging open. "It's not possible. We didn't even raise that much on the dinner."

Sam sat next to me, smiling brightly. "Remember that couple, Mr. and Mrs. Richard Barron?"

"Yes. They were some of the few who actually listened to what I had to say."

"Well, it turns out that Mrs. Barron is a freelance writer with a pretty successful blog. She called the next day for an interview and then did a write-up on the Hartsford Foundation. Donations have been pouring in ever since." Sam took the paper out of my hand slowly. "Now, some of this money will be redirected to the New York center, but you'll get the additional staff and renovations as promised."

My heart pounded as tears of joy sprang to my eyes. I looked up at Sam's happy face and smiled. "Thank you. I know you only gave me this job as a favor to my dad, but I'm so glad you did."

Sam's face softened, his eyes watching me closely. "I didn't do this for your father. In fact, he didn't speak to me for a week after he found out you were moving. I did it for you, Gracie." He reached up and lightly touched my cheek, then lowered his hand. "I wanted to see that smile back on your face."

I sighed and fell back against the couch, putting some distance between us. For some reason his touch felt intimate. "Well, it worked." I eyed the paper that was now on the coffee table. "That there makes me very happy, even if you tormented me with it."

Sam laughed and returned to his casual demeanor, a relief to me. "Well, I have more news that will make you happy."

My back shot straight up. I was eager to hear whatever it was. "Spill it."

"I'm promoting you." He stood after that announcement and leaned back against my desk, facing me and looking very much the savvy CEO.

"What do you mean?"

"It's all taken care of. I cleared out that office next to mine, and your mother has loved spending a fortune getting it ready for you. You'll take over the Hartsford Foundation, running both the New York and Asheville centers. It's perfect."

I shook my head, my heart beating in my ears. "Sam, I can't leave these kids."

"You can visit them anytime. You'll have free rein with my jet whenever you need it. Just think what a partnership we would make. I mean, come on, Gracie. Look what we've already done together."

I couldn't wrap my mind around his offer. Couldn't even imagine going back to New York after having changed so much since being in Asheville. Matt's face filled my mind. I wouldn't leave him, couldn't leave him.

I stared at Sam, hoping he would somehow understand. "It's more than just the kids, Sam. I have a life here."

He scowled. "No, Gracie Belle, you had an escape. I gave you that, and now it's time for you to come home."

I jumped up, anger coursing through every inch of my body. "Is this my friend talking or my boss?"

He matched my hardened stare, fully expecting me to back down the way I always had in the past. "It's both." His expression eased up just a little when he saw tears threaten my eyes. "Just come home, Gracie. Please. If not for me, then for your family. We miss you. You have to know it was never my intent for you to stay here indefinitely."

"What are you saying?" I could barely choke out the words.

He hung his head. "I'm not saying anything . . . yet. There's still plenty of time to decide while we get the renovations started." Disregarding my defensive stance, he walked over and pulled me into a hug that I didn't respond to. "You've grown into a beautiful, talented woman, Gracie." He kissed the top of my head. "Just promise me you'll think about it. You've already accomplished everything you needed to here."

Tears were streaming down my face the moment he walked out. Sam's promotion didn't sound like an offer—it sounded like an ultimatum.

Matt could sense something was wrong the minute he saw me.

"Hey, what's with the frown?" He pulled me out of my chair and into a sweet hug. My door was open, but that didn't stop him. As usual, he knew when I needed to be held.

"It's nothing. I'm just lost in thought." I eased out of his embrace before the tears came again. I'd already shed way too many.

My second conversation with Sam hadn't gotten me anywhere. He acted as if the discussion was closed, telling me he'd be back in two weeks to meet with the architect. He even had the gall to invite me to see the new condo he purchased so he would be comfortable in Asheville during the renovations. Funny how three months ago his buying a condo would have seemed normal, expected even. Now it just felt insane.

"A little birdie named Marcus told me Sam is back in town." Matt's words were careful, but I didn't miss the look in his eye. There was no love lost between Sam and Matt, and neither of them attempted to hide their disdain for each other. "I think that kid's more possessive of you than I am."

I tried with all my might to find a smile, but I just couldn't. "He had the final numbers for me."

"And they aren't good?"

I shook my head, sitting back down at my desk. "No, just the opposite. They're amazing. Almost twice what I expected."

"Grace, that's awesome! So what's the problem here?" Matt kneeled so we were eye to eye, his face growing more and more concerned. He'd been so happy lately. The circles under his eyes were gone and he spent more time laughing than scowling. I reached out and touched his cheek, breaking into my first genuine smile all day.

"Nothing. I guess I'm just suffering from the Elijah syndrome. You know, that emotional drop after such a great achievement."

He kissed my hand and scooted closer. "Then we'll go celebrate tonight. Anywhere you want, just name it."

My head screamed, "Tell him!" But my mouth remained silent. To tell Matt about Sam meant that I would have to tell him about Stewart, and I couldn't handle that yet. Couldn't stomach the idea that I would wipe away the smile I'd come to adore on his face. He would believe what Sam had so crassly implied today, that my being there was an escape. That being with him was no more than a stepping-stone in my quest to find independence.

No, I would wait until I knew Matt would believe me when I told him the truth.

Forcing myself to relax and enjoy the incredible man in front of me, I leaned in to kiss him quickly before anyone saw. "I heard about this amazing Japanese garden, with running water and a hammock. Not to mention the chef serves a seriously mean piece of steak."

Matt beamed. "Funny, that's exactly the place I had in mind."

CHAPTER 31

MATT

It felt wrong to be this happy, this content with my life. The nightmares were gone. I was sleeping for long stretches of time and had the pleasure of spending every evening with someone who inspired, excited, and challenged me all at once.

Grace was so unexpected. Beautiful, smart, kind. That playful laugh she would let loose on occasion. Those gorgeous blue, understanding eyes that never judged or ridiculed.

I heard a snort of laughter next to me before the ball was knocked out of my grip. I'd been standing there staring into space, the ball still in my hand, with a stupid grin on my face. Shaking myself hard, I let out a long breath.

"You got it *baaad*!" Marcus teased as he caught Grace in my line of vision. "Dude, just marry the girl and get it over with. Your drool is starting to wet the floor."

I narrowed my eyes at the sassy ten-year-old. He'd become more relaxed around me, which was a start, but that mouth of his never turned off. He'd need a lot more meat and skill to back up half the things he spit out. But that was a lesson for another day. For now I'd work on consistency and trust. I assumed his wounds had healed, since he no longer winced when he shot the ball, but I knew from experience that they'd be back and probably worse the next time. If I could just get him to open up, let me help him, then maybe there wouldn't be a next time.

"You've got a big mouth, you know that?"

He laughed again at my feigned irritation. "I just call it like I see it. And you, Matt, are in *looove* with Ms. Covington." He began making kissing noises as he held the ball near his face. I moved quickly, but not fast enough to catch the agile little brat who wouldn't stop laughing.

Grace saw the commotion and walked over, her heels clicking on the gym floor. I was beginning to love that sound.

"Looks like you boys are having fun over here."

Marcus almost blew snot out his nose, he was laughing so hard at the warning stare I shot him. The last thing I needed was for him to declare my love for Grace in front of hundreds of kids. I'd barely accepted the idea myself, and if anyone was going to tell her, it would be me.

"Oh yeah," I replied dryly. "Marcus is an all-around comedian."

She smiled warmly at him, not hiding any of the affection she held for the kid, before turning back to me. She looked slightly nervous. "I was wondering if you might be willing to take off early tonight. I need to talk with you about something."

Any thoughts of Marcus flew from my mind as I watched her brow furrow with worry. This wasn't like Grace; she rarely let things get her down. "Sure. Let's go now."

Her smile brightened a little. "Okay, good. Let me just finish and close up my office. Fifteen minutes okay?"

I nodded but didn't miss the apprehension on her face. Whatever she had to talk to me about had her tied up in knots.

"So you're going to bail on me for a girl. Man, that blows." Marcus's voice sounded hurt, but I could see the twinkle in his eye. He was just as smitten with Grace as I was, and looked for any excuse for the three of us to hang out. "Of course, you could let me tag along. It'd help with all that guilt you're probably feeling about leaving your little brother hangin'."

I rubbed his short, coarse hair. "Not this time, buddy. Come on, let's put some action to that mouth of yours. Twenty-one, your ball."

We played hard until Marcus suddenly stopped and scowled toward the door. "Man, I thought we were done with that mess," he whined.

Turning to see whom he was staring at, I knew immediately what had him on guard. Another young business type was coming toward us, looking around as if he was scoping out the place as he walked.

Still scowling in the man's direction, Marcus whispered, "He looks like he belongs on one of those TV commercials, the ones that sell stuff only rich people can buy." I had to agree with him. If a guy were to be called pretty, this one definitely fit the description. He was tall and decked out in what must have been a five-thousand-dollar suit, and I knew immediately from what I saw at the banquet that Grace must have felt a final tour was necessary to reel him in. He screamed Fortune 500.

"Be nice. You won't complain so much when you get another basketball court in here."

Marcus just shrugged off my warning. "Yeah, whatever. I still don't like it. They're always checking out her butt."

"Enough," I demanded, feeling my temper start to sizzle.

The man stepped closer, all polish and ego, and flashed his million-dollar smile our way. "Is Grace Covington here? I was told she'd likely still be around this time of day." His voice was silky smooth, laced with an arrogance that made the hair stand up on the back of my neck.

I'd be polite, for Grace, but I could already tell I didn't like the guy. "Are you here for a tour? She didn't mention an appointment." I threw the last part in for me. I wanted this guy to know I was well versed on Grace's schedule.

His brow furrowed and lifted, as if I'd said the most ridiculous thing. "A tour? No. This visit is personal."

Marcus took the words right out of my mouth. "Personal? What you want with Ms. Covington that's personal?" I would have found his snotty tone amusing if not for the icy chill that was clawing through my body.

Barely fazed, the yuppie tycoon squatted down until his eyes met Marcus's hateful ones. "Ms. Covington is my fiancée, and today is kind of an important day for us."

I was stunned into silence, the chill turning quickly into raging heat inching up my neck.

"There ain't no ring on her finger!" Marcus's hostile but practical words calmed me a little.

I took a deep breath, needing to regain some control. The man was crazy, obviously, and I wasn't sixteen anymore. My days of uncontrollable rage were over.

When the man smiled, I felt sure a sparkle came off his excessively white, capped teeth. "You're right, sport. A problem that will be rectified today."

The ringing in my ears began just as my hands started to ball. I pictured grabbing him by his Armani suit and shaking the life out him. Instead, I folded my arms, with fists clenched, and reminded myself that Grace would never lie to me.

The clicking sound across the floor both eased my racing heart and elevated my pulse. Deliberately, I unclenched my fists before I could use them on something, or someone.

I met her eyes.

"You ready?" she began before noticing the tension thick around her.

At the sound of her voice, the man stood, but I didn't watch him. Instead, my eyes stayed glued on the one person who could destroy me. Her expression said it all as she looked between Armani guy and me—guilt, unmistakable guilt.

"Gracie Belle . . ." His words were etched with longing, and then he wrapped his arms around her. "Baby, I missed you."

And just like that . . . the tight grip I had on my rage snapped.

CHAPTER 32

GRACE

NO, NO, NO! OH, PLEASE GOD, NO! This couldn't be happening. But it was. Stewart and Matt were standing just a few feet apart, and the look of murder on Matt's face was enough to send a punch right to my gut.

My brain finally making contact with my body, I eased out of Stewart's firm embrace. "What are you doing here?" I demanded, my voice low enough to keep others from hearing it. We were already creating a scene, and I heard the gym grow silent around me.

His shoulders slumped, signaling surprise that somehow I wasn't about to welcome him back with open arms. The nerve!

"It's August twenty-fifth, Gracie. I had to see you."

Our supposed wedding day.

Until then the date hadn't registered on me, not even once. Feeling slightly less furious at my former fiancé, I truly looked at him for the first time. He was tall, bronzed, and very nearly beautiful, but some of the sparkle was gone from his eyes. He also looked tired and thin, as if he'd dropped weight since I saw him last.

I pointed to my office. "Can you wait for me in there? I just need a minute."

He nodded and went to step past me, but stopped to lean in and whisper, "You look beautiful, by the way," before softly pressing his lips to my cheek.

I didn't watch him leave but kept my eyes on Matt, who was watching the exchange with a mixture of hurt, anger, and betrayal. I understood that look; I had felt it myself not too long ago. But this was different.

Stepping near him, I cringed when he deliberately stepped back, keeping a safe arm's length from me. "I can explain."

"Let's hope so." His words were harsh, cold and felt like daggers ripping at my skin.

I turned to see Stewart walking toward my office, then slowly faced Matt again. "I just need ten minutes. Can you please give me ten minutes?"

"I don't know. Are you engaged?"

My eyes pleading, I shook my head. "No . . . but I used to be."

His voice was low and furious. "How long ago?"

I didn't want to tell him like this. The tension was too high and he was already starting to doubt me. I could see it on his face. "It doesn't matter." I looked around at the small audience that had gathered, and lowered my voice. "Please, I can explain everything but not here."

He glanced toward my office as Stewart disappeared. "Somehow I doubt that." I stood motionless, not sure what to do or say. "Well go on. Your fiancé waits." The sarcasm didn't mask the anger or the hurt.

"Ex-fiancé," I shot back before walking away. We'd get past this. He'd listen to me and would understand why I kept the sad saga from him. Our relationship was stronger than this misunderstanding. I felt certain of it.

Taking a calming breath, I stepped into my office and shut the door. Stewart was standing and looking around the small space. "I can see it, Gracie. This place fits you."

"You should have called."

He dropped onto the couch, tugging at his tie. "Would you have answered?"

"No, probably not."

Stewart watched me, keeping a mild, negotiating smile on his face. "Your father told me that Sam offered you New York. That's incredible. Not that I'm surprised. You've always been a ball of determination."

The sadness in his voice resonated, and it was hard to stay angry with the man I'd known intimately and believed I loved for so many years. Allowing us this closure, I sat in the chair across from him on the couch. "Sam offered, but I didn't accept the position yet."

He nodded, sucking in a chuckle. "But you will. Sam has a way of getting what he wants. Even you."

I dismissed his last comment, unwilling to fall back into an argument we had beat to death. Like Matt, Stewart wasn't comfortable with Sam's closeness to our family, and he was always making comments about Sam's intentions. If only he knew how many times Sam had comforted me and reassured me when Stewart let me down. Stewart should thank him a million times over. I suddenly felt guilty for having been so snotty to Sam lately. He really was a good friend. A little pushy recently, but still.

Stewart's hand on my knee brought me screeching back to the present. I subtly adjusted my position so his hand would fall away.

"Is this why you came? To ask me about New York?"

"I told you. I needed to see you today." He took my hands in his. "You'd be waiting for me in a gorgeous white gown right now if I hadn't screwed everything up." He fell to his knees in front of me, moving closer. "Please, Gracie, give me another chance. I'll never hurt you again, I promise. I can't eat. I can't sleep. I'm lost without you, Gracie Belle."

I felt trapped by his pleading gaze. This behavior wasn't like him. He was usually so pressed and polished. Despite the compassion flowing through me, though, I couldn't find one ounce of the love I once thought I felt for him. "Stewart, please don't do this. My mind has not changed."

He hung his head and moved back to the couch. "I wish I knew how you did it."

"What?"

"How you fell out of love with me so fast." The way he said those words, as if somehow he was the victim in all this, as if I'd been the one to cheat repeatedly, lit a fire in my gut.

I stood, inflamed. "Seeing your fiancé in the arms of your best friend tends to speed up the process." As soon as the words left my mouth, I regretted them. They made me sound bitter, and I wasn't anymore. "I'm sorry. That was rude of me."

"No, Gracie, don't apologize," he demanded, standing, too. "I want you to yell at me, to do something that shows you actually cared for me at all. You've been nothing but cold emptiness since that night, and I can hardly stand it!" He gripped my arms, forcing me to look at him. "Nine years, Gracie! I have loved you for nine years. And yes, I messed up, but I swear, I never will again." He searched my eyes, begging. "You can't tell me you don't feel anything."

Tears swarmed my eyes as I looked at the man I had been ready to spend my life with only five months ago. I couldn't explain it, and no one seemed to believe me when I tried, but I just didn't love him. "I'm sorry," was all I could choke out.

He lowered his forehead against mine and squeezed his eyes shut. "I can't accept it's over."

I eased away from him. "I really do wish you the best, Stewart." I pulled at the door, unwilling to spend any more time with him. There was another man who needed my comfort and reassurance. A man whose love had shown me exactly what I'd been missing all those years.

Stewart met my dismissal with a curt nod and stormed through the door without another word. Knowing his wordless exit was probably more about his bruised pride than his bruised heart, I didn't allow myself to feel guilty. Instead, I grabbed my keys, shut the door, and looked around the gym for Matt. Spotting Marcus in the TV room, I hurried over to him.

Before a word left my mouth, he spat out, "He left."

Keeping my voice calm, I stepped closer. "Do you know where he went?"

"Where do you think he went? To punch something." The disgust on his face was as clear as his contempt for me.

I didn't have time to change his opinion or even explain myself. I just shot out of there as fast as I could and headed straight for Matt's gym. Sentimentality washed over me as I dashed toward the front doors. That first night seemed so long ago. We were strangers back then, and now? Now I couldn't picture my life without him.

A teenage boy with dark blond hair and squeezable cheeks eyed me suspiciously as I approached the desk.

"Yeah, uh, this gym isn't really coed. There's a fancy fitness center just a few minutes from here." I would have laughed at his discomfort if not for the urgency I felt surging through me.

"I'm looking for Matt Holloway. Is he here?"

The kid didn't commit with words, but I saw his eyes glance quickly toward a hallway across the room.

"Thank you," I muttered before heading that way.

"You can't go back there."

His calls fell on deaf ears as I followed the sound of pounding rock music. The thick door muffled the lyrics, but the bass vibrated in my chest. Finding the courage I needed, I tugged at the door only to be blasted by the volume and a heavy scent of sweat. Everything about the room in front of me screamed rage and aggression.

The door shut behind me, but the man beating repeatedly on the bag in front of him never once looked my direction. I'd never seen Matt without his shirt on before and found I couldn't peel my eyes away from the muscles that rippled every time he landed a powerful punch.

Tattoos that stayed hidden under his clothing were now visible. The pattern of chaos stretched up his arm, across his shoulder, and ended with claws along his neck. The nails were designed to look as if they were tearing into his flesh. Knowing why he had chosen that design made my heart break for the young boy he had been, until he turned and I clearly saw the cross on his chest. The word *Marcie* etched across the center.

Every pattern, every picture that stood against the surface of his tan skin told a story, and I realized that I knew the meaning behind every one of them. I knew him.

He spotted me and stopped cold. The wall I had met with the first time we ever spoke was back in place, cracking my confidence a little. He pulled off his gloves and wiped his face and arms with a towel before turning off the noise blaring from the stereo.

"You left," I squeaked out, trying to apply some volume to my voice.

He nodded and picked up his phone before turning his cold, hard eyes to me. "It's amazing what you can learn from Googling a New York princess. I should have done it months ago and saved myself a lot of pain."

I caught the phone he tossed my way and glared at the engagement announcement for Stewart and me from over a year ago. My mother had written the story for the paper, so the article detailed our long love affair through time and distance. My stomach turned.

"Is that what you needed to talk to me about so urgently tonight, Duchess? Or did you just plan on lying to me indefinitely?"

I flinched at the use of the nickname he hadn't uttered since we became a couple. From him it wasn't an endearing term, but a reminder that he saw me as a cold, snobby socialite.

Setting the phone down carefully, I started to walk toward him. His hand shot up, halting me. "Nope. You don't get to touch me. Not anymore. Any closer and this conversation is over."

I didn't recognize this person, those cruel, accusing eyes. The hard set of his jaw and the defensiveness of his stance. I wanted my Matt back, the one who looked at me with adoring eyes, who would slay a dragon for me if I asked him to.

Tears filled my eyes at the loss. "I never lied to you. I just didn't tell you everything. I knew you would think the worst of me, that you would assume . . ."

"Assume what?" he yelled, his cold calm wavering. "That you decided to go slummin' for a while so you could win back your precious Prince Charming? That coming here was nothing more than a daddy's girl trying to prove herself?"

I was shaking my head as he screamed at me, tears pouring down my cheeks now. "You know that's not true, Matt. You know me better than that!"

"I don't know anything about you, a fact you have made certain of." He backed away, even though I hadn't moved, and stood next to the bag. "So you were engaged. For how long? Exactly why did this fairy-tale romance between you two end?"

His voice was calmer, but I could still sense the temper boiling right beneath the surface, just waiting for release. "We broke up in March after I caught him with my best friend."

Matt shook his head. Each word dripped with venom when he replied, "The falling out you mentioned. How very vague of you. I guess that explains your sudden need to take a job hundreds of miles away."

The timing condemned me, and no matter what I could say to him, it wouldn't change the fact that I had ended a long, serious relationship only two months before I met him. He crossed his arms, still staring at me with contempt. "What else? What else haven't you told me? Since you seem to think lying only comes with a direct question, I'm asking now."

I began to step forward, needing so much to be near him, but the warning glare stopped me once again. Hugging myself, I tried to find some comfort as the pit in my stomach grew. "Sam offered me a promotion when he brought the numbers for the banquet. He wants me to go back to New York and run both centers from there."

I flinched as Matt slammed his fist into the bag twice before dropping his head to it with a frustrated curse. The air was thick, and thundered with a tension that seemed to get heavier and heavier. I felt helpless, lost. He was hurting right in front of me and I couldn't do anything about it.

"Go to New York, Grace." His defeated words echoed through the silence. "Go home to your dream job and the love of your life."

"Matt, please, don't be like this!"

"What do you want from me?" His calm was completely gone, the hurt in his eyes so extreme that I felt sobs fill my chest. "I gave you everything. I ripped out my heart and laid it open for you just so you could tear it to shreds! I should have trusted my gut, should have never let you in."

I rushed to him, the tears choking me now, and grabbed his arm. "Don't say that! I love you! I don't want New York or Stewart. It's always been you. I'm sorry I was afraid. I'm sorry I ever hesitated."

He went rigid at my touch, his body shaking with emotion. Very carefully, as if he would break me by making contact, he removed my hand and then stepped away. His voice, laced with ice, was matched by his cold, dark stare. "Don't you dare say those words to me now. They mean nothing. You loved another man enough to accept his ring and then lied to me about it. Whatever excuses you come up with don't matter. I won't let myself feel like this ever again."

I stared at his bare back as he pushed through the door, never stopping. My legs wobbled as I slid to the ground, sure of only one thing. He'd never come back.

CHAPTER 33

MATT

It had been three days, and I couldn't avoid the center forever. Marcus's ability to understand had a limit and would soon turn to a sense of abandonment if I wasn't careful. Pulling my legs over the side of the bed, I wondered why I still felt so exhausted. I'd been sleeping more these past few days than I had in months, finding that it made the time go by quicker, made the pain in my chest less noticeable.

Sam's words filled my head as they had every day since I met Grace's fiancé. "Growing pains." Well, at least his actions made sense now. I shook my head. To think I was worried about Sam's intentions. Little did I know Grace had someone waiting in the wings until she found her way back home. That trip would probably happen sooner rather than later.

I pressed my fingers to my eyes and then let them drop. I should feel relieved that she'd be out of my life for good. But somehow I just felt numb.

The day went on with me going through the motions. The nuances of my life were so conditioned that I could exist in a mechanical state with everyone unaware of the hollowness I felt. Well, everyone except Bruce, but he honored my request not to ask and left me alone in my brooding.

Grace called several times, and despite my mind telling me not to, I listened to every one of her pleading messages. At least they gave me the full story. Total disclosure seemed to be her approach, although too little too late. Truthfully, I reasoned, she was probably right that it wouldn't have mattered. Knowing everything just made all my hesitations more justified. Had I known, I would have never let myself fall so hard. Would have never let myself believe we had a future when we were so absolutely different. I was a phase, and now we were over. Plain and simple.

Dread filled my chest as I rode to the center. I looked toward the metal doors. I could do this. I could be cordial and professional when I saw her. Taking a few deep breaths, I swung my bike over to park it and locked my gear before trudging slowly up the stairs.

Noise echoed around me the minute I entered, reminding me that nothing had really changed. Sneakers squeaked across the gym floor, followed by the sounds of bouncing balls and kids yelling at their teammates. I spotted Marcus and walked his way, attempting to put a smile on my face. He was sitting on the bleachers, which seemed odd. Usually if he could have a ball in his hand, he did.

"You ready to give it a round?" I asked, dropping to sit next to him.

He shrugged but didn't look at me. "I didn't think I'd see you again." The hurt in his voice was unmistakable.

"Hey, my taking a few days off had nothing to do with you." He shrugged again and I put my arm around his shoulders, squeezing to reassure him. It had taken several weeks, but we were finally at a point where he'd let me touch him. Not today, though. He practically leapt from the bench, fighting back tears.

But it wasn't anger on his face. No. It was pain, physical pain.

"Marcus." My voice was low, calm, despite the anger I could feel creeping up my legs. "Let me help you."

He shook his head no, still not saying a word.

I whispered in his ear. "I can wrap you up so it doesn't hurt so bad, okay? I won't tell anyone. Just let me look at it." With that level of pain, there was probably something broken, maybe even internal injuries, but I wouldn't mention a hospital to him. Hospitals meant questions, and questions led to cops and social services. Like me, the kid had only seen the failures of the system. I understood.

He finally spoke. "You won't tell?"

"You have my word."

He followed me to the backside of the bleachers.

Once out of view, Marcus allowed me to lift his shirt, and my anger turned to all-out murderous rage. Despite Marcus's light brown skin, I could see the ugly purple-and-green bruising that began at his armpit and moved across his left side, down past the waistband of his jeans. I recognized the pattern of the bruising. Someone had kicked him repeatedly while he lay on the ground trying to protect himself. The image enraged me more, but I kept my fury locked behind calm eyes.

"When did it happen?"

"Yesterday."

"At home?"

"No, and don't you go tellin' anybody it did!" Marcus's face said it all. The look of shock and outrage that I would even consider his aunt confirmed her innocence.

"I would never do anything to get you taken from her, Marcus. I just want to know who's doing this to you."

He shrugged, looking away. "Just some guys around the hood."

"Why?"

"I don't know, man! Are you gonna make it stop hurting or what?" His defensiveness told me he was lying, but I didn't push.

I very gently pressed on the swollen areas, watching Marcus wince in pain. "You definitely have a few broken ribs, but I don't think there's anything more serious. I'll go to the gym and get some wraps. It'll cut the pain a lot."

He nodded and I lowered his shirt, then stood. That's when I saw Grace, eyes wide and mouth open. She had seen everything.

"Marcus, why don't you go back to the gym? I'll find you when I get some supplies."

He hadn't seen Grace, thank God for that. But the way he limped back to the gym broke my heart in two. When he was safely out of sight, I turned to look at Grace, motioning toward her office. She followed.

I thought I'd already passed through the hurt, but it sprang back the minute I saw her, full-blown and with lightning speed.

"You need to stay out of this," I told her as she shut her office door.

She stepped forward, planting her hands on her hips. "We have to call someone. Something has to be done to help him."

"Your system isn't going to help him, Duchess."

She recoiled at my words and sent me a fiery stare. "But you can?"

"Yes."

"How? By covering up his bruises? Wrapping up his ribs so he can't feel the pain? That's not going to keep it from happening again." I was surprised by the resolve from Grace, who rarely ever fought back.

For some reason her stiff back and demanding eyes made me more angry, as if I could heap all the blame onto her as well. "Stay out of this, Grace. It has nothing to do with you."

"Of course it does! We have to do what's best for Marcus." Her eyes were bright with determination and so unspeakably blue that I wanted to curse.

"You think you know what's best?" I demanded, torn between wanting to shake her or wrap her up in my arms and beg her not to leave. The confusion made me madder.

"Yes, I do. It's my job to help these children, protect them when I have to. If that means we use the system, then we do. Just because it failed you doesn't mean it fails everyone."

"Your *job*?" I hated how loud my voice was, how harsh each word sounded as it left my mouth. "You got a college degree and a title. I'm the one who lived it! You haven't been there. You have no idea what it's like to get your face smashed in and not be able to stop the beating. You want to hand him over to some bureaucratic jerk who's gonna pull him from his home and put him in hell, just so you can ease your guilty conscience. No way, Duchess. I won't let you do it."

Her tears had started during my rant and continued to flow. I looked down at my shoes, unable to stomach the hurt on her face. I had hit her where she was most vulnerable and I knew it.

I looked up when I heard her weak voice, commanding myself to keep an emotional distance.

"Okay, we'll do it your way . . . for now. But if it happens again, I will report it, with or without your support."

And just like that, she walked through the door, leaving me standing with a heart full of regret. It wasn't how I planned on our first encounter going. I guess I wasn't as ready to be there as I thought. I'd get the supplies, wrap Marcus, and then come up with another place to meet him for a few weeks—or at least until Grace chartered her private jet and flew out of my life for good.

CHAPTER 34

GRACE

I couldn't sit still. The restlessness was so extreme that I found myself pacing across my office. Matt had taken our relationship completely out of my hands, ignoring any attempt I made to explain, much less reconcile. Now he wanted me to let go of Marcus, too. Well, I wouldn't, couldn't. All the heartache had to be for a purpose or I wouldn't be able to handle it. The pain would be too much to bear.

I grabbed Marcus's file, glancing quickly at his address. I'd go see him, talk to him without Matt or the center distracting him. Maybe I'd even get to talk to his aunt, see if she was aware that Marcus was being abused.

The center would be closing in half an hour, giving me plenty of time to go over there and wait. I didn't want Marcus to avoid me, and he probably would if I were to follow him home. Feeling determined, I locked up my office, told Darius I was leaving early, and tried not to look for Matt as I left. His bike wasn't in the parking lot, which filled me with relief and sadness all at once.

Marcus lived just three blocks from the center, but I drove anyway, not eager to trek around in my heels. When my GPS announced that I had arrived at my destination, my stomach flopped. The house, if it could be called that, was leaning from obvious foundation issues. The steps leading to the front door were discolored and showed various stages of rot and mold. I thought of the ten-thousand-dollar dress my mom sent me for the banquet and immediately felt shame. Matt was right. I'd never understand.

I squared my shoulders. *I can still help, dang it!*

Stepping over a few rotting boards on the porch, I knocked hard on the door. No answer. I knew Marcus's aunt worked the swing shift, but I was hoping she'd be home. Resolved to wait, I turned, ready to sit in my car for hours if necessary.

My heart stopped when I looked back toward my black sedan. A man, tall and built, with hard eyes and a sneering grin, was leaning casually against the hood. I stepped forward, forcing my body and face to remain calm. He didn't move when I approached, but looked at me from head to toe in a way that sent shivers down my spine.

"Ms. Covington. We finally meet." His voice was smooth and calm, but still slit my stomach open with fear.

"I don't believe I know you," I choked out, keeping a solid distance between us.

"You can call me King. How's that?" His question appeared to be rhetorical, so I didn't answer, just willed my beating heart to remain steady. He continued, "Did you get the message we sent the other day? I thought we made ourselves very clear. We expect our boys back in the center."

I struggled to keep my breathing slow and steady while my heart pounded like a jackhammer against my ribs and in my head. Somehow finding strength, I faced the eyes of a man I knew could hurt me at best and kill me at worst. I wouldn't let fear stop me, though. "I'm afraid I don't know who your boys are. Maybe if you give me a list of names we can take a look at their behavior and see."

His sinister smile widened, exposing a row of gold-capped teeth. "Don't get smart with me. See, we have our own rules on these streets. Rules I enforce. If you mess with one of us, you mess with us all. That means, Ms. Covington, you mess with me. I'm afraid that don't look so good for you."

His threat hung in the air. I looked around, planning an escape, as if it were possible. We had gained an audience. I recognized some of the boys who were blocking each side of the sidewalk with their arms folded. I was grossly outnumbered, not that I could have taken on even one of them. Matt's words mocked me: "I won't always be here, and you have got to learn to protect yourself." I had failed him. Yet again.

"Now, I'm not an unreasonable man. We could come to an agreement. In fact, you and I could get along just fine." His suggestive expression made my skin crawl. "But let's start with the easy stuff. I want my boys back at the center."

My chin rose as a strength I didn't know I had came pouring from me. "That will never happen."

His smile disappeared. "Then we have a problem."

Before I could find a reply, a man who made even Matt look small pushed through the crowd. He was huge, probably six foot five, and built like the offensive line of the New York Giants. Muscles bulged in every direction, and the hard set of his face elevated my fear even more.

"I've told you before she isn't to be touched!" the man hollered, standing in front of me like a steel wall.

I could only see a little through the small space between his back and his arm. King approached, his face contorting with rage. "And I've told you I own this neighborhood now."

"Not quite." I looked around and saw more men approach, each apparently ready for a fight. I was standing in the middle of some territorial war, and the thought dawned on me that I wouldn't make it out of there alive.

King checked out the mass of men approaching and smiled, an evil, conniving smile. "I ain't in the mood for this now, anyway. You enjoy your little lady. Enjoy her good, because next time I see you in my face, you're dead."

He looked toward his men and walked away, surrounded by those who would die protecting him. My heart broke when I saw Trey move in behind him, his eyes void of any of the innocence that had once been there.

When they were out of sight, my protector spun around to face me. He must have seen the terror on my face, and instead of yelling at me like I expected, he gave me a sympathetic smile. "A lady like you shouldn't see those things. It's time for you to get on home."

I couldn't respond, my body starting to shake from the adrenaline.

"I think it's best if you go on and don't come this way again." He wrapped his arm around me and slowly walked me to my car, taking the keys so he could open the door. "You okay to drive?"

I nodded absently and he opened the car door, ready to tuck me safely inside. Suddenly I found my voice. "Wait. Who was that?"

"Nobody you need to get tangled with. Now go on home." His voice was getting firmer.

"Who are you? Why did you do that?" I still couldn't process what had just happened. Was that real? Did this stranger almost start an all-out gang war to keep me safe?

"It's just what we do around here, Duchess."

My eyes widened and I met his nod. He didn't have to say his name or tell me why. I knew right then that Matt was involved somehow. He shut the door once I'd lowered myself into the driver's seat, and he watched me carefully as I drove off.

As soon as I got home, I called Matt, begging him to pick up. He didn't. I listened to the cursed voice mail greeting and hung up, wanting to smash my phone against the wall. At last allowing myself to crumble, I lay facedown on my bed—the bed he'd bought for me—and sobbed. Never in my life had I felt so completely alone and afraid.

CHAPTER 35

MATT

Grace had called twice. Once last night and again this morning. Each time my finger hovered over the "Accept" button, but in the end I couldn't press it. Yesterday had completely set me back. Seeing her face, watching those tears, was like ripping flesh off my body. I knew she was dangerous, that she brought on an emotional avalanche in me, but I never expected so much heartache.

Marcus and I decided to meet outside the center at five and then walk to the community courts just a few blocks away. He thought my reason was to avoid Grace, which was part of it, but really I wanted to be out in the neighborhood. Something kept Marcus from confiding in me, but that kid was as transparent as glass. I felt certain I'd be able to read his fear clearly if he saw whoever was hurting him.

I waited patiently for ten minutes outside, did a quick check inside the building, and then started to worry. Maybe he misunderstood and thought we'd be meeting at the courts. The idea of him alone out there unsettled me, and I started to quickly jog in that direction. My eyes searched for Marcus as I passed the vacant lots and boarded-up crack houses along the way.

I saw his scrawny form before noticing the man gripping his T-shirt. Rage shot through me like a searing bullet. The jog turned into an all-out sprint until I disengaged the man's grip and slammed him up against a nearby building. Trapping his arms behind him, I turned toward Marcus's stunned face. "Go to the center and wait for me there." He hesitated, still staring blankly at me. "NOW!"

My voice startling him into action, Marcus took off and I watched until he disappeared. Leaning into the man who was unsuccessfully trying to struggle out of my grip, I whispered, "Why don't we see how you do when you face someone your own size?"

That guy was at least my height if not taller, and didn't look like the type to miss a meal. He'd obviously been chosen to intimidate others for a reason. All the same, I released him, doing a quick check to make sure the observers nearby were keeping their distance.

The man wiped blood off his cheek from where his face met the brick, and sneered at me. "My pleasure."

Despite his gruff appearance, I knew from his first swing that this fight was laughable. Easily ducking his poor attempt, I landed two hard punches on his face before slamming another into his stomach. He staggered, watching me with contempt. I smiled back, hoping to infuriate him more. Emotional fighters were sloppy fighters.

His hand slid into his pocket and came out just as the blade sprang free from its holder. I smiled broadly, daring him to come at me. He lunged like a fool, and within seconds I was twisting his wrist until I heard the sharp snap of bones beneath his skin.

I continued twisting until he fell to his knees. The knife clattered to the ground, the screams of my opponent muffling the noise.

"I'll kill you and that kid, I swear!"

Pushing him until his face was planted on the sidewalk, I kneeled on his injured arm while the other lay immobile underneath him. I picked up the knife and held it to his neck, ensuring I had his attention.

Very calmly, I leaned in close. "Let me explain something to you. I have friends as high as the DA's office and as low as your worst nightmare. You so much as look in the kid's direction again, I'll be back and I won't be so forgiving next time. *Capisce?*"

He didn't say anything, so I put more weight on his broken arm and pressed the knife against his neck until his flesh began to bleed.

Between multiple expletives I heard him eke out a "Yes," so I stood and left him on the ground writhing in pain. Slowly closing the blade, I looked at the group of boys who were watching wide-eyed. Most of them were on the list of banned kids, but a few were older.

"You boys are better than this, and you know it." They sneered and backed away. But a couple stayed. I knew one as Trey but didn't know the other boy's name. "You keep this up and you'll end up dead, or at best locked away for life. Is that what you want?"

They didn't respond. Their friends called them over and they left to follow the crowd. Trey glanced back but turned quickly again. The boy was only fourteen years old and was sealing his future already. Tragic.

Backing away so no one could take me from behind, I slowly made my way to the center. Marcus stood as soon as he saw me, and ran into my arms. He was crying. "I thought he would kill you," he sobbed, letting go of that tough-guy exterior. It was a reminder that deep down he was still just a little boy.

"It's going to take more than an idiot with a knife to take me down," I assured him, rubbing his back. "Is he the guy who's been hurting you?"

Marcus nodded, still huddled against my chest.

"You gonna tell me why now?"

He nodded again, but then looked around in fear. "Not here."

I pulled him toward my bike, tossed the extra helmet to him, and had us on the road in seconds. Knowing we'd need to be somewhere no one could hear us, I drove to the plateau where Grace and I first kissed. That place seemed to have a way of lowering one's defenses, and I needed Marcus to trust me.

He leapt off the bike when I parked, and ran to the edge of the plateau. "Oh wow, you can see the whole city from up here!" His excitement was a far cry from the fear that had tormented him just minutes earlier, and I knew we'd come to the right place.

"Yep. Makes you realize how small it all is in the big picture."

He nodded and gazed out at the view.

"Are you ready to talk to me, Marcus?" I stood next to him, hands in my pockets as we both looked toward the city.

He shook his head absently, but then turned to face me, his eyes weary. "Why do some people have it so easy, like those guys who tour the center, while the rest of us have it so hard?"

"Everyone has it hard, Marcus, even those who look so put together on the outside. But just like you're seeing a huge city looking small, God sees our problems and knows exactly what we need."

Marcus crossed his arms. "Yeah, well it doesn't feel like it sometimes."

Kneeling to face him, I turned his hurt eyes toward mine. "He sent me to you, didn't He? I'm here because Liz asked me, and when I prayed for guidance, God told me clearly that you needed me."

Marcus swiped his hand across his nose and sniffed. "You mean like He talked to you?"

"Well, not in words so much, but in a feeling. You know, He sent me someone a long time ago, too. Someone I've been able to tell all my secrets to, someone who has never let me down. Will you let me be that someone for you, Marcus?"

He lowered himself to sit on the ground, pulling his knees up and hugging them to his chest while he looked out over the plateau. "You think you want to know, but you are going to think I'm bad when I tell you."

Sitting next to him, I rubbed his head. "There is nothing you can tell me that will change what I think of you, Marcus. I promise."

He shook his head, unconvinced.

I took a deep breath and tried another tactic. "Do you remember when you asked me if I killed my father?"

"Yeah."

"Well, I didn't, but I wanted to. In fact, I was seconds from pulling the trigger. And you know what, that fact has haunted me for years. I tried to hide it or push it down. I thought I could get away with not facing my past. But I can't, and neither can you. Our mistakes may shape who we are today, but they don't have to define who we are going to be."

He hesitated and then tears filled his eyes. "I only did it at first because I wanted some extra money."

"Okay."

"Aunt Mave already works so hard, and I knew we couldn't afford the new basketball shoes I wanted. These guys were putting the word out in the neighborhood, looking for kids who would make deliveries for them. All we had to do was bring a backpack into the center, exchange it for one that was exactly the same, and bring that one back out. They'd give us fifty dollars for each exchange."

My stomach dropped. Drugs in the center. It all made sense now. "Marcus, we check your bags."

"They sew them in the panels, I guess. I peeked inside once. I wanted to find out how much money was in there, but I never saw nothing."

"Who would you exchange them with?"

"It changed from time to time, but mostly a big brother or a coach. That guy you saw today would give us the bag, tell us what to look for, and that was it. He didn't tell us nothing else. Anyway, lots of kids wanted in on the action, so I only got to deliver a couple times a month. But then one time, the money came up short. They said the kid was stealing from them and they beat him up pretty bad. When he still didn't come up with the money, they went after his sister. Well, that freaked me out because I didn't want anything to happen to Aunt Mave. I never would have done it if I thought they'd come after her. I promise." He looked up at me, his eyes pleading.

"I know, Marcus. Go on."

"Well, after that, they made everyone who delivered sign some piece of paper. They called it a loyalty agreement. It was like we was in a gang. They told us about a guy named King, that he would have our backs, but I never saw him. And I ain't stupid. I know all about gangs. I wanted nothing to do with it. But they kept bugging me to join them. I kept saying no, and then they said they'd go after Aunt Mave if I told." He glanced at me sideways. "Then you guys suspended everyone. If they couldn't get in the center, they couldn't deliver, and King didn't like that. Suddenly they were all about me doing deliveries again, said they'd even up my payment. But I was freaked out, you know, after Eric and all, so I said no. They told me I either took the drugs or a beating. I tried to stay strong, but sometimes I just couldn't."

He hung his head. "They said if I ever told, I would be arrested, too. That I would go to jail right along with them. I don't know what to do, Matt. I don't wanna go to jail."

Marcus started crying silently and I pulled him into an embrace, trying to comfort him as best I could. "We'll figure something out. I won't let anything happen to you." But even as the words left my mouth, I wondered how I could keep him safe. The situation went well beyond Marcus's part. Drugs had infiltrated the center, the one place we claimed was safe and secure for the kids. Coaches and big brothers entrusted with those little hearts and minds were now our enemies.

How was I going to tell Grace? She would call the cops for sure, making me break the promise I made to Marcus. They'd threaten him, force him to tell, and retaliation would soon follow. No, I would have to find another way. Somehow.

CHAPTER 36

GRACE

Neither Matt nor Marcus showed up at the center today, their absence leaving me agitated, moody, and virtually impossible to be around. Sam called and I snapped at him. I snapped at Darius. And then I snapped at my mother, too, although she set me straight pretty quickly.

I tried to justify my behavior to myself. I was afraid and hurting and I had no one to talk to. A voice in my head reminded me that keeping secrets got me in this mess to begin with. Then I snapped at the voice in my head as well, making my conscience go silent.

The sounds of basketballs banging and kids shouting penetrated my shut door, and I realized that silence was all I wanted right then. I wanted to escape the nightmare I had woken up in and go back to before, when every day with Matt felt like a Hallmark card. Glancing at my watch, I realized I only had fifteen minutes left. Relief stretched through my aching body. If there was ever a night for respite, this was it.

My phone rang as the clock hit 7:55 p.m. and I wanted to scream "NO!" But I answered it anyway.

"Hartsford Center." My voice lacked its normal cheery tone.

"Well, I guess I have my answer. I was hoping you would have simmered down since the last time I called."

Hardly. "What do you want, Sam?"

"I want to talk to you, and since you cut me off this morning, I'm not really giving you the option now." Sam's voice moved from cheery to authoritative in a heartbeat. "I'm worried about you, Gracie. You haven't been the same these last few days."

Feeling a sense of indignation well up in me, I heaved a sigh before returning with the curt tone I'd mustered earlier in the day. "Honestly, I'm having a hard time bouncing between the guy who strolled in here, demanding I leave, and the doting lifelong friend who wants to comfort me. You can't be both."

"That's where you're wrong. I am both." His voice softened a little. "We've always been so close. Why are you shutting me out now?"

"I'm not. I don't have anything to tell you." Even as the words came out, I wanted to cry. Sam wasn't the enemy, yet I was treating him like he was.

"Really." I could hear his disappointment through the phone. He knew I was lying. "Well, since you obviously won't tell me, I'll tell you. I got a visit last night from an irate Stewart, who seems to think I stole you away from him. He was rather dramatic about it, too. Idiot. He still takes no personal responsibility for what he did. Even worse, he was wearing the same watch I bought yesterday, and now I'm going to have to take the blasted thing back."

A small laugh escaped my lips, reminding me why Sam and I have always been so close.

"So he ambushed you. Want to talk about it?" His tone was soothing just like all the other times he had comforted me.

Tears filled my eyes. Oh, if only he knew what damage his flyby at the center did. "Not really."

"You're hurting, Gracie. I can always tell because it's the only time you get so snippy. Do you want me to fly down? I can be there in just a few hours."

I was hurting, but not because of Stewart and his horrible timing. No, I was hurting because I missed Matt. I missed talking to him and having him wrap his arms around me and make me feel loved and safe.

Forcing the tears to stop, I tried to keep my voice as calm as possible. "Sam, thank you, but I am fine. I need you to stop trying to protect me. I'm not a little girl anymore."

His voice sounded strained. "I know that, Gracie. Believe me, I know that. But being self-sufficient doesn't mean you shut out the people in your life who care about you. And I care about you."

"I know, Sam."

"No, Gracie, I don't think you do. Listen, I have a few things to wrap up here today, but I'll come down tomorrow and we'll talk."

I knew he wouldn't hear me if I told him not to come. "Okay."

I ended the call feeling more frustrated than I had before I took it. When had I become such a pushover? Or maybe I've always been one. Maybe that's why Stewart thought he could stray and still marry me. Or why Sam thought he could strong-arm me into moving back to New York though I didn't want to.

And then there was Matt. One mistake and he walks away? I don't think so. He wanted me to toughen up? Well, so be it. I wasn't letting him walk away without a fight.

Cleaning up for the day went quickly, and Darius, Jeff, Steven, and I were all out of there in thirty minutes. Darius locked up and reminded me to be safe. His words prickled a little fear in me, but I brushed them off. All the same, when I approached my apartment complex, my stomach fluttered.

Remembering the vicious look on King's face, I did a quick loop around the complex as Matt had insisted. Stepping out of my car, I kept my eyes alert, constantly looking around me. The door was secure, with no sign of a break-in, so I checked my surroundings one more time before putting the key in the lock.

The roar of an engine startled me and I glanced toward the road just in time to see a motorcycle streak away. Sadness hit me. For a moment I thought it might be Matt.

An hour later, after rehearsing my speech a hundred times, I texted him.

Me: I need to talk to you, tonight. Please. It's important.

I waited for a reply, only to be met with silence. Then suddenly the shrill ring of my cell phone startled me. Sure it was Matt, I felt my heart sink when *Unknown Caller* showed up on the screen. I answered anyway, hopeful.

"Hello?"

The voice at the other end of the line was young and panicked. "Ms. Covington, you have to come now. Right now. I need you. Please!"

I tried to place the voice, knowing I'd heard it before. "Who is this?"

"It doesn't matter. You just have to leave, right now. I'll be at the center waiting. Please, Ms. Covington, I need you to come."

I considered my options. This could be a trap that would make me an easy target. But when I thought of Marcus's bruises and how Eric looked after so many others had jumped him, I knew I couldn't live with myself if something happened to one of the kids. Some risks were worth taking.

"Are you in danger right now?" Even as I asked, I grabbed my purse and headed to my car, locking the door to my apartment behind me while still clutching my cell phone.

"I will be if you don't leave right now!" His voice was desperate, broken.

I threw the car into reverse and peeled out of the parking lot. "Okay, I'm leaving now. Can you at least tell me what this is about?"

The line went dead and fear gripped my heart. Driving faster, I pulled into the center parking lot. It was empty. Although the doors of my car were locked, I rechecked them to make sure. I'd wait, I decided. If he came, I would be there.

CHAPTER 37

MATT

I couldn't get my mind to shut off. I weighed options over and over in my head and kept coming back to the same reality—Grace was the director. If the drug dealers were threatening the kids, it wouldn't be long until they went after the staff. In my gut, I knew that handing the information over to the cops was right, that the situation was much bigger than I could control, but I kept thinking about Marcus and what could happen to him. When guys like King made threats, they backed them up.

Maybe I'd start with Darius. See his thoughts and reaction. Darius was a good blend between street-smart like me and system-driven like Grace. Maybe we could come up with a plan.

Feeling a little more settled, I shut down the computers as the cleaning crew finished up at the gym. I needed a shower. My workout clothes were still damp with sweat, and I could practically taste the salt on my lips.

Cody and I had gone long tonight, but it was time well spent. I needed a distraction and he was on fire. No doubt that kid would be ready for varsity tryouts the next week. I still couldn't get over how far he'd come during the summer. Even the kids at school didn't recognize him the first day. Just wait until they saw what he could now do on the mat. I smiled. *Oh, to be a fly on that wall.*

"We're done," the night crew manager said, approaching me. The cleaning company had completely switched out its cleanup team after my complaints, and the difference had been remarkable.

"See you tomorrow, then." I waved as the crew filed out the door, distracted still by the war going on in my head.

The buzzing sound that signaled an entry jolted me back to reality, and my head jerked up. Devon was pushing in like a man on a mission. He did a quick check to make sure no one else was around and then approached the desk.

"How do you expect me to protect your girl when she's set on getting herself in trouble?" he snarled, crossing his massive arms.

Forcing my heart to calm, I stood straight. "What trouble?"

Devon stared at me. "She didn't tell you?" He paced across the floor, my pulse jumping with every step. "King's after her, man. Confronted your Park Avenue beauty right out in the open. What was she doing in the neighborhood, man?" He pointed at my stunned face. "You have to do your part, too! I lost two men last week, and a third yesterday. A message from King that rang loud and clear."

Leaping around the counter in a panic, I grabbed Devon's shirt even though he was probably one of the only men besides Bruce who intimidated me. "When? When was she in the neighborhood?"

Putting me off but seeing the desperation in my eyes, Devon's voice calmed. "Yesterday. But word on the street is he's going after her. Tonight. I've done all I can, Matt. I can't afford to lose anyone else over her."

I stumbled, my balance completely rocked. Rushing back to my bag, I dug around until I could find my phone—and her text:

Grace: I need to talk to you, tonight. Please. It's important.

My empty stomach heaved, my palms suddenly covered in sweat. I was reliving my worst nightmare, only this time it wasn't a dream. It was real, and it was about Grace.

The next few minutes were a blur. I rushed Devon out of the gym, locked up, and sped toward Grace's apartment, praying the entire time that she would be okay. I begged and pleaded with God until I spotted the flashing blue lights. Two police cars were in front of Grace's apartment and her door was open with that horrific and all too familiar yellow police tape across the entry.

Terror gripped me. I had seen her go home. Watched as she stepped inside that very door.

Ignoring the crowd and the warnings to back up, I ducked under the tape, my eyes wild as I searched for her. I couldn't believe I would experience such mayhem twice, but the scene before me was too much to wish away. Total destruction. Every dish, every piece of furniture, and every picture she had hung on the walls was shattered. The beautiful entertainment center she had spent weeks refinishing was spray-painted with vulgarities, its doors hanging from their hinges. Clothes were ripped to shreds and scattered over every inch of floor space.

My legs buckled, my breath escaping at an alarming speed. A searing pain rocked me backward until I fell against the wall closest to me. I struggled to take a breath deep enough to fill my aching lungs. The room began to spin, colors swirling as the trashed apartment became one big blob in front of me.

I scraped my knees on the hard floor beneath me as I tried over and over to pull in some oxygen. My head throbbing and ears ringing, I could only see Grace's face, looking like my mother's did before she died.

"Sir. Sir!" The sharp tone of a female voice made me look up. Her dark blue cop's uniform was a blur, but the shiny silver badge shimmered in the kitchen light.

Somehow I was able to push out one word. "Grace?"

Saying her name was like opening the floodgates, and finally my chest expanded with fresh air, making it possible for me to breathe again.

The petite cop slid her hand to her holster, her eyes hardened from years on the beat. "Sir, I'm going to need you to stand, slowly."

Having been arrested before, I did as she asked, pulling myself together with each movement. I was at least a foot taller than she was, and I made sure she could see my hands clearly.

"Your name, sir," she demanded.

"Matt Holloway. The girl who lives here, Grace, is she okay?" I didn't know where the calm came from, but somehow I was once again in control.

"How do you know the victim?"

Victim. The word almost took me back to my knees. "I'm her boyfriend," I somehow managed to say through the tears that came out of nowhere.

Ever since I was a boy, I had seen the system as my enemy. Which was confirmed when I was arrested as a teenager. But somehow, in one compassionate move, the police officer—who was ready to pull her weapon at a moment's notice—changed everything.

Her hand softly touched my arm. "She's fine. She wasn't home. Fortunately, she was smart enough to call us when she saw the lock had been tampered with."

My head drooped as I attempted to regroup. "Thank you, Lord."

The cop removed her hand when we heard cursing from the back room. The expletives got louder as her partner pushed a tall, scrawny man down the narrow hallway. His hands were cuffed behind his back, but he was still jerking and fighting the cop as they moved. The man's eyes were wild. The eyes of a druggie. My gut clenched as I imagined what he might have done if Grace had come home unawares.

"Look who I found hiding under the bed," the male cop said, still being jerked around by the aggressor. The cop and I made eye contact and he stiffened. "Who's that?"

"The boyfriend," the female officer explained.

The strung-out druggie in handcuffs looked my way and smiled, exposing two missing teeth, then shouted the vulgar things he planned to do to Grace.

My fists clenched instinctively and I lunged. The tiny female cop blocked my way, staring at me with eyes that dared me to move farther. "Don't make me arrest you, too," she barked. When I backed down, still keeping my eyes rigid on the man being removed from the apartment, she continued, "We sent your girlfriend home with friends. I suggest you go find her before you get yourself into trouble."

"Friends." I knew exactly who and bolted to my bike, barely getting "Thank you" out before running through the open door. The crowd had thickened, all neighbors and others interested in the crime that took place on their doorstep. I would never let Grace come back there. If I had to stick her on that airplane myself, fine. She didn't belong in this world.

Forcing myself to stay under a speed that would get me pulled over, I finally made it to Jake's condo and spotted her car immediately. Relief, anger, terror, frustration. Every emotion I'd felt in the last twenty minutes washed through me as I banged on the door.

Jake opened it only a crack and took in my determined face and panting breath. "If you are coming to fight with her, now is not a good time."

Pushing the door with force, I glared at him, sending a look that only another man could understand. "Do you really think I care? Where is she?"

He stepped out of my way, understanding my desperation. He'd been in my shoes at one point with Naomi.

"Back bedroom. But let me warn you. Naomi's not your biggest fan right now."

I stormed ahead, pushing down the guilt. Naomi was probably thinking the same thing that plagued me all the way there. That if I had just answered her call, just swallowed my pride a little, this might not have happened. Then fury rose again. Grace was the one who lied. Not me.

The women were sitting on the bed praying when I opened the door. Grace's eyes met mine and instinct took over, dashing all my fury with one cold splash. Within seconds she was in my arms, my grip so firm I was probably close to hurting her. At some point Naomi slipped out, and all I could do was take in the softness and smell of the woman in my arms.

"Thank God you're okay," I whispered, kissing her head as I gripped her tighter.

Her face burrowed into my chest, the wetness of her tears leaving patches. "You should see my apartment. They ruined everything." She choked up over the last word. I knew her pain wasn't about the stuff she lost but the security ripped from her. A home is supposed to be a safe place, and although I knew that run-down dive wasn't, to Grace it had been her statement of independence.

"I know. I just left there."

She nodded, probably assuming I went in response to her text, and continued to weep softly in my arms.

We stayed that way until the panic was gone and my heart was convinced that she was safe. Eventually she pulled back and wiped her face. She looked calmer than I would have expected after such an ordeal.

"I got a phone call from one of the kids at the center. He begged me to meet him. Said he was in some kind of danger, so I went and waited, but he never showed up. When I got back to the apartment, I checked the door like you showed me and saw scrapes right next to the lock. I think they set me up. That's what hurts more than anything."

The anger came slow, starting in my toes and creeping up along the edges of my skin. I stared at her, my voice getting louder with each question. "You went to the center? At night? Alone? Have you lost your mind?"

She stood straighter, her tone matching mine. "Yes, I went, and I will the next time a kid calls, regardless of the circumstances. Some people actually believe I can make a difference, Matt, even if you don't."

Fear fueled my fury. My hands flew to the top of my head. "When are you going to realize that you are not bulletproof? You don't belong here! You think just because you picked an apartment like theirs or live off a meager salary that you have any idea of what their life is like? You will never know that kind of desperation, Grace! Despite your efforts, the fact remains that you are one phone call away from help, and you always will be."

Tears shimmered against the blue of her eyes and spilled over when she blinked. "You have always underestimated me, Matt. You're right. I don't know their world. Maybe I was foolish in thinking that living that way could help me understand them. But that doesn't mean I can't make a difference. It doesn't mean that I have to know their pain in order to help."

I crossed my arms, ready to say anything that would open her eyes. "Were you helping when you went into the neighborhood yesterday? You think provoking King did anything good for anyone? Wake up, Grace. Devon lost a man last night because of you, and tonight you were King's next target. Tell me how that is helping!"

Her hand flew to her chest. "He killed someone?"

"Yes, Grace. That's their reality. Violence, retaliation, loyalty to the point of death."

She shook her head in disbelief. "I just wanted to help Marcus."

I clasped her arms, forcing her to look at me, the words pouring out in a hot stream. "You don't get it! It's all connected. This neighborhood. Those kids. King's a reality. But when he goes down, another one's gonna rise. It's a never-ending battle. A battle you are completely unequipped to fight."

She stared at me without a word and I released her. The woman was completely hardheaded. Running my hand over the short hair on my head, I sighed. "You need to take that job in New York. It's time for you to go home."

When Grace's face fell, I wanted to reach out and hold her, wanted to tell her I loved her and that everything would be okay. But I couldn't. Our worlds had crashed, just like I expected them to.

She nodded and then faced me with sadness. "I texted you tonight because I had every intention of fighting for you. For us. But how stupid I am, because I realize now that all my efforts are useless."

I shook my head, dismissing her words. "Our breakup has nothing to do with this conversation."

"It has everything to do with it!" She fisted her hands and rapped them against her temples. "What made me think I would ever get through to you? Why do I even try? You don't see it!" She gripped my shirt in frustration. "Despite everything you've overcome in your life, despite all the ways that God has grown you, you are still completely unwilling to trust. You don't trust me. You don't trust the system. I don't even think you fully trust Bruce. But more than anything, you don't trust God."

She let go of my shirt when I didn't say another word, and walked a few steps before turning to glance back at me.

"You spend every minute getting ready to fight the battle all by yourself. Forget everyone else. They'll only disappoint you or let you down, right? My not telling you about Stewart was wrong, yes, but wrong enough to end things like you did? No."

She walked back up to me, her voice lowered, her eyes ablaze with a temper I knew was rare. "It was an excuse, Matt. An excuse to run because you are the one who's afraid, not me. I'm not afraid of you and I'm not afraid of us. But more importantly, I'm not afraid to be vulnerable to whatever situation comes next. God put me here. If that means I deal with bricks through a window, or torn-up clothes, or worse, then so be it!"

With that she walked to the door and opened it. Her face was set, her mouth grim. "I want you to leave."

The tears I could handle, but when Grace turned on the chill, it was like shards of ice slicing through my skin. There was a line between us now, very thick and darkly drawn. Her accusation hung in the air, challenging me to respond. But I couldn't find the words. They stayed jammed in my throat, choking me.

I did as she asked, stopping for just a moment before I stepped out the door. I wanted to reach out, to try to convey what I could in a touch, but tucked my hands into my pockets instead. "I'll leave, but we're not done talking about this." I couldn't even recognize my voice. It was raspy with repressed emotion.

"Yes, we are." She looked tired and fragile, and much too worn-out to argue anymore.

Maybe she was right. Maybe I was afraid, because in that moment when I should have stayed and fought for our crumbling relationship, I just walked away.

CHAPTER 38

GRACE

I woke up thirty minutes before my alarm went off after a terrible night's sleep. As much as I talked a good game to Matt, I felt completely terrified. Kneeling beside the bed, I bowed my head and prayed fervently for God's protection. I prayed for courage and for strength. I prayed for the families of those who'd already lost their lives in this mess, desperately searching for some peace or purpose in all the horrors that had taken place.

Then I prayed for Matt, even though my heart broke all over again. I prayed for God to help him learn to trust and forgive.

Taking a deep breath, I bowed my head even lower. "Please, God, just bring him back to me."

Tears poured and I continued praying until my phone began dinging with my wake-up alarm.

I stood, feeling exhausted, and turned off the sound. Grabbing the clothes I had worn last night, I made my way to the guest bathroom, thankful Naomi had loaned me some pajamas. I'd have to pick up some essentials today, but luckily I kept a makeup bag in my purse, and Naomi had supplied anything I was lacking. I thought of the shampoo the intruders had dumped all over the floors and across the walls of the apartment. No way I was getting that deposit back.

The tears threatened again, but I pushed them away. Matt was right. One phone call, and there I was. Roof over my head with all my basic needs met. What if I hadn't had the option of calling anyone? What if I was forced to stay where I had been victimized? I suddenly understood what Matt was saying about desperation. He must have felt that way every day of his life. A cold chill snaked through my body. For the first time since coming to Asheville, I didn't want to understand, didn't want to know firsthand.

Getting ready went quickly. I folded Naomi's pajamas and placed them on the bed I had already made. Leaving her a quick note of thanks that also promised a phone call, I slipped out the door as the sun was starting to peek over the horizon.

As I drove I pondered what my next move might be. I couldn't tell my parents about the break-in—they would flip out. But at the same time, I wanted to. All the secrets were weighing on me. Sam didn't know about any of the threats and then the personal attack on me. In my gut, I knew that was wrong.

I parked and then gathered my things. Halfway out of my car, I saw Trey sitting on the steps and my stomach tumbled. Immediately looking around for others, I started to retreat.

He stood. "I won't hurt you, Ms. Covington. I promise. No one knows I'm here." Approaching with his hands raised, I could tell he was trying to show me he wasn't a threat.

A bystander would never understand my fear. Trey was only fourteen, gangly, and still had a baby face. His dark hair needed a trim and hung in his brown eyes more often than not.

Searching my heart, I chose to believe him. Matt would be livid at the risk I was taking, but I couldn't consider Matt's opinion anymore. If he had his wish, I'd be halfway back to New York. No. My gut told me Trey was just a lost boy in need of guidance.

When I'd exited the car and shut the door, he got closer and whispered, "Can we go inside? I don't want anyone to see me with you."

I nodded, letting him follow me into the quiet building. Fear made me question myself. Was I making a terrible mistake? Locking the door behind us brought me some comfort, but I still felt shaky as we walked over to my office.

Trey's hands were tucked into the pockets of his fraying shorts, and he walked with his head down, watching his feet move across the gym floor. My heart softened. He looked so lost.

"Let's sit here." I pointed at the couch once we moved into my office. He nodded and sat, still not making eye contact.

I waited, but when he didn't talk, I asked him the question that had to be answered before we could move forward. "Were you the one who called me last night?"

He nodded, still looking toward the floor.

"Did you know they wanted to hurt me?"

He nodded again.

"Were you trying to help them?" I could hardly get that last question out.

His head jerked up. "No! I was trying to help *you*. I promise. They wanted you home. That's why they waited until after the center closed. I knew if I could get you out of there, then maybe you'd have a chance." He tried to hide a wayward tear and turned away. "Even you think I'm a horrible person now."

He'd been trying to protect me. That changed everything. I realized that most of my sorrow came from believing that one of the kids would turn on me. Scooting closer, I reached out to touch his arm, offering comfort and the reassurance that I believed him.

"Thank you."

My touch brought sniffles, and I pulled Trey into my arms when he began to cry.

"I don't know what to do. I can't get out now." He wept harder and I did my best to let him grieve. "I just wanted a family, you know? Someone who cared about me."

He suddenly sat up, pulling himself together. "But I won't let them hurt you. That's why I came here. It's too late for me, but you have to get out of here. King's dangerous, and he's mad. He won't stop at nothing."

Sighing, I prayed for the right words. "I'm not leaving, Trey. But if you tell me what's going on, why he's got such a problem with our rules, then maybe I can help you."

"I can't. It's too big."

I thought back to how Matt dealt with Marcus's injuries, promising the boy protection to end his fear. "Trey, no one will know we talked."

He narrowed his eyes. "Promise?"

"I promise."

Though hesitant, Trey told me everything. How King was using kids in the center to deliver drugs. He told me that several of our coaches and big brothers were actually dealers from other cities. The way he made it sound, King had the largest distribution in the area, and all because he could pass large amounts of narcotics without any suspicion. Worse, there was no link to him. He never dealt with the kids. In fact, Trey explained that until recently most of them didn't even know what he looked like. King only came out of hiding when Devon started to threaten his turf.

"You really messed things up for him when you kicked us all out. Now he only sells half what he used to."

My stomach turned. Even with the suspensions, kids were still delivering. "Do you know who all is working for him?"

Trey shook his head. "They don't tell us nothin'. You do like you're told and you don't ask questions." He shivered as if he knew firsthand what asking questions would mean.

"Would you be able to point out the volunteers who picked up the drugs?"

Trey hesitated and searched my face. I knew I was asking a lot. "Just the ones I passed off with. We never know when a delivery happens or who gets it until right before we come in here."

I took a deep breath, already knowing the answer to my next question before I asked it. "Trey, would you be willing to tell the cops what you've seen and who King is?"

He shook his head vehemently.

"Okay." I paused, even more careful as I said the next words. "I want you to know that I have to. I won't tell them your name, just like I promised, but I am going to tell the police what's going on here. I can't let this continue."

"Why?" He stood, his eyes filling with tears. "They'll come after you again. They'll kill you!"

"Maybe they will, but I'm not afraid. Sometimes doing the right thing is dangerous." Waiting again, I felt that familiar tug when I knew God wanted me to be a witness, and I couldn't waste this opportunity. "Do you believe in God, Trey?"

He crossed his arms and shrugged. "Ain't seen Him do nothin' good for me. What's the point?"

I smiled at him, and patted the couch so he would sit back down. He did but still looked suspicious. "Well, I do believe in God, so I trust the things He says in the Bible. There's a verse in Joshua that says, 'Do not be afraid. Do not be discouraged. Be strong and courageous.' Joshua was the leader of an army that was about to go fight hundreds of thousands of men. They were probably pretty scared, too. But do you know what happened?"

Trey's eyes widened in anticipation. He shook his head.

"God helped them win their battles. In fact, even though the odds were stacked against them, they still won. So no matter what happens, Trey, I'm not afraid because I know God is going to take care of me. If that means I get hurt, it's okay. I trust Him."

"Well, I don't." He lowered his head and crossed his arms.

I rubbed his back gently. "I understand. But if you decide you want to, just come see me, okay? I'm not going anywhere."

Trey sank back against the couch. "My granddad was right. All you women are stubborn fools!"

Laughter escaped me and I stood. "That's very true." I picked up my purse and keys. "Are you sure you don't want to come with me?"

"To the cops?"

I nodded.

"No way." He stood, too, his face hardening.

"Okay. Do you want me to take you somewhere?"

He thought about it for a while. "Could you bring me to my granddad's house? He lives too far to walk and I don't want to go home." Fear filled his eyes, and my heart ached.

Desperation. It's all he had left.

It didn't take long to drop Trey off and get to the police station. Once I was there, though, I panicked. What was I supposed to say? I had no proof. Nothing but the words of a boy who wouldn't even come forward. Then, there was Sam. Could I really go to the cops without even giving him a heads-up? No.

Taking out my phone, I fought the urge to run and hide.

"Be strong and courageous."

Weren't those the words I had just preached to Trey? Talk about being a hypocrite.

Swallowing my fear, I called Sam, knowing that in minutes I would lose not only his respect but probably my job as well.

"Hey, Gracie Belle! I was just thinking about you. I'm probably going to take off in the next couple hours. Dinner at six work for you?" The warmth in his voice made my eyes sting.

"Not really, Sam." I paused, searching for the right words to say. There were none. "I have to talk to you about something."

"Anything, Gracie."

"I haven't been honest with you," I began, my voice shaky.

"I know, Gracie. This thing kind of snuck up on me as well."

What was he talking about? "No, Sam. I haven't been honest with you about the *center*. In fact, when you hear me out, you may never speak to me again."

He laughed lightheartedly. "Don't be dramatic. What's going on?"

"After the incident with Eric, Darius clamped down hard on the rules. We banned a huge group of kids and started being more intentional about safety."

"I know this, Gracie. Darius and I talked about it before I left."

Feeling more empowered with each breath, I continued. "Well, there's more. After you left, the center was vandalized. They threw bricks through all the windows with a pretty direct message painted on each. Basically, they were threatening us. Darius and I decided it was best not to tell anyone . . . including you."

"Gracie—"

I cut him off, closing my eyes. "There's more. Recently, one of the boys at the center showed up with severe bruising and probably some broken ribs. His big brother tried to get him to say who, but the kid refused. If I hadn't happened to see them looking at his bruises, I wouldn't have known, either. I don't know if there is a connection, but it feels suspect in light of what I know now."

"You reported it, right?" His voice was noticeably harsher.

"No, I decided to wait."

"Gracie! We are required by law to report any suspicion of abuse. You know this!"

"I know. I should have, but I didn't. We didn't think the abuse was coming from his home, but he wouldn't tell anyone who was hurting him. So I went to his house in the hopes of talking to both him and his aunt. I never got the chance. Instead, I was confronted by someone in the neighborhood. Someone dangerous. He threatened the center. And he threatened me personally if we didn't lift the suspensions."

"My God."

"Last night they came after me. I wasn't home, but they broke into my apartment and trashed everything." I shivered, thinking for the hundredth time how I never would have checked the door if Matt hadn't drilled it into my head to do so. "Thankfully, I noticed the break-in before I walked into a trap."

I could hear Sam's breathing catch at the other end of the line, and I could almost feel his anger through the phone.

"Are you safe now?" Hard and frightfully calm, Sam's words fed my guilt.

"Yes, but there's more. This morning I went back to the center. One of the kids who had been suspended was waiting for me. He came to warn me to leave. Then I got him to tell me what's been going on." Silence. I couldn't figure out how to say the words. They were too heartbreaking.

"Gracie?"

"They're using the center as a distribution point for narcotics, Sam, and have been for a long time. Months, if not more. That's why they're so angry about our rules. We cut their deliveries in half."

I heard a loud bang at the other end of the line, and a few choice words that Sam rarely ever said. Next I heard him tell his assistant that he wanted to leave for Asheville immediately. Then he came back on the line.

"Where are you now?" There was panic in his voice.

"I'm sitting outside the police station. I didn't know how to go in there alone. I'm so sorry, Sam."

"We will talk about all that later. Right now, I want you to go to my condo. The security guard will let you in. Do not call anyone. Do not tell anyone. Do you understand? No one can be trusted."

"But I need to tell Ma—"

"Gracie! No. One." The pure authority in his voice shut me up. I'd known Sam a long time, and I'd never heard him so angry. Only when he heard about Stewart's cheating had he even raised his voice around me.

Tears started to flow. "Okay. I'm sorry."

CHAPTER 39

MATT

I couldn't get Grace out of my head. As terrified as I was by the thought of her staying and being vulnerable, I was equally tortured by the thought of her heeding my advice and leaving. There was no good solution, no matter how many ways I looked at the angles.

Giving up on the idea of accomplishing anything, I stuck my head into Bruce's office and told him I needed to take care of something important. He nodded and gave me the look he had all week—one that clearly showed his concern.

I couldn't blame him. I'd been all over the map. Depressed, then angry. I was both antsy and agitated. In a span of only a few months, I had gone from having a steady, mundane existence to being a whirlwind of emotion.

Love. It's the one thing that can bring even the strongest of men to their knees.

Her car wasn't in the parking lot when I pulled up. Again, I was caught up in a mix of emotions. I was happy to get a chance to speak to Darius about the deliveries, but my mind was racing with questions as to where she could be. Unable to stand not knowing, I pulled out my phone and texted her.

Me: I'm at the center. Where are you?

No response. I waited only a few minutes before calling. No answer. The knots in my stomach twisted until they multiplied, the what-ifs bombarding my mind. Forcing myself to calm down, I locked up my gear and went inside.

Marcus was racing around a group of boys as he jumped up to make a layup, a smile on his face. My heart steadied a little, reminding me who mattered in this situation. The kids. We had to find a way to make the center safe once again.

Darius was in his office when I found him, laboring over some spreadsheet laid out on his desk.

"Can't talk now. I'm knee-deep in numbers and completely unable to do two things at once." He never looked up. Just waved a hand at me.

Dropping into the chair across from his desk, I ignored his dismissal. "They're using the center to deliver drugs."

Darius's head slowly rose, and he met my stare with the look of disbelief I'd felt when Marcus told me. He said only, "No."

"They're using the kids to bring in backpacks and make exchanges. No trail. Some of the volunteers are behind it. Admittedly, the idea is brilliant. The problem is, I have no idea how we're going to stop it."

Before Darius could respond, we heard whistles blowing frantically as Steven rushed into the office.

"You better get out here now." Distraught, he gripped the doorframe while his chest heaved frantically. "Sam is shutting us down."

The pit in my stomach grew. Sam. Grace. There had to be a connection.

The scene in front of us was like a police bust. Jeff and Steven were rounding up the kids, blowing whistles and shutting down the electronics. Sam was yelling, pointing to the door as if the kids' lives depended on immediate evacuation.

I spotted Marcus, who was gripping his backpack. His head darted back and forth as he watched the chaos unfold. He looked lost and afraid. Infuriated, I stormed toward Sam.

"There's a better way to do this," I hissed when he was close enough. "Can't you see they're terrified?"

Sam stopped yelling long enough to turn to me. The center was half-empty, with kids still grabbing their stuff and heading for the door. His face said it all. Accusation, distrust, and blame.

"I want you out," he demanded. "I knew from the start that you were bad news, but this is a new low."

His words stopped me cold. Crossing my arms, I met his hard stare. "I'm not a scared little boy you can push around. You want to throw accusations at me? You'd better be ready to back them up."

The space between us tightened as we stood face-to-face, neither of us willing to stand down. My temper was getting hotter with each passing second.

His eyes dark and eager, Sam stepped forward and started to remove his tailored suit jacket. "Well, then, come on. I've been wanting to hit something for the last three hours."

Knowing I could take him down with one good punch, I clenched my fists. But I wouldn't. Even though he had it coming, Sam was "family" to Grace. I would never be able to step back over that line once I had crossed it.

I pulled my eyes off Sam for a second to see if all the kids had left the center. We were their mentors, grown-ups who set examples for them. The coast was clear and I turned back, determined to end this thing. "Instead of starting something we both know you can't finish, why don't you tell me what this is really about."

Sam stepped closer, his anger visible to anyone watching. "Why don't *you* tell me about the drugs."

I flinched, completely unprepared for that response.

He shook his head, his eyes ablaze with disgust. "Yeah. That's what I thought. So you figured you could prey on her while she was vulnerable, right? Make her believe you're her knight in shining armor, to distract her from the fact that all along you've been the enemy."

Violence pounded in my head. His words were setting off a chain reaction in me that I could no longer stop. My first shove was meant to be a warning, but I found no satisfaction in it. I wanted more. I wanted blood.

Sam swung, making contact just above the jaw. I could have moved, avoided the blow, but instead I found energy in his attack. I knew the law. It would be hard to charge me with assault when he had taken the first swing.

Barely affected by the punch, I smiled at him, narrowing my eyes. "You feel better now?"

His breathing was ragged and his body was shaking from the adrenaline. "I won't feel better until Grace is as far from you as I can get her. You've done nothing but put her in danger since the first moment you met."

I froze, my mouth dropping open in disbelief. "*I* put her in danger? Are you blind?! You guys sent her down here completely naive and raw. You practically handed her to King on a silver platter. She's been living in squalor, sleeping on the floor in the rattiest apartment in the city, because she thinks it's the only way to prove herself." I pounded my chest. "I've done nothing but take care of her and protect her since she got here. *I* am the one who followed her home every night to make sure she stayed safe. *I* am the one who put a 'no touch' order out in the neighborhood, and *I* am the reason she didn't walk into a trap because *I* taught her how to protect herself.

"You want to stand there all high and mighty and judge me? Then fine. But don't you dare imply that I've done anything less than love that woman with every ounce of my being!"

My words echoed through the empty gym, and I glanced around to see Darius, Jeff, and Steven looking at me with wide eyes.

Sam didn't respond. He picked up his jacket and turned to Darius. "You keep those doors locked until I say otherwise, and I suggest all three of you get your résumés in order." He spun around and left without another word.

Darius picked up a wayward basketball and threw it into the bleachers with a curse, then stormed back to his office.

CHAPTER 40

GRACE

I had taken to pacing. Back and forth. Back and forth. Ignoring Matt's texts and calls was the hardest thing I ever had to do, but I was determined not to disappoint Sam any more than I had already. Glancing at the elaborate clock above his mantel, I questioned again where he could be. The jet should have landed by then.

I walked back to the kitchen, opening the fridge for the twentieth time. The large steel appliance was stocked with all my favorite foods—Sam knew me so well—but I just couldn't make myself eat. Closing the door roughly, I strode back to the bedrooms, one on each side of the hallway, and looked around.

The master bedroom embodied all that was Sam. Masculine, rough-edged wood was used for the oversize king bed, which was adorned with brown sheets and a white-striped duvet. The other bedroom had been designed in stark contrast. Obviously decorated for a woman, the room had a smaller bed and was intricately detailed with multiple layers of color and large, fluffy pillows. It reminded me of my room back home, and I wondered if that's where Sam had gotten the idea.

Striding back to the living room, I attempted to sit and wait. That lasted less than five minutes. When the door handle jiggled, I shot forward, meeting Sam as he stepped in. He paused when he saw me, and stood staring as the door slowly closed behind him.

I'd never seen him look so unkempt. His jacket hung over his arm, his shirt halfway untucked. Not bothering to say a word, he threw his coat onto the buffet in the entryway and veered toward the freezer to pull out a pack of frozen vegetables. My eyes followed him as he dropped the pack onto his red, swollen knuckles.

"Oh my gosh, Sam, what happened?" I rushed toward him to inspect his hand myself.

"Your boyfriend and I had a little chat." Disdain dripped off each word and my breath caught, my eyes searching his body for damage. I didn't see any.

"He didn't hit you." It wasn't a question. I knew without asking that Matt must have forced himself not to fight. I'd seen him deliver a blow, and I knew Sam wouldn't be standing there if Matt had hit back. A feeling of pride swelled within me. Once again Matt had proved to be the better man.

Sam, on the other hand, took my assessment as an insult. "How do you know?"

I raised an eyebrow at him, thinking, *You're alive.*

He pushed past me and headed toward the master bedroom. "I'm going to take a shower."

"You're not going to talk to me about this?" My voice was laced with desperation. I'd been anticipating this confrontation for hours.

He didn't turn, and his clipped words lingered behind him. "I'm not ready yet." The door slammed before I could mutter another word.

Twenty minutes passed. Twenty minutes of anxiety and regret. I felt like that kid whose parents made him find a switch and wait for them. Just when I didn't think I could take the silence any longer, Sam emerged, looking completely transformed. His wrinkled suit had been replaced with jeans and a loose collared shirt. Even in those casual clothes, Sam still was a formidable presence. The only other man I knew who commanded so much space with his demeanor was Matt.

I stood, wringing my hands, as he watched me. "I'm sorry, Sam. I should have told you about the threats right away. I was so sure I could handle it all. Now I realize it was way too huge for me to tackle alone."

He didn't move. "Where have you been living?"

I was surprised by his question, and my voice faltered a little. "Why?"

"I had my driver take me by the three worst complexes in the city. I want to know which one was yours." His hard eyes awaited my reply, challenging me to lie to him again.

"Raintree Apartments. They're only a few blocks from the center."

Sam's lips pressed together into a hard line, his jaw twitching as he clenched his teeth. "I shut the center down. I'm taking you home tomorrow, and then will come back and officially file the police report."

Disappointment flooded me. Closing the center wasn't an option. "Sam, I'm sorry I didn't tell you sooner what was going on. I should have. But please don't make a rash decision about closing the center just because you're mad at me. Think of all those kids."

Sam looked toward the ceiling and took a deep breath. "Gracie, I'm not closing the center because I'm mad at you. I'm closing it because what has been going on ruins every dream I had for that place. It was meant to unify the community, not tear it apart."

He walked over to his desk and picked up a notebook and pen. "I will need the names of anyone you know who is connected to the drug trafficking."

He was talking to me like an employee, the wayward director who had single-handedly ruined his father's dream. Guilt and defeat burdened my heart as he sat there, still watching me. I took a breath and settled into a chair. "I only know of King, the one who approached me in the neighborhood. I won't give the name of the boy who confided in me. Darius still has the bricks they hurled through the windows. I also believe there was an arrest of someone after the break-in. They found him hiding under my bed. We can let the cops know the incidents are related."

Sam shot off his chair, his cool facade melting away. "Gracie Belle, you could have been killed! Do you have any idea what that would have done to your parents? To me?"

I lowered my head, unable to face him. His emotions were like a Ping-Pong ball—bouncing from those of angry boss to caring friend so fast, I didn't know how to respond. Instead, I did as I always had when faced with an emotional conflict: I backed down and waited. Surely it wouldn't take him long to calm down.

But he was just getting started. "It's like you didn't even take into account how any of us would feel. I mean, you purposely choose to live in a war zone, decide to date a guy who's the poster child for domestic violence, and worse, lie to all of us, your family who loves you, about everything! What is going on with you?"

"What's going on with me?" I hollered back, springing to my feet as well so we were face-to-face. Maybe it was the hours of anticipation or maybe the cruel way he sliced at Matt's past, but I was done getting yelled at. "What's going on with you? You're all over the place, Sam! I get that there's problems, real problems, but that has never stopped you before. We haven't even tried to include the authorities and you're shutting it down? And what's with this sudden overprotective vibe? Punching Matt and demanding that I go home? What is that? You're being completely irrational."

He ran his hand through his hair and massaged his neck before lowering it. "You're right."

I resisted the urge to say, "I am?"

Sam stepped closer, getting that look that made butterflies flutter in my stomach, but not in a good way.

"Gracie Belle, lately, when it comes to you, that's exactly how I feel. Irrational, confused, excited. My head's a mess." His voice had calmed and he took my hands in his. Somehow I knew I wasn't going to like what he was about to say.

"I had hoped to handle this better, but I guess we may as well deal with it now. Then we can figure out where to go from here." He paused as if mentally searching for the words. "Something happened when I came to see you, Gracie. I don't know. It's like something clicked or someone turned on a light that had previously been dark. But all of a sudden, you weren't a little girl anymore but a confident, beautiful grown woman." He stepped closer. "Now when I look at you, I see Christmases and Thanksgivings. I see family and long nights working together on something we both love. I see a future."

Wow. That was seriously the only thought in my head. *Wow.*

"I need to sit down."

I backed away from him and dropped back into my chair. Sam followed and sat in the chair next to me, resting his arm over the back of mine.

"It is really so shocking?"

Eyes wide, I nodded, trying to get my brain to form a coherent thought.

As the seconds ticked by without a word from me, Sam started to get irritated. "Seriously, Gracie, say something. I mean, come on.

I know you've noticed me in that way before. Heck, you and your friends called me 'Hottie Pants' up until graduation."

Suddenly I was laughing, and not politely. Like the gasping for air, snot coming out of your nose, hissing because your vocal cords can't keep up kind of laughing.

Sam bolted up to his feet. "Now who's being irrational?"

I threw my hands over my face, trying to calm down. "I'm sorry," I said between gasps. I knew my meltdown wasn't just because of Sam's confession. It was everything. All the stress and emotion and agony I felt over the past week just spilled out of me with a vengeance.

He walked into the kitchen, opened the refrigerator, and then slammed it shut. "Maybe I was wrong about you being a grown woman," he muttered in the distance.

That made me get my hysteria under control. I wiped my eyes and walked to the kitchen, but still had to consciously hold back my giggles. He eyed me suspiciously when I stood next to him and leaned back against the counter.

He handed me a bottle of water. "I guess I got my answer." His voice was flat, but he didn't seem angry.

"I'm sorry I laughed. It was an emotional reaction to all the stress lately. But I have to admit I wasn't expecting you to say that." I eyed him. "Is that why you hit Matt? Some kind of territorial guy thing?"

"Give me a little credit, Gracie. I hit Matt because he preyed on you. He exploited your vulnerabilities so he could make some money."

I grabbed his arm. "Wait a second. He would never. Matt loves those kids. Even more than the two of us do."

He pulled his arm from my grip. "Don't put me in the same category as him. So maybe things between us got a little muddied, but I have always put your best interest first. Don't forget that we're here right now because you lied to me. You put his advice above my rules. Rules I put in place for everyone's protection."

I crossed my arms, the desire to laugh completely gone. "You're wrong. Matt's a good guy, and I love him."

Sam snorted. "Love him? You've known him for like two minutes. Besides, I think we both know from your track record that you don't pick the best men." He walked away, looking more annoyed than angry, and went back to the living room to grab his cell phone. "We leave tomorrow morning, ten o'clock."

I stood in the kitchen replaying the day's events. The old Gracie, the pushover, would stay put, do whatever Sam said to keep the peace. But I didn't want to. I wanted to see Matt and at least tell him good-bye before I headed home. I needed to promise him that I would be back.

I walked over to my purse and picked it up slowly, waiting for the reaction I knew was coming.

Sam approached. "Where are you going?"

"I'm going to stay with some friends. I think in light of everything, it's best. I'll be back in the morning by nine, ready to leave."

He dragged his hand through his hair. "Gracie, that makes no sense. You have a room here. Heck, you're the only reason I bought a place with two bedrooms to begin with. We'll hang out, watch some TV. I don't know, talk. Come on, Gracie. If you leave now, it's going to be awkward between us."

I leaned in and gave Sam a hug good-bye, one he barely returned. "You and I will be fine. I'll see you in the morning."

Exiting his building, I felt an odd sense of freedom. Or maybe just spunk.

The sun warmed my face, and I stood with a goofy grin and closed my eyes. The air was thick with moisture, and sweat beaded on my skin almost immediately, but I didn't care. For the first time in my life, I decided what I wanted and then had the courage to do it. Suddenly everything felt possible. Matt and even the center. In my heart I knew we'd find a way.

I opened my eyes and it was like God agreed, because perfectly positioned in my line of sight was the tall silhouette of the man who had changed my life. He stood, looking off in the distance with his arms crossed, leaning against my car.

He turned my way as I approached, his dark sunglasses blocking any emotion I may have been able to detect from his eyes.

"What are you doing here?" The words were a good front for what I really wanted to do, which was to throw myself into his arms.

He didn't move as he kept those shielded eyes on me. "Waiting for you." When I didn't respond, he stepped closer, the brush of his thumb like feathers across my cheek. "Do you have time for a ride?"

My life was a mass of uncertainty, but I knew one thing for sure. When it came to being with Matt, my answer would always be yes.

CHAPTER 41

MATT

The heat generated from her body pressed against mine was almost enough to distract my driving. She hadn't hesitated. Hadn't even asked how I'd found her. I guess she knew I was the kind of man who'd snoop through every paper in her office if it meant finding Sam's address.

I thought I was strong enough to let her go. Let her have her polished life back. But when Sam walked out the door, it hit me that I might never see her again. No matter what had happened or what would happen, I knew I couldn't live with that. Selfish as it was, my life was forever entwined with hers.

Stopping just feet from the plateau, I cut the engine and enjoyed that she didn't rush to let go of me. But seconds later she did and I longed for the contact again, needed it more than my next breath.

She slid off the bike, but before she could even step away, I caught her arm, folded her into me like a man starving for affection.

"I'm sorry," I whispered, kissing her head, cheeks, eyes—everything I could touch on her face—before lowering my head into the soft crevice by her neck. Could she sense my desperation? My need? "I want you to stay. I love you so much."

Her heart's steady rhythm sped up as she held me tighter. There was no beginning or end to us, just a reconnection that never should have been severed in the first place.

"You were right. I was afraid. When I saw Stewart hug you. When I realized that you had loved someone like him, I couldn't breathe. He could give you the world and all I had was a damaged past and a shaky future. And then there was Sam saying things like 'growing pains' and that I wasn't good enough for you. I'm ashamed to admit it, but I ran before you could."

She pushed back and I loosened my arms just enough to let her look at me directly. Her eyes pooled with tears, one escaping when she blinked. I swiped it away, never wanting to be the reason for her tears. Leaning in, I put my forehead to hers. "Can you ever forgive me? Give me another chance?"

I waited for her answer, my palms sweating in anticipation. She hadn't said a word, but I saw love in her eyes.

"Forgiveness is needed when someone wrongs you, Matt. You never did. I know all about fear, so I'll never fault you for feeling it. You and I will face a lot of ups and downs. And I can't always promise that Sam or someone else isn't going to say something rude. We do come from very different worlds, but that's what makes this so sweet. The key is trusting each other enough to make the journey." She stepped back, her eyes catching mine, challenging me. "Do you trust me?"

The question held more weight than she realized. I didn't trust easily, but even so my answer was instant. "Yes, I do."

She smiled and the world felt whole again. I couldn't wait another moment to feel her lips against mine. Restore all we had been and more. She poured into me as freely as ever and this time

I did the same. Giving my heart, holding nothing back, no matter the cost.

"We'll find you a place to live and a new job," I whispered, still touching the softness of her lips with mine. With just an easy breath, I was back to kissing her, imagining the day when I could completely make her mine.

She stiffened and broke away.

"What's wrong?"

"I'm leaving in the morning for New York."

The knocking of my heart battled the ringing in my ears. "What do you mean you're leaving? Why?"

Easing out of my arms, she took my hands in hers. "I need to go home. Hug my parents and reassure them that I'm safe. Matt, I have no clothes or money. They ruined everything. It's just not practical for me to stay here, especially when I need to keep pushing Sam to reopen the center."

"Then we'll go together. I'll drive you myself and then bring you home." I wouldn't let her go. Not again.

Her sympathetic smile matched the look in her eye. She didn't want me to go.

Touching the bruise that Sam's punch had left behind, she continued, "I don't think you being there is going to help me change Sam's mind. He has a big heart but an equally big ego. What happened in the center was like a slap in the face."

She wanted trust, but how could I be okay with her leaving? She would never come back once she tasted the freedom of her old life. Free from all the sacrifices and broken people, myself included.

"You won't come back," I choked out.

Her hands on my face forced me to look at her. The kindness in her eyes, the glossiness of her skin, the way her hair framed her dimpled cheeks did more to torture me than reassure me.

"You said you trusted me." She searched my eyes for confirmation.

"I'm trying to, but you're walking away from me." What had I expected? I had driven her to this moment, telling her over and over again that she didn't belong here. I had pushed her away.

She moved forward, pulling me back to her until we locked together again. The kiss was different this time. It felt like our last one. Desperation consumed me. "Please don't go. I want to spend the rest of my life with you. We don't need Sam or your family. Marry me. Now. Today." I dove in deeper, kissing her until she had to stop and catch her breath. She tried to push away, to break free from my embrace. I wouldn't let her. Wouldn't let her say the words I knew were coming.

"Matt." Her voice, so soft, so fragile, ripped through my fear and I slowly released my grip, giving her the space she wanted. Again her eyes searched mine. I didn't know why. My feelings were already exposed. I'd laid it all out and she was about to reject me.

"It's not a choice between you or them. My parents are wonderful people. I want them in my life. Sam's a good man. I know you don't think so, but he is. They aren't our enemies. They're my family."

I turned away. I couldn't stomach any more.

"Matt, you're my future. I know this. I even think deep down they know this. But I can't run off with you, forgetting my obligations to them and to the center. That's no way to honor God or start a life together. I need to leave, but I promise you I'll come back."

Turning to her, I held her face in my hand. I had no choice but to believe her. No choice but to wait, even though I was terrified of losing her forever.

"You say the word, and I'll have a plane ticket waiting at the airport."

She smiled, leaning into my hand on her cheek. "It won't come to that."

I tugged, forcing her close to me again, the intensity of my stare meant to seal my oath. "But if it does, I will come for you."

She didn't speak but wrapped her arms around me in a fierce hug. I had gotten all I had hoped for—reconciliation, and reassurance of her love. Yet why then, when I held her, did it feel like the beginning of the end?

I took Grace home earlier than I wanted to because I had promised Cody a victory dinner. He not only made the varsity team but was also guaranteed to be a starter.

We lingered in front of Jake's condo, neither one of us wanting to be the first to say good-bye.

"What time do you leave tomorrow?" I asked, still holding her.

"I have to be at Sam's by nine. He wants to be in the air no later than ten."

I reminded myself for the hundredth time to trust her. To fight against the part of me that wanted to throw the shield back up over my heart.

Kissing her one final time before letting her go, I willed myself to look confident. "You'll call me when you get there?"

"Of course."

She turned the knob and mouthed, "I love you," then disappeared behind the door.

Using all that was left of my willpower, I walked back to my bike and headed to meet Cody at the Pit Stop. He'd earned a barbecue dinner—that was for sure.

Timely as ever, Cody was already waiting at the entrance when I pulled up to the small restaurant. He stood straight, with a relaxed smile on his face. His newly confident posture wasn't the only thing that had changed during the six months we'd been working together. Cody had easily dropped sixty pounds of fat and put on about twenty pounds of muscle. The bullying had completely stopped, just as I expected it would as soon as he knew how to defend himself.

"So how's it feel to be the newest member of the Trojans varsity wrestling team?" I asked, grabbing his shoulder in an affectionate squeeze.

"Surreal, actually." He smiled like a man who had just conquered the world.

I slapped his back and pushed him through the door. "Come on. I want to hear all about it."

Cody started telling me details but turned quiet when Carol charged toward us with a big smile on her face. "My love! Where have you been? And where is that lovely lady friend of yours? Still around, I hope."

I hugged the boisterous Carol, catching the shock on Cody's face. She had a way of stunning people. "She's very much still around. I just thought I'd take this guy here out for a little celebration dinner. He made the varsity wrestling team today."

Carol turned her penetrating eyes to Cody, who squirmed shyly under her stare. "My, my, aren't you a handsome feller. Ohhh, my girls would go crazy over that baby face." She grabbed some menus and then turned. "Come on. Let's get some food into those bellies."

My phone buzzed in my pocket as we talked, but I silenced it quickly. People who chatted on the phone during dinner annoyed me to no end.

Carol took our orders and disappeared, but not before embarrassing Cody a little more. She got a twisted pleasure out of doing that sort of thing.

"Okay, so give me the play-by-play." The phone vibrated again in my pocket. Silencing it before he noticed, I leaned in, giving Cody my full attention.

He relaxed and then went over the whole tryout process. "Well, I walked into the gym, and I swear you could have heard a pin drop. For a moment, I strongly considered turning around and walking right back out. But then I realized I was more scared of you than them, so I stayed."

I rested my elbows on the table, not at all amused. "Good, because I would have killed you."

Cody laughed and then continued, "So they started by pairing all of us new guys against each other. I guess to kind of rank us early on. My nerves were going crazy because the first guy had about two inches on me. But as soon as they blew the whistle, I don't know, something in me snapped and I had him on his back in three moves. That caught the assistant coach's attention, so he paired me with Blake Mason." Cody's eyes got big, as if I should have known the significance of that name.

When he saw my confusion, he clarified for me. "Blake Mason is the best junior on the team. Everyone knows he will make captain next year. So we paired up and he was harder, of course, but still I had him flat the minute I used that side hold and twist move you showed me. Well, now everyone was watching, and all the other pairings were stopped. Coach Taylor, the head coach, called me over and started asking me all these questions. What team I'd been on before, who I trained with. He couldn't believe that I'd never competed. So then he brings out the big guns. Joshua Fedder, senior, all-American, state champ runner-up last year."

Pride for him radiated in my smile. "Let me guess, you had him on his back, too."

Cody shook his head. "No, he got me, but it was a tight match. Three full rounds. In fact, at the end he shook my hand and said it was the hardest match he'd had in a year."

I knew I shouldn't focus on the loss, but I didn't want Cody to get comfortable. "Well then, it looks like we have a new goal."

"New goal?"

"Before the year's out, you'll have that Joshua kid on his back. I guarantee it."

Cody shook his head again and laughed just as Carol slid the food in front of us. "You can't give a man a break, can you? Even for one night?"

I cut my meat but kept my eyes locked on Cody. "People who get comfortable get passed up by those who are hungry. Always be the hungry one, Cody."

He agreed, eyes wide, and cataloged every word I uttered as gospel. A good reminder that my influence was way too significant to be taken lightly.

We continued to eat while he went into more detail about the holds and stances that he used in the matches. I ignored my phone two more times until I couldn't stand it anymore.

"Can you excuse me for one second?" I asked, getting up from the table. "I'll be right back."

Whoever was calling me had done so five consecutive times. Accepting the call as I walked outside, I silently prayed it wasn't a solicitor, because they were going to get a piece of my mind.

"Hello?"

"Matt? Is that you? Sheesh, man, why do you even have a phone if you're not going to answer it?"

I could pinpoint that snotty tone anywhere. "Marcus? What's going on? Are you hurt?" I'd given him my phone number months ago, but he'd never used it before.

"Listen, can you come to my house? We want to talk to you."

"Who's we?" My instincts were on fire, my gut clenching as I sorted through the possibilities.

"Does it matter? Please, Matt. You told me I could trust you. Well, I need you to back that up." Marcus's voice fell a little, no doubt expecting me to let him down.

I glanced over at Cody finishing up his meal, and despite knowing I'd disappoint him, decided to go with the greater need. "All right, Marcus. I'll be there in ten minutes."

Slipping the phone back into my pocket, I walked over to our table. "Hey, I'm so sorry to cut out on you early, but I have an emergency I need to take care of."

His face immediately looked worried. "Is everything okay?"

"Yeah, I'm sure it is. I just need to check or it will bother me all night." I tossed two twenties on the table, easily covering our meals and leaving Carol with a generous tip. "Listen, you take your time and enjoy a night of rest. Be wary, though; when Carol sees you sitting alone, she'll have you a girlfriend before the end of the night." I smiled, winking at him.

He turned red, a remnant of the bullied, overweight kid coming out.

"Cody"—he clasped the hand I offered—"I'm proud of you. You set a goal, you worked hard, and you accomplished it. That makes you more of a man than most out there. But I still expect you in the gym on Monday morning."

With a handshake and a smile, Cody nodded in agreement. "I'll be there."

I hastily left the restaurant and raced to meet Marcus. Lord knew what trouble that kid had gotten himself into this time.

The porch light was the only thing visible as I drove through the dark streets. I hated being there at night. It put me on edge, took me back to juvie and the mindset of kill or be killed.

I parked my bike and scaled the steps to pound on the door. It flew open, but Marcus wasn't the one on the other side of it. A sturdy woman, who had to be his aunt Mave, smiled and stepped aside so I could enter. She looked tired and weathered, but her eyes were kind.

"Matt Holloway, so happy to finally meet you," she said as she shut the door behind her.

Considering the rough neighborhood, I was surprised by how well kept the living room was. Though the furniture looked second-hand, every surface was cleared and polished, reflecting a woman who took pride in the little she had.

I offered her my hand. "Aunt Mave?"

She grasped it, her dark cheeks rising with a smile. "That's me, all right." She let go of my hand and shouted, "Marcus, get in here!"

A loud "Yes, ma'am" came from the back of the house, and Aunt Mave offered me a spot on the couch, then sat next to me.

"Marcus told me what's been goin' on. The drugs, the fights." She shook her head in disgust. "I can't believe they'd use little kids like that."

I nodded. "I know. And with the center now closed, I've got to be honest, I don't know what's gonna happen."

Marcus shuffled into the room, his posture exuding shame.

Mave raised her head, looking annoyed. "Now don't you go looking like a victim in all of this. You knew what you was doin' was wrong. Fifty dollars. Dumb. That's what it was."

I stifled a laugh. I could definitely see where Marcus got his sass.

She turned back to me and I straightened, not wanting to get my own tongue-lashing.

"Well, I'm just tired of all this. That center was the only good thing this neighborhood had, and I'll be damned if I'm going to let them run us good folks out of here. So we got a plan, but I need your help."

"Sure, whatever you need."

Glancing back to Marcus, she pinched her brow. "You talk to those boys?"

He nodded, still looking ashamed. "Yes, ma'am."

"Good." She stood up and looked between us like a general about to give orders to her men. "Matt, I need you to bring Marcus and his friends to the police station. I've got a car, so you can just leave that bike of yours here."

I stood, too, suddenly feeling protective of Marcus. "Don't you think that's a little rash?"

Mave crossed her arms and stared me down. No wonder Marcus was cowering—that woman was more intimidating than a three-hundred-pound man. "If he was man enough to do the crime, he needs to be man enough to confess it. And I told his little hoodlum friends the same thing."

"Listen, Mave, I appreciate what you're saying, but if we do this, there's going to be a big target on your back. They will retaliate."

She set her jaw and those dark eyes of hers got real serious. "I ain't afraid. We've let those bullies have too much freedom as it is. That center is ours, and I ain't gonna let them have it without a fight. Now, you boys get on out of here. I got some phone calls to make."

I turned to Marcus, who looked terrified and for good reason. "Come on. You heard the woman. Let's go."

CHAPTER 42

GRACE

My phone started chirping an hour before the alarm was set to go off. I rolled over, half in denial that morning had arrived. I'd stayed up way too late talking to Naomi and Jake, and then spent another hour tossing and turning as I contemplated the talk I would have to have with my parents.

More chirps sounded from the cursed device and finally I pried my eyes open enough to glance at the screen.

Matt: I need you and Sam to come by the center before you leave today. IMPORTANT!

Matt: Did you get my last text? Call me.

I did as he asked but got his voice mail. "Hey, Matt, it's Grace. Okay, I'll try to get Sam out there. What's going on?"

Hanging up, I pulled myself out of bed and called Sam, letting him know that I would be early so we could stop by the center and pick up some of my things. He begrudgingly agreed, still short with me. I wondered how tense the flight home would be now that there was such a distance between us.

Unwilling to fret any longer, I texted Matt that we'd be there at nine. I pulled out the jeans and T-shirt I'd washed last night and hurried to the shower, smiling that I'd worn the same outfit three days in a row. Oh, how much I had changed. My mother was going to be mortified.

Sam was grumpier than I expected when we loaded into his town car. He grunted instructions to the driver and sat back with his shades blocking his eyes. Apparently, his night was even more restless than mine.

"What all do you need from the center again?" he mumbled without making eye contact.

"Just some personal items. It will only take me a second to grab them." Setting my hand lightly on his arm, I forced my tone to soften. "Sam, are you okay?"

He jerked away. "I'm fine. Just ready to get home."

Resigned to the silence, I laid my head against the headrest and stared out the window as buildings and streets blurred past us. Soon I recognized the neighborhood and sat up when suddenly the street was packed with car after car along the curb. Still blocks from the center, there were hundreds of people lining the street. Sam sat up straight, looking out at all the commotion.

"What's going on?"

Shaking my head, I just stared as we moved closer to the building and even greater crowds of people. "I have no idea."

When we were as close as the crowd would allow, the driver parked the car. Sam insisted that I get out his door, and clasped my hand the minute we were free from the car.

We moved forward, stopping every few feet as someone shook our hands or hugged us. They thanked us for the center and for all we had done for the community. They begged Sam to reconsider and told him how much they wanted the building reopened. With each step Sam's tough exterior started to melt, and I even caught a single tear escape past his sunglasses.

My own eyes were teary, especially when child after child hugged me and begged me to stay. After what felt like an hour, we at last reached the entrance to the building. Still gripping my hand with an iron hold, Sam led me up the stairs to face Marcus, Trey, and Eric, who stood the minute they spotted us. I looked around for Matt but didn't see him anywhere.

The boys looked unified, the last of my composure disappearing as tears tumbled down my cheeks at the sight of them. Trey stepped up first.

"Mr. Hartsford, we all messed up. You trusted us. But we did some bad stuff—stuff we're not proud of."

I looked from Marcus to Eric, who both had their heads lowered in shame. They must have been delivering the drugs, too. My heart ached. No wonder they would never come forward. They were probably terrified.

Trey continued, "We know you can't let us in here again. We get that. But please don't go punishing the whole neighborhood 'cause of us. We told the cops everything last night." Trey looked up at me, his brown eyes blazing. "Strong and courageous, right, Ms. Covington?"

"That's right, Trey," I choked out, barely able to speak.

Trey stepped back and Marcus looked up, taking a deep breath. As he watched Sam, I knew the kind of courage it had to take to address him. Marcus was instinctively gun-shy around men.

"Mr. Hartsford, please don't do it. We'll do anything you want. We need a place like this." He turned to me and smiled. "And we need Ms. Covington, too. Even though she brings those stuffy suits around all the time, we know she's doin' it 'cause she cares about us. We need someone to care about us."

Sam squeezed my hand and I could feel his wall crumbling. There was no way to look into the eyes of those boys and not be affected.

Eric was the last to speak and seemed the most ashamed. "I didn't tell you the truth, Ms. Covington, because I didn't want you not to like me. They targeted Melissa and me for a reason. We both chose money over doin' what was right. That's why I wouldn't come forward. Why I wouldn't press charges. I'm sorry."

Unable to stop myself, I pulled Eric in for a hug, letting go of Sam's hand in the process. Then I grabbed Trey and Marcus, too. "I'm so proud of you boys," I cried as I held them.

When I released them, they all quickly swiped their eyes before anyone noticed they were crying, and turned again to Sam.

"So, Mr. Hartsford, will you open us back up?" Marcus's shaky voice resonated in the air.

Sam cleared his throat. "I'll think about it, son. What you did here today matters, though, so thank you."

Marcus looked ready to beg some more, but then glanced at something behind me and slumped his shoulders, choosing instead to keep his mouth shut. I turned to see who he was looking at and spotted Matt right behind us, watching. He was wearing the same clothes from yesterday and didn't look like he had slept at all.

Sam turned as well, and he and Matt made eye contact immediately. I watched Sam's reaction. He stiffened but didn't attempt to stop me when I ran down the stairs and threw myself into Matt's waiting arms.

"Thank you," I whispered. He held me tightly, giving me all the strength he had left.

"They arrested King last night and three other ringleaders. I'm even working on a deal for Devon, so he's going to testify as well."

I couldn't believe it. I knew how Matt felt about the system. How he felt about letting anyone help. In a span of twenty-four hours the situation had gone from hopeless to possible.

"Did you do all this, too?" I asked, looking around at the mass of people gathered.

Matt shook his head. "Nope, this was all Aunt Mave. That woman would scare the skin off a tiger."

I laughed, hugging him tighter, and silently thanked the Lord for His miracle. Only He could do something so powerful in the hearts of those surrounding the place.

Sam cleared his throat. "Gracie, we need to go."

Though I didn't want to, I pulled back. "I love you," I promised, then let go of Matt to join my old friend.

I saw the anxiety in Matt's eyes, but he didn't stop me. Instead, he let me walk away with Sam, trusting that our love was strong enough.

The fighter finally let go.

It wasn't until we were away from the neighborhood, and halfway to the airport, that Sam started to smile. He shifted to gaze out the window so I couldn't see it.

"You're not fooling anyone, Sam. I know they got to you."

"Maybe." He turned to look at me, stretching his arm out as an offer for me to scoot closer. I did, happy that the tension between us was melting.

He squeezed my shoulder. "You know, you're the only girl who's ever laughed at me when I poured my heart out."

I stifled the giggles that threatened to come again.

"I shouldn't have assumed Matt was involved. I guess that was a little judgmental."

"You think?" My sarcasm was met with a warning stare.

"It doesn't mean I like him, though. I still don't think he's right for you."

I stiffened and sent him a challenging stare. "And I still don't care."

He shook his head but squeezed me again affectionately. "I don't know what I was thinking. With this new attitude you've picked up, we'd fight nonstop."

"That's just because you have an ego the size of Manhattan and are used to getting whatever you want."

"Ouch!" He pushed me away, feigning hurt.

I let the giggles come and pushed him back. Soon we were in an all-out war, each vying for dominance until Sam's driver cleared his throat.

"Sir, we are approaching the airstrip."

Sam pushed me one more time and straightened his jacket. "Thanks, Richard. I'm so ready to get home."

He didn't say it, but somehow I knew everything would be okay.

CHAPTER 43

MATT

Marcus lunged at me again, almost getting me to drop the ball, but I made it around him with two side steps and sunk the fadeaway.

"That's game, buddy," I announced proudly as he muttered excuses about losing. Truth was, I rarely got a shot on the kid, but today I was on fire.

Grace was coming home.

It had been a month of late-night phone conversations and Skyping, but in the end it was all worth the separation. Sam reopened the center a week ago and even reinstated Grace as the director. Security was tight, and the cops came once or twice a day with drug dogs just in case, but the kids still kept coming, filling this place up even more than before.

Marcus grabbed the ball and vowed victory in a rematch, but I was quickly distracted when the woman who had completely turned my life upside down entered. Dressed in a light blue sundress that wrapped and flowed around her body, she was tan and looked as stunning as ever. My mouth went dry.

Grace was flanked by a man and woman who were obviously her parents, making my heart beat faster as I slowly approached them. Sweat trickled down my back, and I wished I were dressed in something better than the ratty T-shirt and shorts I'd put on to play basketball in. This was not how I envisioned our introduction.

Before I could mutter a hello, Grace flung herself into my arms and held me as if I were her life support. "I missed you so much," she whispered. I wanted to hug her back with the same fury, but I felt paralyzed by the stare of the man in front of me.

Aware of my unease, Grace let go and turned to her parents. "Mom, Dad, this is my boyfriend, Matt. Matt, my wonderful parents." Her smile lit up the room, and she seemed to be the only one undaunted by this monumental moment.

Grace's father approached. His face was calm and unreadable, his eyes an exact replica of his daughter's. He stretched out his hand and I returned his firm handshake, fully aware that the tattoos on my arm would be the first impression I made.

"My daughter says I need to get to know you. That you're going to be around for a while." His voice gave no indication of his thoughts.

"Yes, sir. I hope so." Okay, I would have gladly stepped into the ring any day with a man twice my size. Anything would have been less intimidating than that moment.

He kept a firm grip on my hand and turned it slightly to examine the ink on my forearm.

"You know, my dad was a tattoo guy himself," he said, letting go of my hand before a grin appeared. "Most proper man you'd ever meet, yet his back was completely covered. He called it his guilty pleasure."

Before I could get over being stunned by his admission, Grace's mom pulled me in for a tight embrace. "Matt, we are so happy to meet you. Thank you for taking care of our baby." She stepped back and examined me from head to toe. "You're right, Grace. He is very handsome."

Her mother looked around the building with a smile before clapping. "Oh, I can't wait to see the renovation plans." She grabbed her husband's arm and tugged him along. "Come on, dear. Let's give these lovebirds a minute alone."

Grace's father looked back and forth between the two of us and smiled before following after his wife. I watched with my mouth open, completely unprepared for them to be so gracious.

Marcus soon had Mr. Covington engaged in a basketball game while Darius showed her mom around the building.

Grace's small arm snaked around my waist. "I told you they were wonderful."

"All the same, a little heads-up would have been nice."

She turned to me and smiled. "I wanted to surprise you. Besides, I couldn't wait one more minute."

Without hesitation, I swept her into my arms and held her tightly, the month of anxiety already slipping away from me. "Never again, Grace. I'm not letting you leave ever again."

She held me close, burying her face in my chest. "I'm not going anywhere."

I held her face in my hands and looked deep into her eyes. She was my future, my forever.

"Now that your dad's here, I plan to ask him a very important question."

She smiled playfully, knowing exactly where this was going. "That's fine as long as you realize I still want a grand spectacle of a wedding. You can take the girl out of New York, but you'll never take the New York out of the girl."

Matching her smile, I wondered how I ever got so lucky. "Sweetheart, you can have whatever you want. Just don't think I'm waiting eighteen months to make you mine."

She saw the intensity in my eyes and knew I meant it. If I had my choice, we'd be married tomorrow.

Her eyes grew big, a small pout forming. "Six months?"

What could a man do? How could I ever say no to this beautiful woman? "Not a day longer. I mean it."

Her arm encircled me again, pulling me tight against her. "I love you so much."

I kissed her head, relishing the wonderful smell I'd been longing for all month. "I love you, too."

"Ah, man! Are you at it again?" Marcus hollered from across the gym. "Mr. Covington, that's all those two ever want to do."

Grace and I burst out laughing at the stunned expression on her father's face. We approached hand in hand until I let go to take Marcus in a friendly headlock.

"Boy, your mouth is way too big," I scolded.

He laughed and disengaged the way I'd taught him. His eyes were as bright as his smile, and for the first time ever, I saw that glimmer in his eyes. Hope. Trust. Joy.

I'd seen the Lord do amazing things, but nothing touched me more than seeing His mercy in the eyes of a child.

Another victory.

ACKNOWLEDGMENTS

A heartfelt thanks to:

The entire Waterfall Press team, especially Tammy Faxel, Daniel Byrne, and my amazing editors, Gail Hudson and Robin Cruise. It's an honor to partner with such wonderful professionals.

Josh Webb of Root Radius—for your continued guidance and strategic coaching. I'd be lost without you.

Mandy Hollis of MH Photography—for allowing me the use of your beautiful photograph for my cover design. Your talent for grasping emotion is remarkable.

Debby Wade of ACTSolutions Counseling Center—for giving me guidance and insight into the minds of those dealing with trauma.

My sister, Angel—for always reading my first draft with keen eyes and wise words. Your invaluable input continues to make me better.

My faithful beta readers, Abby, Karen, and Suzy—for your attention to detail, advice, and ideas.

My wonderful writing critique partners—Conni Cossette, Janice Olson, Patty Carroll, Jackie Castle, Ann Boyles, Dana Red, Lyndie Blevins, Keisha Bass, Michelle Stimpson, Jan Johnson, and Lynne Gentry—for helping me elevate my writing and for always pushing me to dig deeper.

My wonderful readers—for your continual encouragement, e-mails, and reviews. You are the reason I love writing so much!

And finally, to my amazing husband and children—for all the sacrifices you make, allowing me to pour my heart and soul into every word.

ABOUT THE AUTHOR

© 2013 Karen Graham

T.L. Gray serves as a pastor's wife in Ennis, Texas. It was her desire to help young girls know and experience Christ's unconditional love that led her to write her debut novel, *Shattered Rose*. Her books are about flawed characters who struggle in the world. She loves writing stories that offer hope to the broken, with the intention of taking the readers on a journey where they both cheer for and want to shake the hero/heroine. She aims to depict culturally relevant settings while presenting an inspirational message that will stay with readers long after the book is closed. Follow her on Twitter @tlgraybooks or visit her at www.facebook.com/tlgraybooks and www.tlgray.com.